W9-CYG-469

Rejection. Cool and complete—like a rope being severed by a well-honed blade. Rejection of a proposal she had not even known she had made. But thank the gods for his good judgment, for in her mourning she had apparently grown weak and lost her own.

No, Intef had said simply, and inside this dark place his meaning had been as bright as day. *No*, the kiss they had shared the night before had meant nothing. *No*, they should not give in to this inexplicable lust. *No*, for he was the self-proclaimed robber of Pharaoh's tomb, and she was Pharaoh's only defender. *No, no, no, no*. They were enemies, after all. They had become allies only by necessity. They could never, ever be more.

She watched his torch float down the corridor and felt a wave of relief. His clarity of his thought was astounding; the content of it unimpeachable. The only feeling they should be allowing inside their hearts was the simple will to survive.

Author Note

In the ancient Egyptian language, there is no word for *queen*. Though ancient Egyptian women had more rights than their foreign contemporaries, the highest rank a woman could achieve in pre-Ptolemaic Egypt was chief wife. There are three verifiable exceptions: Sobekneferu, Hatshepsut and Tausret—women who ruled as pharaohs.

This story takes place just after Tausret's reign. Though little is known about her, she lived in a time of corruption, invasion and civil strife. It is this historic milieu that informed my best guesses about her life.

The heroine of the story is Tausret's adviser. She, too, must come to terms with Tausret—both how to serve her memory and how it may serve her. Trapped inside Tausret's tomb, she must finally learn to live.

In addition to Tausret, I reference these historical figures: Rameses II (the Great Ancestor), Merneptah, Seti II, Amenmesse, Bay, Siptah, Setnakht, Suppiluliuma II and Rameses III, who is considered Egypt's last great pharaoh.

I recently had the opportunity to visit Tausret's magnificent tomb and would like to thank Alaa Aly Taie, the wonderful host of Villa Al Diwan, and the excellent guide Hassaan Alazzazy, for their inspiration.

I hope you enjoy the story!

GRETA
GILBERT

—

Saved by Her
Enemy Warrior

HARLEQUIN
HISTORICAL

If you purchased this book without a cover you should be aware
that this book is stolen property. It was reported as "unsold and
destroyed" to the publisher, and neither the author nor the
publisher has received any payment for this "stripped book."

HARLEQUIN®
HISTORICAL™

Recycling programs
for this product may
not exist in your area.

ISBN-13: 978-1-335-50538-5

Saved by Her Enemy Warrior

Copyright © 2020 by Greta Gilbert

All rights reserved. No part of this book may be used or reproduced in
any manner whatsoever without written permission except in the case of
brief quotations embodied in critical articles and reviews.

This is a work of fiction. Names, characters, places and incidents
are either the product of the author's imagination or are used fictitiously.
Any resemblance to actual persons, living or dead, businesses,
companies, events or locales is entirely coincidental.

This edition published by arrangement with Harlequin Books S.A.

For questions and comments about the quality of this book,
please contact us at CustomerService@Harlequin.com.

Harlequin Enterprises ULC
22 Adelaide St. West, 40th Floor
Toronto, Ontario M5H 4E3, Canada
www.Harlequin.com

Printed in U.S.A.

Greta Gilbert's passion for ancient history began with a teenage crush on Indiana Jones. As an adult, she landed a dream job at National Geographic Learning, where her colleagues—former archaeologists—helped her learn to keep her facts straight. Now she lives in southern Baja, Mexico, where she continues to study the ancients. She is especially intrigued by ancient mysteries and always keeps a little Indiana Jones inside her heart.

Books by Greta Gilbert

Harlequin Historical

Enslaved by the Desert Trader
The Spaniard's Innocent Maiden
In Thrall to the Enemy Commander
Forbidden to the Gladiator
Seduced by Her Rebel Warrior
Saved by Her Enemy Warrior

Harlequin Historical Undone! ebook

Mastered by Her Slave

Visit the Author Profile page
at Harlequin.com.

For my beloved aunty Kathy,
our family's reigning queen, who has
loved and inspired me all my life.

Chapter One

1189 BCE
—*Valley of the Kings royal burial ground,
west of Thebes—modern Luxor—Egypt*

Aya was kneeling in prayer when she felt the guard's hand cover her mouth. She tried to cry out, but his large palm muted the sound. 'Do not scream,' he muttered in her ear. 'Remember your dignity.'

He tugged her head backwards and she felt the cool of a blade against her throat. 'It will be over soon,' he assured her. 'Close your eyes.'

Aya did as she was told. *Quickly*, she thought. *A merciful death.*

A bronze voice sliced the silence. 'Cease.'

Aya opened her eyes to discover the High Priest of Amun standing over her, the torchlight flickering on his powdered face. He blinked at the guard. 'No blood may be spilled inside a house of eternity. Use rope.'

There was a rush of movement into the burial chamber. Aya was seized by her arms and lifted, and her feet were pulled out from beneath her.

'Behind the shrine,' the High Priest directed and Aya was carried across the chamber like a goat.

'Holy One,' she said. 'What is happening?'

She was tossed to the floor beside the hut-sized golden container that had been constructed around Pharaoh's sarcophagus. She tried to sit up, but the guard's large palm held her down.

'Pharaoh's Most Beloved Advisor is irrelevant now,' he muttered, his sour breath in her ear. 'She will follow Pharaoh to the fields of paradise.'

Aya perceived a rope being threaded between her bound arms and wrapped around the shrine.

She heard the sound of men heaving. Her wrists rose up above her head, suspended by a rope she could not see.

'The pectoral,' the High Priest intoned. Aya felt the weight of her golden pectoral necklace—the most valuable thing she owned—being lifted off her chest.

She tried to kick, but her feet were already bound. They were being lifted above the floor like her wrists had been.

'I beg you to cease!' she shouted at last and, when she heard the High Priest's bemused grunt, she began to sob. 'For the love of Isis.'

'Silence her,' he snapped and Aya felt a blow to her stomach.

'Holy Ones!' she shouted. Another blow. 'Guards!' A blow to her side, her head, her face...nothing.

When her wits returned, Aya heard the sound of bricks being stacked in mud. If death had a sound, this was it. *Scoop, swish, set.* Her head throbbed and her heart filled with dread. She moved to cover her ears, forgetting that her wrists were tied.

She opened her eyes.

If death had an aura, it was the quality of torchlight. It flashed across the painted ceiling, illuminating the garish yellow stars. She was lying on her back, her ankles also tied, and now she knew why the men had bound her this way.

Tied beside the shrine of the deceased, she could not show herself to the priests standing at the entrance to the chamber. She could not display her tears or appeal to them for mercy. She could not see them and they could not see her. She could only whimper in misery and stare up at those terrible stars, ablaze in the mocking torchlight.

Myrrh.

Its scent was everywhere. The priests had filled the chamber with its anise-tinged smoke. 'The Breath of Isis', it was called, because it was supposed to invoke the divine protectoress. But it only clogged Aya's lungs, giving her the unusual sensation of drowning. If death had a scent, surely it was that of myrrh.

She was seized by a spasm of coughs. She strained against her bonds, forgetting that she could not cover her nose. She could do nothing but let her lungs clear themselves in the sanctified air of the tomb, feeling all the while that she was despoiling it. She should not be here, but she was tied. *Tied.*

She filled her voice with deference. 'Is this some manner of test, Holy Ones?' She pictured them lingering in the shadowy corridor just beyond the chamber, their bald heads gleaming in the torchlight. 'Surely you do not mean to leave me here?'

The practice of burying living servants with dead kings had been forbidden in Egypt for thousands of years and the men at the entrance to the chamber knew it. It was an abhorrence, an offence to *ma'at*, the principle of order and justice. Yet not a single voice responded to her query.

'Venerable priests,' she began. 'I beg you. Do not condemn me thus. I have never stolen. I have never cursed the gods. I have never harmed an elder, or a child, or spoken ill of anyone. I have served the Living God in all...' she paused '...in most things.'

She awaited a response, but there was only the diminishing torchlight, the thickening air and the dogged rhythm of the bricks, as if the jackal-headed god of death himself were stacking them.

Her voice cracked. 'I refer you to Pharaoh's funeral papyrus,' she said. *And to your own humanity, by the gods.* 'I am to be freed from service! It has been written.'

But it was as if she were talking to the paintings on the walls.

Scoop, swish, set.

'If you do not free me, you defy the will of a god!' she shouted. 'You place Great Egypt in danger.'

So why were the priests not responding? Aya searched her heart—the centre of all her thoughts—and a dark knowing descended. The priests did not care whether or not they offended Pharaoh Tausret, because they had never believed in Pharaoh Tausret at all.

Because Pharaoh Tausret had been a woman.

'I can pay,' Aya lied. 'There is a cache of gold hidden in Pharaoh's Temple of Millions of Years. I can show you where it is.'

She thought she heard someone grunt, followed by a breeze of whispers. Perhaps her lie had found some adherents among the priests and other officials. Perhaps the High Priest himself was considering her offer? She had long suspected his designs on the Horus throne.

The High Priest was not the only man with such an ambition. General Setnakht, a rebel general with his base right there in Thebes, had sought the double crown throughout Tausret's reign. It was rumoured that he, too, was gathering his army and that Setnakht and the High Priest would soon face each other in battle, with the Horus throne as the prize.

There was only one problem with their efforts. Neither of the pretenders could prove a link to the royal bloodline. Without royal blood, none could win the loyalty of all the people. Royal blood was divine blood and only a god was allowed to sit on the throne of Egypt.

Whichever man succeeded in taking the throne would claim a link to Pharaoh's bloodline and Aya was the only person who could prove him wrong.

Which was why it seemed that she was doomed.

'You may save yourself,' the High Priest said suddenly. The sounds of bricklaying ceased. 'Tell me where I may find Tausret's heir.'

Aya bit her tongue. She did not know exactly where the heir resided, but she knew enough. It was a secret that Pharaoh had shared with Aya alone. How did the High Priest know she kept it?

Perhaps he had only guessed that Aya knew about the heir. Perhaps he thought that the threat of entombment would be enough to coax her secrets from her.

'Speak now, woman!' the High Priest thundered. 'Or be silent for ever!'

It was her chance. If she would reveal the location of Pharaoh Tausret's only living son, she could save her own life.

But it was a confession she could not make. She

had been a poor counsellor and an even poorer protector, but a traitor she was not. She would keep the heir's existence hidden for ever, for that had been Pharaoh's dying wish.

Scoop, swish, set.

Now it was Aya who said not a word and the moments seemed to stretch into years. She had failed Pharaoh in many things, but she would not fail her in this.

'I will find him, you know,' snapped the High Priest. 'And I will kill him.'

Aya heard another brick slide into place and the sound of voices moving further and further away. 'You will not find him,' she whispered, as if merely saying the words could somehow make them true.

She would not allow herself to cry, though tears seeped from her eyes anyway. She needed to remember her dignity, as the guard had said. She had begged and grovelled and debased herself enough. Now it was time to quietly accept her fate.

'The will of Osiris,' she whispered and a stream of tears dribbled into her mouth. They tasted of kohl and brine, of sour and salt. They were the taste of suffering, of a long, slow, terrible death.

There was not a single sound now and even the painted stars had ceased to shine. And Aya was alone.

Chapter Two

Intef held his breath, testing the quiet. It had begun only moments ago, when the voices had faded and the sound of stacking bricks had ceased. Bless the gods for the peace. The woman's grief-stricken ravings had been almost too piteous to bear—and so very loud.

'I am to be freed from service,' she had cried, betraying her advanced age. It seemed that the old woman had served Pharaoh all her life, for her freedom had become so precious to her that she was threatening to remain in the burial chamber if she did not receive it. She had even offered to lead the priests to gold in exchange for it.

She had obviously been overwhelmed by grief and in the end they had had to bind her limbs with rope just to extract her from the chamber.

That had been at least an hour ago, but Intef knew he could not yet emerge from the stuffy chest in which he huddled. The tomb was not yet empty. A whole gang of servants were currently filling its long entrance corridor with earth. He thought he could hear the faint spilling of their buckets. If he could hear them, then they would be able to hear him.

Another hour, he decided.

He exhaled, forcing his breath through the layers of
linen surrounding him and reminded himself to stay
calm. He had nine days, after all. That was how long
the tomb workers had assured him that one man could
survive inside a tomb before the spirits of the Underworld claimed him.

Intef turned away from the morbid thought. He had
more immediate concerns, such as how to adjust the
angle of his throbbing neck. He was not sure he could
wait much longer. He was wretched with hunger and
thirst and both his legs had gone numb.

How many hours had it been since the priest Hepu
had stuffed him inside this wooden prison? Twenty at
least, for it had been late the previous night when Intef
had met the priest outside Tausret's mortuary temple.
He thought back to the strange encounter.

*'You are Setnakht's beetle?' Hepu asked. Like Intef,
the priest had been working in secret for the rebel
Generals—first Amenmesse, then Setnakht—for most
of his life.*

*'I am indeed, Holy Brother,' Intef replied. 'It is nice
to finally meet you.'*

*Hepu looked disappointed. 'You are too tall for the
chest I had planned.'*

*'Do you have another? Something with a rooftop bed
and a view to the river?' Intef jested.*

'You are nervous,' said Hepu.

*'On the contrary, I am delighted to begin my ad-
venture.'*

*The priest shook his head. 'You should be nervous.
I know not of a single living man who would do what
you are about to do.'*

'How difficult could it be?' asked Intef. 'I will relax

inside a chest for the next few hours, then get carried by royal chest bearers into the dusty hills. After another short rest, I will emerge from the chest into a lovely tomb, then chisel my way out through a bit of stone.'

'When you realise what you have done, you must not panic,' said the priest. He gazed at the hammer and chisel Intef carried. 'You think those are your greatest tools, but they are not.'

Intef sighed. How priests loved to give advice. 'What, I beg, is my greatest tool?'

'Calm,' said Hepu. 'Come, we must hurry.'

Hepu sneaked Intef into the pillared staging hall and they stumbled amid the deceased Pharaoh's sacred grave goods. 'I have replaced the beer with water in a dozen amphorae bound for the tomb,' he whispered. 'They will be on the second shelf in the northeast storage room.'

'Remind me again, Hepu, where is that particular room?'

Hepu expelled a heavy sigh. 'Nobody has instructed you in the layout of the tomb?'

'The men in the tomb workers' village said it was very long, with two large chambers.'

'By Horus,' Hepu held out his arm. 'Imagine this is the tomb,' he said. He ran his hand down his forearm. 'This part is simply a long corridor leading down to the chambers. After Pharaoh—and you—are entombed, it will be filled in with earth.'

'I knew that much,' Intef said.

Hepu arched a greying brow, then opened his palms and held them slightly apart. 'This is what you will be left with—two large chambers connected by another corridor.' He raised his left hand. 'Your journey will end when you reach the second or main chamber. It is the deepest part of the tomb.' He touched each corner of his hand. 'There are four storage rooms adjoining the main chamber. Your chest will be placed inside one. In one of the other storage rooms you will find the water containers I mentioned, along with beer and bread.'

'Olive bread?' asked Intef.

Hepu ignored Intef's attempt at levity. 'To reach the first chamber, the false chamber, you must break through the main chamber's security seal and go up this corridor.' Hepu pointed to the space between his palms to indicate the corridor that joined them. 'Just before you reach the false chamber, you will notice two entryways on either side of the corridor. Those are the unfinished chambers.'

'Where Pharaoh Tausret's greatest treasures lie?' asked Intef.

'For the sake of the rebellion, let us hope,' said the priest. He raised his right hand. 'You will have to break through another brick seal to reach the false chamber. It is slightly smaller than the main chamber but is similarly flanked by four storage rooms. It is also where you will carve your tunnel,' said Hepu. 'Ah, here we are.'

They had arrived at Intef's unlikely ferry—a large ebony chest. Hepu opened the lid to reveal a cache of the late Pharaoh's undergarments. 'Get in,' he said.

'You must be jesting,' said Intef.

But Hepu was a man who did not jest and Intef held his breath as Hepu covered him with layers of lavender-smelling loincloths.

'You could not have chosen a chest full of salted beef?' mumbled Intef.

If their mission succeeded, Hepu would be raised to the priesthood of one of the larger temples of Thebes. If it failed, he would likely lose his head.

Hepu arranged the last layer of garments atop Intef and sighed. 'Forgive us, oh, mighty gods,' he said. 'We labour for the good of Egypt.' Then he closed the chest and locked it shut.

Intef thought back to Hepu's strange advice: *'When you realise what you have done, you must not panic.'*

Who was panicking? If there was any cause for panic, it was because he would be smelling like a woman for the next nine days.

It was an ignominious mission to be sure. Instead of marching alongside General Setnakht on his way to seize the empty throne of Egypt, Intef had agreed to be buried inside a tomb surrounded by a woman's delicates.

And that had not even been the worst of his debasement. The processional journey from Pharaoh Tausret's House of Millions of Years to her House of Eternity the following morning had been something akin to being baked slowly in an oven. At one point he had caught himself moaning.

Thankfully, none of the chest-bearers seemed to notice. Nor did the onlookers, whose oohs and ahhs only added to the cacophony. Who could detect a small moan above the jangling sistrums of the priestesses and the shrieks of the professional mourning women?

Then there was the distraction of Pharaoh herself, who had been transfigured into the god of resurrection via a solid gold coffin made in the shape of Osiris. A troupe of milk-bearers purified the ground before her as she floated towards her tomb on a sled borne by six white bulls.

The onlookers obviously revered her: she was the

last direct descendant of Rameses the Great Ancestor, the last person in Egypt to carry that divine blood.

Though to be fair, she no longer carried any blood at all. Just seventy days ago, it had been drained by the embalmers and her cranial matter had been removed through her nose. Four of her organs had been preserved in sacred canopic jars, leaving her heart in its place, and her entire royal body had been smothered in Natron Valley salt.

After thirty-five days in salt, her royal corpse was then cleaned and wrapped in linen strips cut from her own robes. Precious amulets were placed beneath those linens, which were then sealed in place by unguent-scented resins.

Every preparation had been made to preserve Pharaoh Tausret in a journey that—it occurred to Intef—had begun only moments ago, just after sunset.

It was the first of the twelve hours of night and Tausret's soul was journeying through the Underworld while Intef waited inside the chest that contained her undergarments.

Intef might have laughed. It was a humorous situation to be sure. He would retell it to his fellow soldiers one day to riotous applause.

'And it was dark inside the tomb, you see,' he would say, 'and hot as the mines of Hammamat. There was not a single breeze. The air stood as still as death. But I took comfort among Pharaoh's loincloths, for they smelled of lavender and felt like soft clouds...'

He could hear their laughter already. 'Ha-ha-ha!' they roared. 'Ho-ho-ho!'

Not really, though. He was fooling himself. It was not his friends' imagined laughter he heard, it was the pounding of his own heart inside his ears.

Chapter Three

Aya had run out of prayers. The heir was in danger and there was nothing she could do to protect him. She tugged hopelessly at her bonds. Already she was losing her strength. She was failing Tausret in death as she had failed her Pharaoh in life, and the people of Egypt would suffer for it.

No—this could not be. How had she not anticipated the High Priest's treachery? He was the wealthiest, most powerful man in Egypt, with an ambition to match his lands. Now that the throne was empty, he would stop at nothing to seize it.

There were only two things in his way: General Setnakht, the rebel leader in the South, and the true heir to the double crown, whom most did not believe even existed.

But Aya knew otherwise and, apparently, so did the High Priest.

He had meant to scare the heir's location from Aya by tying her here, but it was of little consequence that he had failed. He had informants in every village and spies in every *nome*. He would set his minions upon the North, focusing his attentions on the Delta, where Tausret had made her capital.

Aya could picture the High Priest's spies combing the Delta's waterways and sifting through its cities. *We seek a young man of unusually good education*, they would say, flashing the image of a triangle inside a circle. *He wears this tattoo somewhere upon his skin.*

A bounty would be offered and peasants from Memphis to Avaris would jump at the chance to collect. Eventually, the young man would be found—Tausret's son, the last living god in Egypt—and slaughtered like a bull.

The corrupt High Priest would then only have to defeat the rebel General Setnakht, an easy enough endeavour when he combined Pharaoh's standing army with his own loyalists. And thus a new dynasty would be founded, a new history chiselled into stone. The priest would rob the treasury to build his monuments and neglect the peasants, just as he had done in his tenure at the Temple of Amun. Egypt would be ruined.

And Aya could do nothing about it. She could only stare into the inky blackness and wait for her end to come.

She passed the moments reciting stories inside her head.

This is a tale of two brothers, one from the North and one from the South...

Words had power; they carried magic.

This is the story of the eloquent peasant. He never knew his words were recorded for the pleasure of the King...

When woven into a tale, words could cradle the heart.

This is the story of Sinuhe who wandered far from his home. 'Take me back, long road. Take me home to Egypt...'

Still, there did not seem to be enough words in the world to allay her misery.

Her back ached, her stomach throbbed and her throat scratched with thirst. How long would she survive, bound as she was, without the ability to move? She did not wish to know. Time was passing so slowly, as if it had become a frozen thing, giving her the opportunity to consider all the things she had never done.

She had never ridden a horse or tended a garden. She had never visited her father's homeland, or learned how to properly shoot an arrow. She had failed in her efforts to learn Akkadian and had never once gone swimming in the Great Green Sea.

She had never before fallen in love.

A tear surfaced. Of all the things to make her weep! She had always suspected romantic love to be a kind of madness—a chaotic whirlwind of souls that always seemed to end in woe.

Why did she care that she had never fallen in love? She had certainly enjoyed the pleasures of the flesh. Like all young women, she had attended the Festival of Drunkenness and indulged in its holy rites. She had painted her body with henna and anointed it with frankincense oil and stepped inside the goddess's temple, where she had selected from among the many eager young men.

'Will you make me your Hathor?' she had asked, several different times over the years. Always her chosen partner had accepted and they would share a cup of beer and lie together, helping to ensure that season's flood.

Though now, at her advanced age of four and twenty, even that sacred indulgence had lost much of its intrigue.

Once, Aya had made bold to ask Pharaoh if she had ever fallen in love.

'Long ago,' Tausret had admitted with a mysterious grin. She had pressed her fingers to her lips in the sign of a secret. 'With a Libyan man—a warrior. He had blue eyes just like yours.'

'How did you know it was love? How did it feel?'

'As though my soul opened up and gifts began to flow out of it,' Tausret had said, her dark eyes sparkling.

Aya had frowned.

'As though I could embrace the hippos and kiss the crocodiles,' Tausret had added, laughing.

'You jest, Mistress?' Tausret never jested. She rarely even smiled.

'I merely attempt to describe the indescribable,' Tausret had waxed. 'How I wish that you could experience it for yourself, Aya! One day you will.'

'But how will I know it is love?' Aya had asked.

'You will feel as if you are a heavy stone who has suddenly exploded into a cloud of dust.'

It was true, then—love was madness. Clearly it was, if it could inspire the Living God to spout such strange poetry.

Pah! Life was mad enough as it was. Besides, romantic love usually required the participation of a man and men could not be trusted.

Did you trust your Libyan? That was what she should have asked Tausret that day. Certainly the answer would have been no. For a woman in power, men were as treacherous as a *wadi* in a storm.

Or a priest inside a tomb.

Her stomach continued to ache and she was clinging to each breath as if it were a memory.

'The will of Osiris,' she said. 'Let it be done.'

* * *

There it was again—the whisper. It diffused into the air like a puff of smoke. It was louder this time and he could distinguish the words: *'The will of Osiris. Let it be done.'*

He was hearing things now. He had been stuffed inside this wooden oven for so long that his mind had been cooked.

Unless Pharaoh herself had issued the whisper. But that was impossible.

It would be many hours before Pharaoh's *akh*, her transfigured spirit, would return from its journey. Until then, the only soul inside the chamber was Intef, along with a dried, withered mummy inside a coffin of gold.

And the soft echo of a sigh.

Intef blinked. First whispers and now a sigh? But it could not be so. Surely it was Intef himself who had sighed.

He moved his sweaty brow against the soft linen surrounding him. It had grown warmer inside the chamber since the entryway had been sealed. He would need to break through those mud bricks soon.

Intef recalled how the mad old woman had protested the setting of the bricks to seal the chamber. Did she not understand the necessity of sealing the chamber? Tomb robbery was a veritable plague across Egypt and especially here, in the Pharaohs' royal burial grounds.

Though it was possible the woman had not been protesting the sealing of the chamber itself, but merely its contents. *'You will not find him,'* she had added in a whisper, referring to the fabled heir to the throne.

Perhaps the woman had truly lost her wits. Everyone knew that Tausret had been unable to produce an heir for her late husband, Pharaoh Seti the Second. Tausret's fallow field was so widely known that it had lately become the topic of songs and laments. In a sense it was the very reason Intef was here.

Intef paused, hearing another noise. He was certain that he had not produced it. It seemed to have come from the middle of the chamber.

'*Oouu...*'

Not a sigh, but a strange, plaintive sound that might have been emanating from the sarcophagus itself. He focused his attention, hardly believing his ears. It sounded very much like a woman crying.

Had one of the slaves been left behind? It could not be. To bury a person inside a house of eternity was against the law—slave or not. It was also contrary to every religious text that had ever been written. There could be only one woman inside this House of Eternity, and she was no longer of this world.

'*Oouu...*'

There it was again. Intef's whole body stiffened. *This is not real*, he told himself, and then thought back to Hepu's grave advice. No matter what Intef did, he must not panic. 'The will of Osiris,' he said. 'Let it be done.' He gripped his bronze chisel and wedged it between the wood.

There was the sound of splitting wood, and Aya nearly jumped out of her skin. 'Pharaoh?' No, it could not be. The *akh* of her beloved mistress was well on its way to the Underworld by now.

Was it not?

Aya's heart pounded. 'Pharaoh Tausret?' she said again. She wiped her eyes against her bound hands and peered into the darkness.

'Stand down, wretched demon!' shouted a deep, masculine voice.

Aya shrieked. She strained against her bonds, craning her neck.

'Who speaks, by the gods?' commanded Aya. 'Name yourself!'

There was a loud crash, as if a piece of holy furniture had just been destroyed. 'Mother of—'

'Cease your cursing!' shouted Aya. 'Identify yourself!'

'Identify myself?' gasped the spirit. 'Identify yourself!'

'I am Aya, Pharaoh's Most Beloved Advisor.' Her voice was trembling. 'Speak your name!'

'I am Intef, son of Sharek, soldier of Egypt,' the voice said. 'I—I seem to have lost the feeling in my legs.'

Aya paused. The spirit had a title? And legs?

'Then you claim that you are…living?' Aya asked. Madness was taking her, surely. It was the only explanation for what she thought she heard.

'I know that I am living!' the man—Intef—shouted. 'I should ask you the same.'

'I am very much living,' said Aya. This was the strangest conversation she had ever had.

'Well, now that we have determined that we are living, I can tell you that in this moment, I quite wish to die.'

This was truly odd. 'Why do you wish to die?' she asked.

'Because it feels as though a thousand tiny scorpions are travelling down my legs, stinging as they go.'

Aya nearly laughed. Scorpions! Travelling down the legs of a real man in real pain!

He moaned. 'My legs are on fire.' He seemed to be sucking the air through his very teeth.

'They are merely returning to life,' Aya explained, feeling as if she were describing her own spirit. 'Have patience... Intef.'

Intef, she thought—after that line of old warrior kings. She was not alone. On the contrary, she was accompanied by a warrior. Slowly, her sobs returned, but this time they were joyous.

At length his seething breaths subsided. 'Why do you weep?' he asked.

'I am...grateful to hear your voice.'

'You scold me for cursing and now you are grateful to hear my voice?'

'Are you not grateful to hear mine?'

Another pause. 'I had not expected to find a... woman in this House of Eternity,' he said. 'A living one, anyway.' He laughed then—a deep, gravelly growl that might have belonged to the King of the demons himself.

Aya felt her skin tickle with fear. 'You refer to Pharaoh, the Powerful One, Chosen of Mut, Daughter of Re, Lady of Upper and Lower Egypt?'

'I assume she is the only other woman in this chamber,' said Intef. 'Unless the Powerful One has also brought along her flock of wigmakers?'

Aya stifled a gasp. Did this man have no respect for the sanctity of the deceased? Aya prepared herself to issue another scolding, then paused.

'What, I beg, are you doing in this House of Eternity, Intef, son of Sharek?'

'What do you think I am doing?'

She made her voice meek. 'Have you come to save me from murderous priests?'

Intef spouted a laugh. 'Not quite.'

Aya felt her stomach twist into a knot. He had not come to rescue her, or aid her in any way. Of course not. He had come to aid himself. This man was a tomb robber.

'I fear that you are here for a nefarious purpose,' she ventured.

Intef said nothing in response and Aya's heart filled with horror. Tomb robbers were the lowest and rudest of men. They were desecrators and defilers. They snubbed their noses at the gods and placed the souls of the deceased in peril. And yet it seemed that Aya's own life now depended on one.

'How did you get here?' she asked.

'I should ask you the same,' he said. When she did not respond he said, 'I was smuggled inside a locked chest.'

'And how did you release the lock?' she asked.

'How do you think?'

'Force?'

'I happen to be rather strong. And I carry a large chisel.'

Aya shuddered.

She perceived movement in the darkness. Intef seemed to be straining to stand. She heard another piece of wood slide across the floor and wondered which of the sacred chests he had destroyed.

Whichever chest it was, its contents had been despoiled by contact with the man's skin. And that—Aya realised—was just the beginning of the desecration he planned.

'Call to me,' Intef said across the darkness. 'So that I may find you.' Aya shut her mouth. Suddenly she did not wish to be found.

'You are tied, are you not?' asked Intef. 'The High Priest said something about rope.'

Aya heard his footfalls as he neared. 'It would be helpful if you would indicate your location,' he said and she felt the weight of his body collapse atop hers.

'Get off of me!' she shrieked.

'I am trying.' A groping hand grazed her thigh, then another pressed against her waist. 'Where is the rope?' he demanded.

'Just here around my wrists. Please... I—' She felt a hand graze her breast and gasped.

'Further up,' she managed to say. Her heart pounded as his hands finally found her bound wrists. She exhaled.

'Do not celebrate yet.' She sensed him moving away from her. He called across the chamber, 'I think I have found what is anchoring the rope.'

'What is it?'

'A very large chair.'

The sacred Horus throne. 'You must not touch it.'

He made a loud straining noise, as if he was trying to lift it. 'What you are attempting is sacrilege,' she warned.

'I am not attempting, I am doing,' he said with a heave.

'It is a crime punishable by—'

'Do you wish to discuss levels of impiety or do you wish to be freed?'

She drew a breath. 'To lift the Horus throne requires the strength of four men.'

'Or the strength of one soldier.'

She held her tongue. Between his next series of heaves, he began to whistle a cheery tune. Who was this arrogant demon and how dare he whistle in a place like this? 'Seth's bloody—' he said at last, swallowing the last part of the curse.

Aya supposed she should have been grateful for his restraint, but she could only cringe as he returned to where Aya lay and she sensed him taking his seat beside her head. 'It is only because I have not had any sustenance that I cannot lift the throne,' he boasted. 'I am merely weakened by my hunger and thirst.'

'Of course,' said Aya.

'If only I had a dagger, I could easily sever your bonds.'

'You did not bring a dagger?'

'A dagger would have made me even heavier inside the chest. Besides, I knew I would have my pick of daggers once I gained entry to the tomb.'

'Have your pick of them?' Aya repeated, her anger surging. 'The jewel-encrusted golden ones, you mean?'

'Precisely.'

Aya's heart roared. The audacity of this man! The ribald frankness with which he described his planned pillaging of this sacred house!

'Do you happen to know where those daggers have been stored?' he asked.

'I am afraid I have no idea,' she lied.

He sat puzzling for many long moments and she hoped he would not become frustrated. Surely a man such as him would have a short temper.

'I am grateful for your efforts,' she added out of fear.

'Do you usually offer thanks before it has been earned?' he replied.

Aya swallowed her anger. 'What tools did you bring with you?'

'A hammer and chisel.'

Aya paused. She had been expecting him to say a

shovel, for she assumed that the only way out of this tomb was to dig through the mass of rocks and earth with which the long entry corridor was currently being filled. 'Do you mean to chisel your way out, then? Is that your plan?'

No response.

'What other tools did you bring?' she asked.

'Flint to light a torch.'

'Well?'

Chapter Four

Flint. A flame. He could sever the rope by means of one. It was a good idea and he certainly would have thought of it himself momentarily. It irked him that she had done so first. She was one of those grandmotherly types who seemed to delight in her superior knowledge of things. He could almost sense her smirking beneath her wrinkles.

Yet she was right. By setting fire to the rope with which she had been tied he could not only free her, but fashion a torch with the scorched ends.

But should he free her? It was clear that he was going to have a problem with this woman, whatever he did. From the way she had corrected his use of language to the derision in her tone when she had asked about the daggers, she was going to make his job more difficult.

He should have had the foresight to lie to her. He should have told her that he was indeed sent to save her, that she had hidden allies in the Temple of Amun or some other nonsense.

Though once he chiselled his way out of this tomb, he and his fellow tomb raiders would be taking much more than just a few jewel-encrusted daggers. The sooner this woman—what had she called herself? Aya? As soon as Aya came to terms with this inevitability, the easier his job would be.

Still, he sensed he needed to be careful with her. If she was anything like her monarch, then she was dangerous and even ruthless. It was rumoured that Pharaoh Tausret had killed her late husband Seti's heir, an innocent young man whom Seti had conceived with a harem wife.

If Aya really was the beloved counsellor she claimed to be, then surely she was implicated in that merciless deed. Intef feared that setting her free would be something like cutting the leash off a crocodile.

If only she were a common tomb robber, her treachery would be wholly manageable. The two could take turns chiselling through the limestone and come to some arrangement about the tomb's…harvest.

According to Intef's orders, it was going to take nine days to chisel his way out. With the aid of a partner they could work continuously and it would only take four or five.

But she was no partner. She was the kind of highborn woman who cringed when a lowly soldier set his hands on the golden throne. What would she do when he began to eat the holy breads? he wondered. How would she respond when he filled one of Pharaoh's golden goblets with beer and took a long, gluttonous drink?

He returned to the middle of the chamber and gazed down at the rope. If he did not untie her, he would have to be responsible for caring for her himself. And what then?

He was here to complete a mission—the most important mission in Egypt. General Setnakht needed treasure to grow his ranks and seize the double crown once and for all. If Intef and his fellow tomb raiders could gather enough treasure here, it was possible that the General could buy himself an entire army. He could win the crown with a simple show of force. There might not have to be a fight and Intef was cursedly tired of fighting.

He retrieved his flint from the inside pocket of his kilt and launched his spark.

Flames erupted on the first try and he coaxed them through the fibres of the rope until it was severed in two.

'You may untie yourself now,' he called in the direction of the shrine. He blew on the burning fibres and severed another part of the rope, fashioning a makeshift torch. He rounded the corner of the shrine with his light. The old woman had more than untied herself. She had disappeared.

'Aya?'

He felt a warm breath in his ear and a sharp prick against his back. 'Drop the torch.' He let the torch fall to the floor as a slender arm squeezed around his neck. 'If you make any movement at all, I will kill you,' she said. She moved the sharp object to the base of his throat.

Like a freed crocodile.

'I am a soldier and protector of Egypt,' he said. He was both stronger and smarter than this woman, or so he assured himself. 'Do you really mean to kill me?'

'Precisely.'

He did not believe her, despite her unexpectedly firm grip around his neck. 'It is wrong to take a person's life,' he remarked.

'It is worse to take a person's afterlife.'

Thankfully the torch still smouldered on the floor and he caught a glimpse of the weapon she held—an arrowhead of the finest obsidian. It seemed she could deliver his death in an instant.

'You would kill a man inside a house of eternity?' he asked. He could sense a trembling in her hand.

'I would kill a man who would despoil that house.'

'And when that man's corpse fills that house with the stink of death?'

'The stink of triumph over evil.'

'Only the god Osiris may judge what is evil.' He reached for her arm, but she pressed the flat of the arrowhead harder against his neck.

'I will not allow you to rob this sacred house,' she said. There was fear inside her voice. He could feel the heavy thrum of her heart against his back. She seemed to be trying to gather the will to kill him.

He would have to seize both her arms at once, then quickly duck his head, but he needed to find the right moment.

'You would kill a man before he has done anything wrong?'

'I loathe men like you,' she said. 'You are a stain on the banner of Great Egypt.'

'You cannot escape this tomb alone.'

'I am certainly capable of wielding a hammer and chisel.'

'Of course you are—perhaps for several hours,' he mused, 'but you would quickly tire. You would need to work for months. What you do not understand is that the god Shu does not enter here. After only eight or nine days, the air will grow sour.'

She paused, as if she had not considered that particular truth. 'I will dig my way out, then.' Another slight loosening of her grip.

'Dirty, suffocating work,' he commented blithely, 'and I doubt you could break through the brick seals to the chambers.'

'The mortar has yet to set. It will be easy enough to breach.'

'Easy? The final seal will be as hard as rock by the time you reach it. And even if you could emerge from the entrance, what would you say to the guards of the Kings' Valley? The Medjay are trained to kill intruders. How would you convince them not to kill you?'

'I am confident,' she said with no confidence at all, and that was his cue. In a single movement, he ducked under her grip. Then he seized her wrists.

'Drop the arrowhead,' he commanded, staring at her shadowy fist. 'Now!' She appeared to open her hand, but as he moved to catch what he expected to be the falling weapon she yanked her other wrist from his grasp and placed the arrowhead in her own mouth.

She lurched away from him, writhing and kicking in an attempt to free herself. But he lunged forward, pushing her off balance. Together they went tumbling to the floor.

He landed atop her, crushing her beneath his weight. 'Are you harmed?' he asked, though he could not think of why he was so worried about her well-being. She had just tried to kill him.

She whimpered a small assent. She was unharmed, thank the gods. The fallen torch burned just near her head and, as he lifted his own head, he beheld her shadowy face for the first time.

His breath caught in his throat.

She was no hardened old crone—that was startlingly clear. The flickering torchlight revealed a woman in her prime, with full cheeks, shapely red lips and strange, kohl-stained eyes the colour of the sea.

Seizing on his hesitation, she lurched her head forward and smashed it against his. A sharp pain split across his skull and tiny streaks of light obscured his vision.

He swung his legs astride her and sat up, keeping her wrists pinned to the floor with his hands.

'Spit out the blade,' he commanded, as she slowly came back into focus. Curse the gods, she was beautiful. 'Do it now.'

When she refused, he considered his options. He could attempt to roll her over, though that would require him to briefly release her arms. Too risky.

He could pull her hands together and try to hold them with one of his, thus freeing his other hand to extract the arrowhead. But he doubted his fingers would have enough force to pry open her teeth. Besides, he did not wish to harm her.

He had never been so paralysed by inaction. As he gazed down at her strange blue eyes, he felt an odd kind of humming sensation deep in his stomach. If he were not defending himself against a violent enemy, he might have believed it a twinge of lust.

She exhaled and he felt an unwanted quickening of his blood to his extremities. His heart thumped out a strange rhythm.

Her expression was grim. Her lips were tight and colourless against her face and the flare of her nostrils suggested the depths of her anger.

She obviously hated him—so much so that she seemed unable to calm her breaths. He imagined the arrowhead she held in her mouth, with her just waiting for a chance to use it on him again. There was not a

woman in the world he should have desired less and yet
there it was—that deep hum slowly becoming a roar.

By all the wicked gods.

'Well?' she said.

Chapter Five

'Well, what?' he asked, though his eyes were not projecting the kind of curiosity she might have expected would accompany such a query. Instead, they seemed to be smouldering. At her.

Either he was experiencing some lusty memory, or he could barely contain his anger towards her. She was rather certain it was the latter.

'Are you going to let me go?' she asked.

'Do you think me a fool? Spit out the blade.'

The blade was her only weapon—the only advantage she currently had against him. She could not give it up.

She assessed her situation. He had positioned himself too far down the length of her body for her to be able to use her legs against him. How could she get him to bend forward towards her and expose his holiest, most tender parts? An idea surfaced.

'Are you going to kiss me or not?' she asked.

It was the only thing she could think of to give herself the advantage. In order to kiss her lips, he would have to lean forward and lift his body off of her hips, exposing himself. A quick raise of her knee would be all it would take to send him reeling.

'You wish for me to *kiss* you?'

She nodded vigorously.

So that I may deliver you the ultimate pain.

It was an admittedly unneighbourly plan, but he was an unneighbourly man. Did he expect her to simply welcome the plunder of her mistress's tomb?

She had acted impulsively by threatening him with the arrowhead, but it was too late to turn back now. Besides, if he was capable of plundering a tomb, what other things might he feel entitled to take without asking?

She needed to speak to him in the only language men such as him knew—that of force. She only wished she were better trained to express herself in that particular tongue.

'You have obviously bested me,' she cooed. 'Why not give me a kiss?'

The torchlight flared, illuminating his face, and she beheld him for the first time. His scathing dark eyes perched over a nose that thought itself clever. His brown skin glowed beneath a sheen of villainous sweat. His fiendish eyebrows were so long and sleek they looked like wings.

But of course he would be handsome. All wicked men were. There would have been too much justice in the world if his appearance had actually matched the state of his soul.

'Forgive me for not trusting your intentions,' he remarked. His eyes sparkled with something resembling humour. 'It is difficult to believe you would wish to kiss me after you just tried to kill me.'

His casual tone stirred her wrath. Was her effort so very trifling that it struck him as funny? Very well, she would embrace the role.

'Do you really think I could have harmed you with

this little thing?' Aya stuck out her tongue to demonstrate the arrowhead and saw his expression change. He raised a winged brow and his dark eyes burrowed into her. She felt a pang of heat deep in her stomach.

She sensed that she had just waded into a pool without a bottom. She quickly returned the arrowhead to her mouth and gathered herself. She could not show fear or hesitation. Unscrupulous men feasted on such emotions.

A quick, sharp kick, then into the shadows.

She affected a playful pout. 'If you want the blade, then come and get it.'

It was the most unusual invitation he had ever received from an enemy, though admittedly he had never faced an enemy such as she. Still, he knew he would be a fool to accept it.

She was clearly planning to bite off his tongue. Or worse, she was planning to slice it off with the very arrowhead she cradled gently inside her mouth.

Gods, that mouth. It was the most sensuous thing he had ever seen. When she pursed it in disapproval, it resembled nothing so much as a lotus in bloom. Her eyes, in contrast, gave nothing away. They were as blue as the sky and as distant as the clouds. Together, her lips and eyes seemed to be conspiring against his will. The hot and the cold. The carnal and the sublime.

Perhaps he was still experiencing the deleterious effects of his confinement. It was possible that he had merely conjured her: a vision to explain the weakness in his limbs and the spinning in his head.

Or perhaps she had been sent by Tausret herself— a beautiful, dangerous spirit created to distract Intef from his purpose here.

Yet she did not seem like an enchantress. On the contrary, she appeared to have no awareness of her own beauty and her attempt at seduction had all the marks of a novice. Did she really think him so dull-witted as to take such bait?

He bent forward tentatively and caught wind of her scent—a heady mix of lavender, myrrh and insincerity.

But there was something else in the air around her. Something delicious and womanly. He breathed in more deeply and it was as if the scent alone could quench his thirst. He bent closer. By the gods, she smelled like seduction itself.

This was a bad idea.

'I will not kiss a woman who is beneath my restraint,' he stated, bending away.

'Then release me.'

'Release the arrowhead first.'

Then she did something totally unexpected. She obeyed him. Abandoning her pout, she spat the offending weapon to the floor.

'There,' she said. 'Now will you kiss me?'

She did not know which was more confounding, his hesitation or the way his eyes lingered so long on her lips.

In retaliation, she studied his lips, which were far too lush and generous to belong to a man like him.

Why was he not kissing her? Did men not usually seize upon such invitations? She had spat out the weapon, after all. He was no longer in any immediate danger. Was it her appearance itself that repulsed him?

It would not have been the first time. Egyptian men, especially Southerners, were often repulsed by her strange combination of features. She was not Egyptian enough to desire and not Libyan enough to denounce.

Still, she was a woman and he was a man, and it was quite dark, even with the torch.

Now that torch flickered and they stared at each other—two archers who had run out of arrows. Who would give up first?

Not Aya. Clenching her stomach muscles, she lifted her torso off the floor, leaving only a hand's width of space between their two faces. 'Why will you not kiss me?' she breathed.

His voice smouldered. 'You must kiss me first.'

He was watching her from beneath those impossible brows, his expression full of menace. He lifted his hands from her wrists, pretending to give her the opportunity to escape.

Barbarian man. He was trying to scare her. He was expecting her to run, only to pull her back beneath his control. She would not give him the satisfaction. She was a noble woman—an advisor to a pharaoh. She ran when she decided to run.

She sat up, braced her arms behind her and pressed her lips to his.

His eyes flared and she felt the rush of his breath into her mouth. Good—let him be surprised. He was not the only one who could assert his will. Though in truth her will felt rather flimsy as his mouth encompassed hers. He pushed back at her, tilting his head in order to deepen the kiss. Her stomach flooded with heat.

He moved his mouth over hers, opening and closing in a kind of controlled abandon. Curse his lips. They were softer and lusher and vastly more pleasurable than she had even imagined. They were trembling slightly, as if with nervousness.

Lust rioted through her. It was as if he wanted her after all, despite her appearance.

May the gods forgive me, she said to herself, realising she wanted him back.

Their lips began to move together in a steady rhythm.

She was vaguely aware of the need to lie back on the floor, to draw him down with her and position him for her show of force. But for the moment she could only marvel at how good it felt to kiss him.

This is a trap, he told himself.

There was no other reason for her to invite such intimacy—unless he was mistaken about her feelings towards him. She had said she loathed him, had she not? She had obviously wished him dead. Yet her kiss was like life itself—served up with a generous sprinkling of lust.

How good it felt to kiss her. Their lips danced as if in time to the same propulsive lute. Perhaps she had changed her mind about him. Maybe in the time between now and when she had pressed the arrowhead against his neck she had realised that he was in fact her only hope for survival.

Not likely. Her loyalty for her departed Pharaoh was as fierce as it was obvious. At any moment, she would surely attempt another head smashing, or bite down hard upon his tongue. Still, it was difficult not to feel anything but excitement as they shared the same warm breath.

He gave her lower lip the gentlest of sucks. She sighed and he felt his desire spike. The sistrums of logic sounded, warning him to retreat. He ignored them.

He swept his tongue into the soft cavern of her mouth.

Had he gone mad? He was kissing a woman who had attacked him, who had openly vowed to see him dead.

He needed to get as far away from her as he could. Instead he pushed his tongue deeper.

His tongue was plundering. It moved through her mouth, taking everything it wished. She knew she should stop him, but she did not want to.

He tasted like lavender and beer, fresh and tangy, with a hint of salt. It had been many hours since she had eaten any food. Surely that was reason he tasted so good. His hand moved up through her hair, sending ripples of sensation down her neck. She felt her limbs relax as he gently cradled her head.

This was not part of the plan, though at the moment she could not remember exactly what that plan was. She could only meet his tongue with her own, for it seemed the two appendages had urgent business together.

He pulled her towards him, deepening the kiss. Her whole body seemed to fill with light. She could not recall a kiss ever feeling this right and she doubted her own mind. At the festivals, she had kissed her partners with great passion, for that was what the goddess demanded.

There was no divine spirit observing her now, however, and yet all she wanted to do was keep kissing.

She wondered if it was a simple matter of contrast—that anything would feel good after being left for dead. Surely that was the reason for the pangs of sensation travelling down her limbs, the strange excitement in her heart. She was simply returning to life.

He seemed to be doing the same, for she could feel the length of his arousal pressing against her stomach as his tongue continued to coil with hers. The sensation should have terrified her, but instead warmth rushed through her in a secret torrent.

He was her enemy, yet she had never felt so at ease in the arms of a man. Was this some sort of deception? But it was she who was supposed to be deceiving him!

She fought to recover her wits as he eased her to the ground. She lay back, feeling like a reed bending beneath a mighty lion.

He raised his head to observe her and there was that fire in his eyes. She could practically hear its windy flames. It was a man's passion and it was all for her.

But it could not be. She was not the kind of woman men were passionate for. She was an advisor to a pharaoh.

Though not any more.

She looked around her, slowly realising that he had pushed her into the position she had desired all along. His hips had lifted off hers, exposing the most vulnerable part of him to her waiting leg. She moved it into striking distance.

She had to do it, lest he believe her weak, or easily seduced, or tacitly offering him a gift she did not wish to give. A show of force—that was what was needed now. This was her chance.

'Forgive me,' she whispered.

Chapter Six

Forgive her? What was there to forgive?

Then he felt it—a pain so poignant that it made him lose his breath. It shot up into his stomach and then directly to his head, which seemed to burst into a thousand shards.

He reeled back in agony. She had kicked him, the little croc. She had thrust her thigh into the most sensitive part of his body and delivered a blow so painful that it was sending tears into his eyes.

She rolled out from beneath him as pain coursed through him in unrelenting waves and he watched her disappear into the darkness beyond the torchlight.

He took the arrowhead in his hand and began to laugh. Not since the Battle of the White Desert, when a Libyan spear thrower had stuck him in the back of the thigh, had he felt so much pain.

He collapsed back on to the tile floor, foetal and laughing through his tears. She was not only more dangerous than he had at first thought, she was vastly more interesting.

He tried to think his way through the pain. He put his heart into an imaginary jar and gazed at it from far away. There were endless ways to shield oneself from pain, after all, and over the years Intef had become quite adept at many of them.

There were also many ways to invite pain, including lying helpless before one's enemy. Intef peered around the chamber nervously. There were certainly other arrowheads hidden among Pharaoh's grave goods, along with the arrows to which they were usually attached. As Pharaoh's Most Beloved Advisor, Aya probably knew exactly where they were. She could return any moment with an arrowhead in each fist.

The thought struck him as funnier still. Intef, son of Sharek, the deadliest archer in the southern rebel army, killed by a trembling, terrified servant who had likely never even held a dagger.

'Are you off to find another arrowhead?' he called into the shadows. 'Go ahead, then.' He felt dizzy and his voice was as dry as dust. 'Do your worst.'

He reached for the torch and stood. At the far corner of the room, he could see the frame of a doorway. Crossing to it, he flashed his torch inside to discover a small storage room stacked to the ceiling with wooden chests. Beside the chests was a wall of shelves that had been filled with amphorae.

He could practically feel the cool water running down his throat. He flashed his torch behind him to assure himself that Aya had not followed, then selected one of the containers from the second shelf. He shoved his thumb beneath its wax seal.

He felt vaguely remorseful. It was hot and stuffy inside the tomb and she was probably just as thirsty as he. And while she had caused him a great deal of pain, it had already practically disappeared, yet she was probably still suffering the effects of her failed head blow.

He had killed many enemy soldiers in the line of duty and that was difficult enough, but he had never in all his life had to defend himself against a woman.

A beautiful woman, as it happened, though not in the traditional sense. Her eyes were not the right colour, her nose not the proper length, her skin was too pale and her lips were almost masculine in their fullness.

It was as if the venerable Ennead of Egyptian gods had sat down at their table with a woman from the Black Land of Egypt and a woman from the Red Land of Libya and fashioned someone altogether new.

She was a surprise, this woman, and Intef could not remember the last time he had been surprised.

He removed the seal from the amphora full of water. 'For you, Aya,' he said, raising the container. 'Life, prosperity, health!' He put the jug to his lips and felt his strength increased. He glanced down. Surprisingly, so had his arousal.

He should not have been surprised. He was a lusty man, after all, and he often enjoyed the pleasures of the flesh.

Intef tried to recall the last time he had lain with a woman. Surely after General Setnakht's invasion of Wawat, six months before. A horde of Nubian beauties had descended upon the army's desert camp after a raid, eager to relieve the soldiers of their plunder. Intef vaguely remembered a woman who had offered to rub his shoulders, but could not recall anything more.

He took another long draught of water. Had there been any women from his village lately? Perhaps during the Festival of Drunkenness at the last inundation? But he had not joined in the festival, he remembered now. It had been the second year of drought and the idea of such indulgence had not appealed to him.

A few years ago, there had been the march to occupy the Osiris Temple at Abydos, just after Pharaoh Siptah's murder. A veritable swarm of women had come to greet Setnakht's rebels and Intef was certain that he had taken his pleasure with one of those lusty villagers. But what had she looked like? What had she called herself?

Perhaps his long hours squeezed inside the chest had also squeezed his memory. Or maybe he simply needed a bit of sustenance to stir his recollection.

He looked around the small room and spied a basket of bread atop one of the crates. His stomach roared. Why was he thinking of women at all, entombed as he was in this house of death? He should be thinking of how to drink and eat and avoid losing his life.

Though perhaps it was the very nearness of death that made him consider women at all—lust being one of the more vibrant features of living. So why could he not recall the names and faces of the women with whom he had…lived?

In truth, there was only one he could remember at all…

Her name had been Nebetta. They had grown up together on a temple-owned plantation north of Thebes. Intef did not remember when he had met Nebetta, just as he did not remember when he had learned to speak or walk. He just remembered that she had always been there, like the sunrise or the western hills.

He had liked to tease her. She had been so tall in those early years—much taller than he—and she had never seemed to know what to do with her limbs.

'Be careful not to poke your head in the sky, Nebetta!' he would warn her and she would scold him for being too short to see above the wheat.

He had not really noticed her beauty until his eighteenth year. She had begun to work at her family's date stand in the market at the centre of Thebes and, whenever Intef had visited her, he'd noticed some new miracle. The silken shine in her long dark hair, the flush in her cheeks, the way her green bead necklace seemed to glow against her sepia skin.

'My lotus in bloom!' he would call to her and would know by the tinkle of her laughter that his compliment had hit its mark.

One day Intef had joined his father at a gathering of military recruits in a tavern in the centre of Thebes. Pharaoh Seti's brother, Amenmesse, had been preparing to seize the Horus throne and most of the men of Thebes were joining the fight.

'Amenmesse is the rightful heir!' they had shouted.

Intef had stood beside his father as the recruiting scribe had added their names to the list.

'We are recruiting all over the South,' the scribe had told them. 'We need your help in the search for volunteers.'

When the meeting had concluded, Intef had strolled back through the marketplace, hoping to catch a glimpse of Nebetta. By then he had been so popular among the young women of Thebes that he had been known as The Fisherman, because he always had at least a few young women on his hook.

When he had spotted Nebetta that day at the date stall, he had cast his line in the water. She had been as lovely as a palm standing there, arranging the small fruits.

When she had finally noticed him watching her she had held out a date to him and flashed a grin so dazzling that it had stopped him in his tracks.

'Leave it to you to show up when there are free dates to be had,' she'd jested.

Right then, Intef had realised that he was no longer The Fisherman. He had somehow become the fish.

They had made love that afternoon in the shade of the date palms. When Intef had returned home that night he had been nearly trembling with joy.

'Father, Mother, there is something I must tell you.'

It had been just after sundown and the two of them had been lounging on the roof of their small mud-brick hut, gazing out at the river. The last ferry of the day had just embarked from shore and Intef had watched with strange delight as its big linen sails had caught the wind and headed for the west bank of the river.

'We must pack our kits tonight,' Intef's father had said. 'We leave tomorrow for Edfu.'

'We are leaving Thebes?' Intef had asked.

'Of course we are—did you not hear the recruiter? He needs our help.'

'But it is just a recruiting mission.'

'We volunteered to support General Amenmesse's bid for the throne,' Intef's father had said. 'This is how we do it.'

'But there is no battle. It is a voluntary mission for the able.'

'And we are able,' Intef's father had said. 'Or do you not wish for the rightful heir of Egypt to wear the double crown?'

Intef had frowned. It had seemed to him that it was less a question of succession than it was of the balance of power: Amenmesse's supporters lived in the South, while Seti's resided in the North. It all seemed rather pointless, though he would not tell his father that.

'I need you to come with me, Intef,' his father had added, 'to protect my back.'

Intef had gazed out at the ferry, slowly making its way across the great river. Its passengers had seemed so small against the tide.

'I wish to do what is right, Father.'

He had glanced at his mother, who had nodded gravely. 'I do not need any help in the fields, dear boy.'

'We leave before dawn,' his father had said.

'But it is just a recruiting mission.'

Intef's father had shaken his head. 'You either support Amenmesse or you do not. There is no—'

'Mother, Father, it is Nebetta. I wish to make her my wife.'

Intef's mother had gasped with joy, but Intef's father had frowned.

'You have committed to Amenmesse's army,' he'd said. 'Nebetta can wait.'

The ferry had approached the opposite shore. Intef had seen the pilot pull hard on a line and its sails go slack.

How easy it was for his father to say such things with Intef's mother at his side! he had thought.

'I am so happy for you, Son,' she had said, her eyes full of tears.

'Father?'

His father had stood and crossed to the ladder, then started his way down. 'You are a man now and your life is your own. But remember your duty,' he'd said.

Intef had slept on the roof that night. He'd gazed at Sopdet, the brightest star in the night sky, and decided it was a sign. He would build a hut for Nebetta over the following days and, as soon as it was built, he would make her his wife.

With Nebetta waiting for him in Thebes, he had known he would be able to fight whatever battles awaited him. He would stand strong by his father's side and help put Egypt to rights.

The following day, Intef had woken to the sound of his father's soft footfalls walking away from the hut. He must have sensed Intef watching him, but he had not turned around to look. He'd only walked away slowly across the field and disappeared.

Just a few days later he and his mother had received the news of his father's death.

'They were ambushed by Seti's troops,' the officer had explained. 'They were not even armed.'

'How did he die?' Intef had asked.

'An arrow in the back.'

There had been no Nebetta after that. There had only been the hot sun, the piles of wheat and Intef's solemn vow to ride out with Amenmesse's army.

What he had not done for his father in life, he would do for him in death.

Now, Intef dug inside the basket of food and came upon a small linen pouch. Inside were a dozen perfectly ripe dates. He paused, recalling that day so long ago when he had been offered a date and the promise of love.

There was a reason he did not remember the women he had enjoyed since then. After his father's death, the desire had gone out of him. He felt so little when he lay with a woman now that it usually did not even register in his heart as a memory. He could not even remember the desire to kiss a woman's lips—at least, not until tonight.

Though he knew he should not have been considering Aya as a woman. For his own good, he should be considering her as a dangerous crocodile. There was a reason the priests had locked her in here and they had placed their own souls in peril in doing it. What did she know? Whom did she threaten? Perhaps she had committed some terrible crime. The thought gave him a chill. She was probably stalking him right now, just waiting for him to turn his back.

If she attacked again, he would have no choice but to restore her bonds. He had to stay alive to complete the mission, after all, for the mission was bigger than either of them. He had been a fool to kiss her and to let her stir his lust. Such feelings were more dangerous than they seemed—a lesson he had learned long ago. He was a soldier and a servant of Egypt now. An honourable man. Before anything else, he had to do his duty.

Chapter Seven

She huddled in the shadows, trying to stop her trembling. She feared him, but she feared herself more. Where had the calm, rational advisor to a pharaoh retreated, and who was this panicked, impulsive girl in her place?

She could only thank the gods that the arrowhead had not drawn blood when she had held it to his neck. She had regretted the kick before she had even made it.

She did not wish to harm him. Intef, son of Sharek, a man who had released her from her bonds. A man who, after defending himself against her attack, had worried for her safety.

A man who had treated her with gentleness.

The kiss.

When their lips had touched, it was as if she had stepped into the current of an invisible river. It was not until he eased her back to the floor that she remembered he was her enemy.

And he *was* her enemy. He was a tomb robber, the most wretched of men. His very presence in this sacred space not only threatened Pharaoh's afterlife, but also Aya's current one. How could she know for certain he did not mean to dispose of her at some point, or somehow do her harm? She had already given him ample reason. Besides, crooked men craved conquest. She needed him to know she would not be conquered.

Still, she needed to get out of this tomb and, for that, she needed him. It would not be long before the High Priest's spies found Tausret's heir. If Aya could find him before they did, she could save his life. It was the least she could do for a pharaoh who had given her everything and for an Egypt she loved with all her heart.

The light of Intef's torch emanated from one of the storage rooms. She stood and made her way towards it.

'I see you have discovered the holy amphorae,' she said, glancing at the large jugs lining the shelves all around him.

He did not even lift his head to greet her. 'That is what you have to say after trying to take my life?'

He was concentrating on an open amphora, which he had placed in the middle of his folded legs. Beside him lay a smouldering coal brazier and a half-eaten loaf of bread.

'Forgive me,' she said.

'The last time you said that, you followed it with a rather punishing kick.'

'I apologise.'

'You apologise? Well, that is a first. Scores of men have tried to wound me in my short time on this earth, but none has ever apologised for it.'

'I am not like other men,' she stated.

'Well, you certainly are not,' he said. Finally, he looked up at her. 'Mother of Mut.'

'It is a grave sin to curse. Have you no reverence at all?'

'I curse when something warrants cursing.' He was staring at her brazenly.

'Nothing warrants cursing in this sacred home.'

'Not even the way you look?'

She cringed. People had reacted to her appearance with derision all her life, but most had the decency not to speak their feelings aloud.

'Here, catch,' he said. He tossed her the bread.

She stared at the half-eaten loaf in anguish. It had been spoiled by his lips—it could never be returned to Pharaoh.

'Just eat it,' he said. 'It cannot be made whole again.'

He was right, of course. They would have to eat many more sacred loaves and drink many more amphorae of beer if they wished to escape this tomb.

'Which company did you say you fought for?' she asked.

'I am currently with the mighty Sons of Ra.'

'Currently? Does a soldier not remain with his company throughout his career?'

'I am often called upon to train others.'

'In treachery?'

He ignored the jab. 'Archery.'

So he was an archer, then. He certainly had the chest of an archer—all lean muscle and stark bone. But a trainer? A teacher of men? If he was so accomplished, then what was he doing inside this tomb at all?

'I have not heard of the Sons of Ra,' Aya said, 'and I did not know that soldiers were moved between companies to provide training. You must be quite an expert.'

'I am the very best.'

She scanned his expression in search of the lie and

was instantly thwarted by two formidable defences: handsomeness and conceit.

He was grinning at her even now, trying to distract her. He had probably been using his good looks to his advantage all his life.

'It is strange that I have not heard of you,' she said. 'Being such a distinguished archer.'

'My company is stationed at a fort further south,' he said. 'It is doubtful you would have heard of us.' His eyes shifted a little. 'Your Pharaoh was woefully removed from things in the Delta.'

'The Delta in the North occupies a more strategic position than Thebes does here in the South,' she noted calmly. 'The North is a better place to address the Asiatic threat, as well as the confederation of Sea Peoples.'

He rolled his eyes. 'You do not agree?' she asked.

'There is no disagreeing with a northerner.'

Aya held her temper. 'I will gently remind you that it was Pharaoh Tausret's own grandfather who built the northern palace at Pi-Rameses. Perhaps you have heard of him? He was called Rameses the Second, otherwise known as Rameses the Great Ancestor. He certainly seems to have believed in the Asiatic threat.'

'The Asiatic threat in the North is one thing; the Nubian threat in the South is quite another.'

Yes, the Nubian threat is much less threatening! Aya stopped herself from saying it. She was supposed to be striking a deal with this man, not arguing politics.

'The land of Egypt faces many threats,' she stated neutrally.

'Indeed it does. And yet what concerns me most is the threat standing before me...' He paused. 'The Libyan threat.'

He smirked and her teeth locked together inside her mouth. She was beginning to understand better why she had nearly slit his throat.

'I apologise if my appearance threatens you,' she hissed.

'Then you are Libyan?' He pointed to his own eyes, indicating the colour of hers.

'Part Libyan, part Egyptian.'

People never saw the Egyptian part of Aya, despite her full lips and dark hair. They only noticed her pale skin and blue eyes—features of the enemy.

He squinted, as if studying a scroll. 'I do not believe you are a killer.'

'Why do you not believe it?'

'For one thing, you are a woman.'

'Women are just as capable as men of being killers.'

'And yet they do not kill with the frequency of men. That is irrefutable.'

'Only because they are not allowed to become soldiers or guards.'

'And rightly so.' He glared at her. 'Women should give life, not take it away.'

'The same could be said of men, could it not?' asked Aya. She had had this debate many times before, with many similar men. The next thing he was going to say was that the gods created men to sow the seed and women to cultivate the field.

'You are too beautiful to be a killer,' he remarked instead.

The comment was unexpected—and totally illogical. Had he not just moments before insulted her appearance? She opened her mouth to protest, then felt a strange heat colonising the surface of her skin. By the time she thought of an appropriate response, he was lifting the jug to his lips.

Glug, glug, glug.

She had never heard a man drink so loudly. Nor had she ever wished for a drink of water more. Banish him and his soldier's manners! And curse her skin, which she could feel every second becoming a deeper shade of red.

Too beautiful to be a killer. Ha! 'The beautiful goddess Hathor once nearly destroyed humankind!' she announced.

He placed the amphora on the floor, but his eyes were still drinking—her. 'It is rude to stare,' she said.

'It is indeed,' he said and his eyes said, *Glug, glug, glug.*

She scowled. He grinned.

Surely he was mocking her. Southerners had a particular disdain for Libyans, the people of the Red Land as they called them, and this man was southern to the core. Still, she felt a strange lifting of her spirit. She could count on one hand the times she had been called beautiful in her life.

'You are clearly already experiencing the effects of the beer,' she said. She glanced at the empty amphora beside him, feeling an aggravating thirst in the depths of her own throat.

'It is not beer I drink.' He held the amphora out to her. 'It is water.'

'You are mistaken,' she replied. 'It is unnecessary to provide the deceased with water in the afterlife, for there are rivers and lakes everywhere. There is only wine and beer in this house.'

'And yet I am drinking water,' he insisted. 'Perhaps you are not right about everything.'

He continued to hold the amphora out to her. 'No, thank you,' she said. Accepting a drink would be admitting she was wrong and she did not wish to seem a fool.

'You will need to drink eventually,' he observed.

'I realise that.'

'Well, what are you waiting for? Do you plan to kill me first?' He motioned to one of the chests stacked against the wall. 'Perhaps after I dip into the holy cheese that has been packed into those boxes?'

'You are baiting a crocodile,' she growled. There it was again—the anger. It was bubbling inside her like a spring.

'So the answer is yes? You do plan to kill me?'

She tried to keep her calm. 'I must stop you from robbing this tomb however I can. It is my duty and also my most fervent wish.'

'Well, murder is certainly one way to stop me, though I really do not believe you capable of such a thing.'

'You do not know me,' she breathed.

'And neither do you know me,' said Intef. 'But I will help you along with that. Do you know what I do when a man tries to kill me?'

Aya shook her head.

'I kill him in return.' The mockery was gone from his voice. 'That is how it works.'

Suddenly he was on his feet. She turned to flee, but he caught her by the arm and spun her around. He was standing behind her, squeezing his arm around her neck, just as she had done to him. His other arm was tight around her waist. He spoke gently into her ear. 'Perhaps I should.'

She was like a crocodile stolen from the reeds, well tied and slowly losing its energy to fight. She made one last, writhing effort, then went limp against him. 'Go ahead, then,' she breathed. 'But do it fast. A merciful death.'

The words echoed in his mind and, though he held her, he did not see her, for he was already somewhere else.

He was standing on a vast desert hardpan strewn with bodies of fallen men. It was the aftermath of the Battle of Memphis, and the rebel General Setnakht had prevailed. Behind him, Pharaoh Tausret's men were running for the hills, their blurry images slick in the desert heat.

Before him there was only pain: a field of Tausret's soldiers in varying stages of death. Intef and his partner Ranofer had come to collect their arrows, which had killed all of their victims save one—the man pinned to the ground at their feet.

Intef stared down at the man's smallish figure, a soldier so new to manhood that the stubble remained on his head from his sidelock of youth. He was slashing the air wildly with an imaginary sword, no longer in his right mind.

Intef felt a familiar deadness in his heart. The boy was an Egyptian just like all the rest of the dying—a young man who had found himself on the wrong side of an unnecessary war.

'Whom do you serve?' Ranofer asked the boy, as was the custom.

'I serve Tausret,' the boy said. He slashed his invisible sword at the men's ankles.

'Why do you serve the widow of Seti?' asked Ranofer.

The boy's blood wept from where Intef's arrow still stuck in his thigh. 'She is Pharaoh! A living god.'

'She is a woman,' said Ranofer. 'A woman!'

'Who will bear a divine son!' cried the boy. He had lost all his colour. He would not survive the hour.

'May you walk for ever in the Fields of Yaru,' said Ranofer, and pulled his dagger from its hilt.

'Stop!' cried Intef.

'He will not survive,' said Ranofer. 'He is practically dead already.'

But Intef would not listen. He was digging in his kit for a bandage. If he could just extract the arrow from the boy's thigh, it might be possible to seal the wound.

The boy raised his head one last time. 'May the Devourer of Souls make meals of both of you!' he hissed. 'Now do it. A merciful death!'

Ranofer tossed Intef a glance and Intef turned away. There was a soft gurgle and the sound of the boy's lifeless body collapsing to the ground.

Ranofer stepped to Intef's side, wiping his blade on the cloth of his kilt. 'You are welcome,' he said.

A plume of the boy's blood flowed to the base of Intef's sandals. 'He could have been my own son,' said Intef.

'It is foolish to indulge such a thought,' Ranofer said.

'Egyptians killing Egyptians.'

Ranofer slapped Intef hard across the face. 'Such talk imperils both of us.'

'Apologies,' said Intef, wishing Ranofer would hit him again.

'The boy followed Tausret, the false god,' added Ranofer. 'There was no choice.'

Ranofer was right. There was no choice—not for lowly soldiers such as themselves. In this endless fight for power, they were merely tools.

Intef stared at his bow and arrow, hating it. It was all he could feel any more—hate—and usually not even that. He could not do it any more—this pointless killing. He would not do it. His heart was dying; perhaps it was already dead: What was a united Egypt worth if forged by the blood of Egyptians?

Chapter Eight

'**D**o it now,' Aya was saying. 'Kill me.'

'Kill you?' Intef asked.

'Kill me,' she said, 'and quickly. A merciful death.'

He bent to her ear: 'I am not that kind of man.' He released her, pushing her forward into the low light of the brazier. 'Not any more.'

She stumbled, gathered herself and turned to face him. 'Then what kind of man are you?'

'As I said, I am Intef, son of Sharek, soldier of Egypt and man of honour.'

'If you are a man of honour, then why do you wish to steal from this House of Eternity?'

He paused, imagining how pleasant it would be to admit the truth: *I am here to pillage treasure so that there will be no more killing.*

He sensed a large wall looming between them made entirely of her anger. Judging by the current trembling of her lower lip, Intef knew that it could fall down upon him any second.

'This is the first tomb I have ever entered and I pray to the gods it will be my last,' he said truthfully. 'I come here not out of greed, but out of need. I am here to feed my brothers.' In a sense that was also true.

'Your brothers starve?'

Yes—for victory.

'My father is dead a year now and my four brothers are not yet old enough to till the fields. The grain ration is a pittance. They are always hungry.'

It was a terrible lie, but it seemed to be working. He sensed a change in the quality of the wall between them. It was no longer composed of granite, but of sand.

'Go on,' she said.

'I requested to return to Aswan to help them, but my term of service is twenty years.' That was not true either. Setnakht's rebel army was wholly voluntary. 'I am sure you are aware of the punishment for mutiny.'

'Impalement by a blade through the stomach,' she intoned. 'The same as for tomb robbery.'

'It is a risk I am willing to take. One of my brothers is still suckling at the breast, you see,' he embellished.

His stomach rolled with guilt as he watched a tear slide down her cheek.

'I have not come here to rob Pharaoh of her sustenance in the afterlife,' he explained. 'I have only come to take a few pieces of gold—just enough to see my brothers to adulthood.'

He loathed himself as he watched her produce a cloth from beneath her linen belt and wipe her tears. She was shaking her head. 'I feel foolish for having…acted the way I have towards you.' She hung her head.

Gods, he had never felt so very lowly.

'Where does your commander believe you to be now?' she asked.

'Ah…ill,' he blurted out. 'He believes I am plagued

with the shivering sickness.' A terrible side effect of the lying sickness.

'How much treasure do you plan to steal from this house?' she asked.

'Only enough to sustain my family. I am not the kind of man you believe me to be.'

Nor was he the kind of man he was portraying himself to be, though it should not have bothered him as much as it did. He had lied many times before in the protection of General Setnakht's campaign. It should have been no trouble to do it again now.

'The way I see it, you can kill me and take up my chisel and hope to get out before you perish,' he said. 'Or we can take turns with the chisel and hope to get out before we both perish. But I am telling you now that, unless you attack me directly, I will not kill you. I have seen too many lives lost in my tenure at arms to take another.'

At last—the truth. It was a relief to feel the coolness of it on his tongue. He was weary of life-taking, just as he was weary of the world that contained that life. 'Let us agree to work as allies,' he urged, 'and swear it before the gods, lest our sleep be haunted by demons.'

She stood for many moments searching his eyes. Her beauty was unnerving. It was as if the Lord of the Desert himself had lifted his magic sceptre and created a black-haired goddess with alabaster skin and eyes like secret water holes.

'I am fortunate that you are here,' she said at last. 'I cannot condone your plan, nor can I condemn you for having made it. Let us make our apologies to Pharaoh and Osiris, and pray for your family's health. We shall work together in this. It seems we must.'

* * *

That night—if night it was—Aya found herself inside a memory.

She was standing in Pharaoh Tausret's birthing chamber, gazing out the window at the courtyard below. A remarkably large snake had slithered into view beside the pond. It was dusk and the low rays of the sun were turning the serpent's scaly white skin a haunting crimson.

'Tell me, Aya, what do you see?' Tausret called from her birth chair. She had been labouring since daybreak and still the babe would not come.

'A serpent, Your Majesty,' said Aya. 'A good omen.'

Tausret's midwife rushed across the chamber. 'What kind of snake?' the old woman asked, arriving at Aya's side.

Aya shook her head. The only snakes she knew were the magical kinds that appeared in the sacred stories, or the ones fashioned of gold and posed atop the royal headdress. 'A cobra?'

Together they peered down at the unusually long, white-skinned beast. The midwife gasped. 'Apep,' she whispered. She bent to Aya's ear. 'We must kill it now, lest Tausret lose the child.'

'What is the matter?' called Tausret from across the chamber.

'It is nothing to worry about, Your Majesty,' replied the midwife. 'Aya is going to capture the noble beast right now and return it to the wilds. Come, let us focus on your breathing.'

Aya found Tausret's bow and several arrows and rushed to the courtyard. The snake was moving very slowly into the pond and Aya marvelled at its length. It did resemble Apep, the long, coiling monster that Ra slew each night to save the world from darkness. It was a bad omen indeed.

Aya stepped as close to the snake as she dared and launched her first two arrows. Neither reached its mark. Quickly she launched several more arrows, but it was as if the great snake was surrounded by an invisible shield.

Aya aimed her final arrow at the snake's tail, releasing the projectile just as the beast disappeared into the murky depths. The arrow stuck in the dry ground like the marker of an empty grave.

When Aya returned to the chamber, Tausret lay slumped in her birth chair, the colour drained from her cheeks. The midwife shot Aya a look and Aya shook her head. *I failed*, she said wordlessly. *Apep lives.*

Tears glazed the old woman's eyes. 'Let us move her to the blocks.'

Tausret's hair clung to her face and her eyes seemed far away as Aya and the others carried her to the birthing blocks and placed her feet in the holds.

'I am going to tell you when to push, Your Majesty,' explained the midwife. 'Do you understand?'

But Pharaoh did not even lift her head. 'Leave us,' she muttered.

'Your Majesty?'

'Leave us for a moment, please,' said Tausret. 'I wish to be with Aya alone.'

The midwife shot Aya a look of panic, but seemed to understand. She motioned for the others to follow her as she quietly exited the chamber.

Pharaoh gazed out the window. The setting sun was painting the sky in pink and orange. 'This is what I wish to remember, Aya,' she said at last. 'You and me here, watching the sky. The goodness of the people of Egypt. A man I once loved.'

'Your Majesty, I do not understand,' said Aya. 'You must only—'

'Aya, I am going to die.'

'Your Majesty, just one more push and—'

'Aya, listen to me, for you are—you are my most beloved advisor.'

'I am here.'

'I have a secret to tell you, but you must swear by the Book of Thoth that you will tell no one!'

'I swear.'

Tausret closed her eyes. 'The stories are true. There is an heir.' A feathery grin traversed her lips. 'Right here in Pi-Rameses—my only living child.'

Aya nearly jumped out of her skin. 'Who is he, Your Majesty, that I may bring him to court?'

'No, Aya. Court is no place for a child of mine...' Aya nodded, for there was perhaps no one who understood better. 'I only wish for someone to know the heir exists,' she continued, 'the great-grandchild of Rameses the Great Ancestor, with eyes like yours and the family tattoo—a triangle inside a circle—' Tausret held her belly and cringed in pain. 'Promise me you will tell no one, Aya!'

'I promise.' A pool of blood had formed on the floor. 'Midwife!' Aya cried.

Tausret closed her eyes. 'There is one more thing I ask of you.'

'Anything, Your Majesty.'

'I wish for you to live your life, Aya.' She opened her eyes suddenly. 'Do you hear me? After I go—that is how you may honour me. Do not throw away your days laying offerings at my *ka* statue. Do not punish yourself for imagined crimes. Do not become some selfish man's brood mare.' She gazed down at her bulging stomach. 'Live your life, Aya, in all the ways that I never could. See me off to the next world, but do not turn away from this one.'

Tausret's head rocked backwards and she began to howl in pain.

'Push, Pharaoh,' Aya sobbed. 'Strong Bull! Lady of the Two Lands! Beloved of Maat!'

The midwife and her assistants rushed back into the chamber, but by the time they arrived at her side, Pharaoh was already gone...

Aya awoke in tears. The darkness was so complete that she feared she had died herself. To test her own existence, she folded her trembling hands.

'Aya?' said a man's voice. She tried to respond, but no words came. 'Aya? What is wrong?'

Intef.

'Nothing,' she blurted. She willed her tears away. He had seen too many facets of her weakness already.

'You were crying. It sounds as if you are shivering.'

'You are mistaken.'

She could hear his footfalls as he crossed to the other side of the chamber. She sat up and squeezed her knees to her chest.

She perceived the flare of the torch. He emerged from the shadows, carrying one of Pharaoh's robes, which he gently placed over her body.

Her shivers subsided beneath the weight of the linen and relief flooded her heart. Becalmed, she inhaled the thick garment's lavender scent. It was as if Pharaoh herself had come to comfort her.

'Gratitude,' Aya murmured, but he was already gone.

She closed her eyes. The twelfth hour of the night had surely passed. She prayed for an omen—something to assure her that Pharaoh had successfully made the journey through the Underworld and had been reborn as the god of light.

'Where are you, divine soul?' she whispered. She pictured Tausret in the form of the sun embracing the land of Egypt with her light.

When Aya opened her eyes, she saw Intef's torch. It was coming towards her, a tiny ball of fire, as if he had plucked it from Tausret's fiery head.

He planted himself before her and offered his hand. 'Come. We must begin our work.'

'Just a little more rest,' said Aya. Now it would begin: the desecration of her mistress's tomb, the consumption of the sacred food and drink. The chiselling and the pillaging. The breaking of her very heart.

'Aya?'

'I beg you, just a little more time.'

At last he departed and she was left to contemplate the agreement they had come to hours before. In exchange for Aya's help chiselling, he had agreed to take from the tomb only what was necessary to save his family. Moreover, Aya would be able to choose which items he would take.

She could fill his sacks with gold ingots and silver *deben* and other replaceable bounty, minimising the damage to Pharaoh's cache. His family would be saved and she could spend the rest of her life working to replace what had been taken.

It was a fair solution, which was why she did not trust it. There was something he was not telling her. Something hidden behind that distracting grin.

He crossed the room towards her once again, an amphora in one hand and a torch in the other, and she peered at him through half an eye. The torchlight flickered on the rippling muscles of his stomach, which flexed in rhythm with the bulging muscles of his thighs.

His physique was nearly perfect, despite his advanced age. His short soldier's kilt concealed little. She could see every bump and seam of flesh. His military life had strengthened and hardened him in obvious ways.

But what was she not seeing? Experience had taught her to doubt all agreements—and the men who brokered them. Men who stood close to the throne always wanted to stand closer and, over the years, she had honed the ability to look into men's eyes and discover the nature of their lies.

Intef, however, was an enigma. Instead of discovering the lie in his eyes, she had only discovered the way they seemed to change colour in the torchlight.

He was either utterly sincere, or extremely skilled in concealing his thoughts.

He stood above her now and made a show of peeling the wax off the amphora and tipping it to his lips. 'Pah!' he spat.

'What is it?'

'The beer,' he said. 'It is bubbly and tart, just as beer should be.'

'Then why do you grimace?'

'I was hoping for wine,' he said. 'But tomorrow is a new day.'

'I forbid you to drink the sacred wine!' she exclaimed, then lowered her voice. 'It is the one thing that cannot be replaced.'

'Did we not agree that we will eat and drink from the stores?'

'Yes but not the wine, for it is made from grapes sown—'

'—on the day Pharaoh assumed her reign,' Intef finished Aya's sentence. He started towards the storeroom. 'It is said that the wine of Pharaoh imparts special strength. Thankfully I know right where to find it on the shelves.'

'Do not even think of it!'

'The longer the reign, the finer the vintage,' he called back to her. 'Remind me, how long was Tausret's? She counted Pharaoh Siptah's reign as her own, did she not? Seven years? Eight?' She heard him pull an amphora from the shelf.

Chapter Nine

Aya jumped to her feet and ran across the chamber, forcing herself between Intef and the shelf full of holy amphorae. 'I forbid you from even looking at them!'

He folded his arms and nodded his head, as if congratulating himself. 'Aha! I see that you are able to move after all.'

The realisation hit her all at once: he had never meant to drink the sacred wine.

'Brute!' she shouted. He had outwitted her, though that was not what vexed her the most. It was that terrible, triumphant, god-forsakenly handsome grin he wore. 'Is everything a jest to you?' she asked.

'Is everything so serious to you?'

'My duty is to Pharaoh,' she said, aware that there was very little space between them. She pressed her back against the shelf. 'I must protect her.'

'An honourable sentiment. Perhaps you should have been a soldier.' She could not determine if he was mocking her or not. All she could tell was that he had too many teeth and they were far too white.

'Perhaps you should have been a magician,' she said, 'for you seem to be full of tricks.'

'I had to find some way to get you moving,' he said. 'You were like a half-dead hippo beneath that robe.'

'Ha-ha,' she said. 'You see? I can recognise a jest.'

He shook his head, and stepped away from her. She exhaled, though she could not say why she had been holding her breath.

He gestured to a sheltered area behind a shelf. 'The only thing missing is a good-humoured woman to warm my bed mat,' he said.

'But there is no bed mat.'

He slid her a look. 'A jest,' she said. She forced a smile, then stepped to the side, putting more space between them.

'Such a mirthless grin,' he said. He poured water into a cup and offered it to her.

She stretched her arm to accept the cup and returned to her position several paces away. 'You think me a cold, ill-humoured woman,' she said, staring into the cup.

'On the contrary, I find you full of fire. It is unfortunate that you have no outlet for all that passion.' He poured himself a cup and drank it down.

Was he mocking her again? 'I am advisor to a pharaoh,' she said.

'Such a lofty title! I imagine you have men clamouring to warm your bed.'

She eyed him suspiciously.

'No men?' he asked.

'Your rudeness is as ubiquitous as mud.'

'You allude to the marshes?'

'I allude to your lack of education.'

'But you were thinking of the marshes.'

'I will not dignify your crudeness with a response.'

'You must have wandered them quite a bit in your

tenure at court,' he said, pouring himself another cup. 'How many times? Dozens?'

The audacity of such a question! She considered leaving the room, forgetting the chamber was sealed. 'I will assume that is a yes,' he said.

'It is not a yes!' Aya cried out, though she had no idea why she had even lowered herself to respond to him.

'So you have never wandered the marshes?' he asked.

The man had provoked her last nerve. 'Of course I have. I am a woman, am I not? I go to the festivals. I take part in the rites.'

'I do not believe you.'

'I do not care what you do or do not believe.'

'Which festivals?'

She searched her mind. 'The Festival of Drunkenness, for example.'

'Any others?' he asked. The moments passed like the footfalls of an elephant. 'So the Festival of Drunkenness,' he said at last. 'How many times have you participated in those ecstatic rites?'

'Many times.'

'How many?'

He waited in silence for her response, having apparently suddenly acquired the virtue of patience. She busied herself sipping her cup until all the water was gone. 'Certainly two. Possibly three. I cannot recall.'

'If you cannot recall the pleasures of the flesh, then you certainly have never enjoyed them,' he stated.

'That makes very little sense.'

'Do you at least have someone to love? A child? A pet?'

'I love Tausret. I have served her all my life.'

'And how long is that life so far, may I ask?'

'An impertinent question if ever there was.'

His twinkling eyes slid up and down her body. 'I would say that you have seen at least thirty floods.'

'Four and twenty!' she cried.

'Four and twenty—that is still rather old. And only thrice have you enjoyed the pleasures of the flesh?' He lifted the amphora of beer and held it out to her. 'In that case you should not be drinking water.'

She frowned, once again unable to read his tone. But she allowed him to tip the container to her glass and when he was finished she took a long gulp. 'Pah!' she said, feigning disgust.

'What is wrong?'

'It is bubbly and tart, just as beer should be.'

'Then what—? Aha!' he exclaimed. This time his grin was genuine. 'Well done, Advisor.'

She could not contain her grin. 'Thank you, Thief.'

'Soldier, if you please.'

His expression sobered and he tilted the amphora into his own cup. He was definitely concealing something. 'And just how many years have you served in Pharaoh's army, soldier?' she asked.

'Twelve so far,' he replied then drained his cup. He finished with a loud sigh. 'I was eighteen when I joined.'

'So you are thirty now. A more advanced age than my own.' There, let him feel the sting of his own tongue!

'I am not so very old.'

'There are lines of years at the periphery of your eyes,' she observed.

'That is because I did not sleep last night!'

She understood instantly that she was the reason. 'Apologies,' she said. 'I sometimes cry out in the night.'

'It is unfortunate that I lost so much rest, as I fear it will affect my chiselling.'

'How can I make amends?'

The question seemed to cheer him. 'You can tell me what was in your vision.'

'There was a serpent—a bad omen. I launched an entire quiver's worth of arrows at it, but could not manage to hit the beast.'

'A bad omen? What did it portend?'

'The death of a mother and her baby,' Aya's throat squeezed. 'On the birthing blocks…'

'Pharaoh Tausret?'

Aya nodded.

'Not a vision, then,' Intef said. 'A memory.'

'A tragedy.'

He shook his head. 'It is why a woman should never be pharaoh.'

'Excuse me?'

'If Tausret had been a man, she would have had an entire harem's worth of heirs.'

Aya bit her tongue. She felt like a bed of coals he was currently teasing with a poker. 'Why the scowl?' he asked. 'I am merely being logical. It is nothing against the woman herself—though there was the problem of the corrupt treasurer she kept beside her.'

'You refer to Chancellor Bay?' she asked.

When Seti was Pharaoh, he had employed the Syrian immigrant Bay to help him in the battles against Amenmesse. With each success, Seti had promoted Bay to ever higher offices, until finally Bay was in control of the entire treasury.

Meanwhile, because Tausret could not produce an heir, Seti had named Siptah, the young son of a harem wife, to be his successor, with Tausret to function as the boy's regent. When Seti died and the young Pharaoh Siptah succeeded to the throne, Bay had stepped in to guide the boy and pushed Tausret aside. Worse, he had sent most of the treasury's gold back to Syria.

'Bay is a dirty thief,' said Intef. 'A man in Tausret's position would have seen—'

'A man in Tausret's position?' Aya interrupted. 'A man was in Tausret's position—her husband! Seti the Second was the one who promoted Bay. He loved him like a son.'

'A terrific failure of judgement.'

'By a man!'

Intef was shaking his head. 'Bay did not turn treacherous until after Seti went to the next life and the boy Siptah took the throne. It was Tausret's job as regent to remove Bay's tongue from Siptah's ear and Bay's arm from the treasury. But for how many years did she ignore Bay's treachery? Five? Six? She was blinded by his charm.'

'Bay was not charming.' Aya was feeling her blood begin to warm again.

'How can you judge who is and is not charming to another?' Intef argued. 'Some women are charmed by crocodiles. Some men, for that matter.' He shot Aya a significant look.

Did he mean to suggest that he was somehow charmed by her? Or simply that she was like a crocodile?

Curse him in either case! She would not allow him to undermine her point: 'When Tausret finally inherited the double crown, she set to work restoring the treasury. She had no wealth, yet she defended Egypt and made alliances to ensure the supply of grain. She was one of the best Pharaohs Egypt has ever known.'

'Yet she allowed Bay to bankrupt us! He was a dirty thief and Tausret was complicit.'

Aya smiled to conceal her growing anger. The man knew nothing of the royal court, yet he was judging Pharaoh as if he were the feather of truth itself.

Dirty thief indeed. What an interesting judgement for Intef to make! He was planning to steal from Pharaoh's own sacred store of gold after all. Was he not doing the same as Bay?

'Dirty thief…' she repeated. She shot him her own significant look.

He narrowed his eyes, apprehending the slight. 'You insult me.'

She turned away from him. She had vowed not to lose her temper again. 'I only observe that there are noticeable similarities between—' but now she was speaking to an empty room, for Intef had already departed.

Chapter Ten

Dirty thief. The words were like hot wax on his skin. How dare she deride him so? They had an agreement, after all. A pact. People who made pacts did not hurl insults.

He had left the torch behind, but it was of no matter. He could find the sealed entrance to the main chamber by touch alone. Ah, there it was—the place where the plastered wall gave way to bricks, their mortar still moist. He did not need to see them to know they would be easy to destroy—and he needed to destroy something. He set his chisel and landed his first blow.

How dare she suggest he was anything like Bay? The man who had bankrupted Egypt? It was like comparing a puff of wind to a dust storm. Intef was a thief, yes, but a worthy thief, a necessary thief. Had they not already agreed on that?

He tapped his chisel against the topmost brick until it crashed to the floor. He felt better already.

Why did it matter what she thought of him anyway? She could consider him the filthiest jackal in the meanest desert in Egypt. As long as her considerations did not include a plan to kill him, they should not matter to him at all. Besides, he did not wish to make friends with the woman he was going to betray.

He continued to strike his blows, hoping that the false chamber was as large as the true one, for there were now two people breathing the air inside the tomb, and, instead of nine days, they now had only four or five to reach the surface.

Why had he not done this hours ago, when the bricks were softer still? If he had gone to work the moment he awoke, he probably would not have even needed a chisel.

But hours ago, Aya was deep inside her night vision and he had not wanted to wake her.

As he had watched her slumber, he considered the possibility that at any moment she could have sat up and slid a blade across his throat. Deep in his heart, however, he knew she was not going to attack him again. He had watched her all night because he could not help himself.

Her appearance fascinated him. It was not just that she was Libyan, it was everything about her. Her nose, for example, was too long and seemed to have a personality of its own. Whenever she scolded him for cursing, it would twitch slightly, as if she had just inhaled a bad scent. When she was angry, her nostrils would flare like an angry bull's. It puzzled him that he could find such a nose attractive, yet just the thought of her angry nostrils made his skin flush.

Her lips were even more of a conundrum. Their shape was too curved, too opinionated. It was as if they had been perfectly fashioned to soften the delivery of her stubborn arguments. The Asiatic threat indeed! It was not right that such troublesome lips should be so lush and red. Worse, they often colluded with her eyes to assault him with intensity and colour.

Finally, there was the problem of the gap in the middle of her front two teeth. On the rare occasion that she smiled he could not take his eyes off it, as if it were some kind of door that might welcome him to paradise. It made him make her want to smile again and again.

He had watched her for hours and, as each desirous idea arrowed into his mind, he had lifted his mental shield, reminding himself that not only was she part Libyan, but that she was also murderous and imperious and entirely above him in rank.

She was also a 'Most Beloved Advisor' to a most disastrous pharaoh. The woman represented everything that was wrong with Egypt, or so he told himself as he had gazed at her mouth, wondering what it would be like to kiss again.

The last brick went tumbling to the ground and he felt a pulse of cool, fresh air. He breathed it in and reminded himself of his duty. Perhaps that was the problem: the stuffy air inside the main chamber had muddled his thoughts. He had forgotten the reason he was here.

Another memory surfaced…

'Remind me, which one is this?' General Setnakht asked.

'This is Intef, son of Sharek,' answered the officer. 'The archer, my lord. He fought with Amenmesse at the Battle at Aniba.'

'This is the Assassin of Aniba?'

'The very same,' averred the officer.

'Do you know why you are here, Assassin?' the General asked Intef.

Intef kept his gaze carefully averted. 'No, General,' he said, though the reason was always the same. Someone, or many someones, needed killing.

'Because there is going to be a great battle,' said General Setnakht. He stepped back to address the dozen other soldiers assembled in the room. 'The North against the South, Egyptian against Egyptian, one last time. The pretender Tausret has finally died and she has left our Great Egypt without an heir.'

There was a collective gasp as the men absorbed the news. Intef watched a fly fall out of the air and on to the floor. He was so tired of fighting.

'As I speak, thousands of men march south to join the High Priest right here in Thebes.' The General ran his hands through his greying hair. 'The High Priest means to defeat us and seize the double crown.'

There was a spate of hisses and angry shouts. 'Just let him try!' shouted one officer.

'He will eat the tips of our spears!' called another.

The General motioned to a roundish young man standing with the officers. 'Most of you know my son and heir,' Setnakht continued. 'Many of you have fought alongside him in our raids in Nubia. He is smart, strategic and does not shrink from a fight. Thus I have granted him a new name. All hail Rameses the Third.'

Intef saw the men's eyes flash with surprise as they made their collective salutation. General Setnakht could not claim a single drop of royal blood, nor could any of his wives. His son was not a Rameses. To name him thus was not just a lie, it was heresy.

The newly stamped Rameses the Third stepped shamelessly forward. His corpulent face and large mouth belied no expression, but his small black eyes darted warily about the room, never resting.

'As my father said, you men are being considered for a special mission. If it is successful, we will have the wealth we need to purchase mercenaries for the battle against the High Priest. The South will defeat the North for once and for all, and Egypt will be united beneath a strong pharaoh—my father, Setnakht!'

The men erupted in cheers, though Intef remained unmoved. He had heard a similar speech when General Amenmesse had rallied his southern rebels against Seti only twelve years before. He had heard the speech again when General Setnakht's rebel warriors—Intef among them—had ridden out against Tausret at the Battle of Memphis. Now he would ride out again—against the High Priest. When would it end?

Intef turned to the soldier standing next to him. 'I wonder how many Egyptians will need to die this time?' he muttered.

Rameses paused. 'Excuse me, soldier, what did you say?'

Intef drew a breath. 'I said, my lord, that I wonder how many will die in order to achieve success?'

Intef braced himself for a scolding, but Rameses only smiled. 'Why, none,' he said. 'That is the reason for the mission.' He placed his arms behind his back and began to pace. 'My father and I will choose four men from among you—three ants and one beetle. The beetle will be sent beneath the earth into a tomb full of riches. If he can survive, he will forge the way for the ants. The treasure they extract will pay for mercenaries—enough to defeat the High Priest.'

The men resumed their excited talk, but Intef remained puzzled.

'Why do you shake your head, Assassin?' Rameses asked.

'You said that if the mission is successful, none will die,' said Intef. 'But if the treasure is meant to purchase more soldiers, how is that possible?'

'The answer is simple,' said Rameses. 'If we can purchase enough men, there will be no battle at all. The High Priest will simply stand down. No lives will be lost.'

Something stirred deep inside Intef—the echo of some long-abandoned hope. He had never been to a battle in which the armies did not fight. He yearned to see it.

Rameses stepped next to the man standing beside Intef. 'Tell me, soldier, what do you know of the afterlife?'

'I know that when I reach the Hall of Ma'at, my heart will be weighed against a feather and that I will be judged pure, for I follow the rightful King!'

There was a barrage of cheers, but Rameses ignored them. He stepped before the next man in the line. 'And what do you know, soldier?'

'That the Hall of Ma'at is just the beginning,' the man said eagerly. 'That there are lakes of fire and gates guarded by demons and you must know the spells to pass through them.'

Rameses nodded absently, then returned to face Intef. 'Tell me, Assassin, what do you know of the afterlife?'

'I know nothing, my lord,' said Intef.

'Nothing?'

'My heart is heavy. Why stalk a festival to which one can never be admitted?' Several of the officers laughed.

'Any family?' asked Rameses.

Intef cringed. 'Not any more.'

'Is that why your heart is heavy?'

'I...failed to do my duty once. But never again.'

General Setnakht whispered something into his son's ear. 'No wife, no mistress?' Rameses asked.

'Why complicate things?' More laughter.

'Then what do you desire, Intef, son of Sharek?'

What did he desire? That was simple: 'I desire peace, an end to the wars for the double crown, no more cursed fighting,' he said.

'If you are chosen for this mission, you may discover something worse than fighting. Worse even than death.'

Intef only shrugged. 'There are many things worse than death, my lord.'

'What things? Give an example.'

'Well, life, for example,' he said, expecting more laughter. But this time no one laughed and it occurred to Intef that he had spoken from his heart.

Rameses glanced at General Setnakht, who gave a small nod. 'If you work for my father and me, we will work for Egypt.'

Intef looked into the men's eyes. A father and a son, working together. No more war. His broken heart throbbed, wanting to believe. He bowed his head.

Rameses grinned. 'Men, I think we have our beetle.'

Intef kicked the fallen bricks aside and stepped out of the main chamber into the dark corridor. Now he would begin again. He would cross the long hallway and break through to the false chamber and start chiselling through the ceiling within the hour.

He could no longer afford to indulge in his strange fascination with Aya. He had made an agreement with the future Pharaoh of Egypt, after all—a Rameses who was not a Rameses. But it was no matter. The lack of a blood connection to the throne was of little importance when the unity of Egypt was at stake.

Intef's father had given his life towards achieving such a goal and it was Intef's duty to see it through. He needed to think of this woman for what she truly was: a dangerous distraction from that purpose.

She did not even like him, and thank the gods for that. Although her insult had stung, he was also grateful for it, for it helped him see her for what she was: a mosquito—a noisy and sometimes bothersome presence to ignore and to swat away when necessary.

Hundreds, even thousands, of men's lives depended on Intef's ability to do his duty now. He would not allow a woman to prevent him from doing it.

Aya needed to make amends for the insult she had made. She reminded herself of this purpose as she stepped into the corridor and stood beside Intef. 'Pharaoh's winged *ba* spirit will have a better chance of finding her now that you have broken the seal,' she remarked in her friendliest voice.

'That is not why I did it,' Intef replied.

Aya gazed at the fallen bricks that had once represented her own doom. 'Nevertheless, I am grateful for your efforts.'

'I do not labour to earn your gratitude.' He stepped out of the torchlight and soon she could hear his sandals slapping down the dark corridor.

'Wait!' she called after him. This was not going as she had hoped. 'I did not mean what I said to you. Your desire to help your family is honourable and good.'

A mirthless laugh echoed down the hall. 'Now I am honourable and good? Just moments ago I was a dirty thief.'

She hurried after him down the long hallway, rushing past him and stopping in the middle of his path. 'You are in my way,' he said.

'Why must you always be so rude?' She held up her torch and widened her stance, further blocking the way.

He sighed. 'Would you please do me the kind favour of moving out of my way, my lady? You see, we have a tomb to burrow out of and very little time in which to do it. Millions of thanks.'

'Your sarcasm rather undermines your efforts at good breeding.'

'And you are an authority on good breeding?' He stepped closer. She was overcome by an awareness of his height.

'I ask merely to be treated with decency,' she said. It was more than his height. It was his presence. She found herself leaning towards him, as if pulled by an invisible rope.

'Decency?' he replied, stepping closer still. The twin flanks of his chest now occupied the whole of her vision.

'If you are trying to intimidate me, you are failing,' she said, though her heart was beating as if she had just stumbled into a lion.

'If I were trying to intimidate you, you would know it.' She could feel his thick voice deep inside her belly.

'Would I?'

He exhaled and his warm breath tickled her hair. 'You would.'

She should have let the discussion end there, should have calmly stepped aside and let him pass. 'How would I know it?'

He took her chin in his hand and she gasped. He squeezed her jaw just a little, then slowly tilted her face up to his. 'You would know because you would feel fear.'

By all the holy gods. His musky breath poured over her face. His lips were so close. In truth she did feel fear. She was afraid of how much she wanted to kiss him. 'I certainly do not feel fear.'

He bent closer still. 'That is only because I do not wish for you to fear me.'

Was she mistaken, or was he closing his eyes? 'Yes,' she whispered.

'No.' His eyes flew open. He released her chin and lurched backwards. 'Say what you wish to say and have done with it. We need to get to work.'

Aya could hardly remember why she had stopped him at all. 'I have come to apologise for my bad behaviour,' she managed to say. 'I vow never again to insult you, or seek to do you harm.'

He grunted a laugh. 'And I vow never again to believe a single word you say.'

'I do not wish there to be enmity between us.'

'Then please do not offer me any more friendly kisses,' he said, 'and kindly stay out of my way.'

He pushed past her, but she turned quickly and kept up with his pace. 'I will not cease until you accept my apology. Please! I am sorry for what I said to you. You are not a— I did not wish to imperil our friendship.'

'Friendship?' He stopped again. 'If you are such a friendly person, then why did the High Priest of Amun leave you inside this tomb? There are much easier ways to rid oneself of an enemy without endangering one's holy *ka*!'

She opened her mouth to speak, then shut it again. She sensed that if she did not tell him the truth now, she would lose his confidence for ever.

'The High Priest wished to torture me,' she admitted.

'For what reason? Punishment?'

She had to tell him the truth. If she lost Intef's trust, it was possible that he would break their agreement. Tausret's greatest riches would once again be a risk. 'Information.'

'What information?'

How could she do this? How could she deliberately betray Pharaoh's dying wish? 'Information that only I can give,' she said, stalling for time.

It occurred to her that if the High Priest knew about the heir, then others did, too. Still, she needed a better reason to break the most important promise she had ever made. First and foremost, she needed to protect the heir. What if she could enlist Intef's help in doing just that?

'If I tell you this…secret,' Aya said, 'you must vow to help me when the time comes.'

'Fine, I promise,' Intef said. 'Now tell me, what information was the High Priest trying to extract from you?'

Aya took a breath. 'He wished to know the location of the heir to the Horus Throne.'

'What?' he said. His mouth hung open. Aya cast her eyes to the floor. 'Apologies, but I am not sure I heard you correctly. Could you say that again?'

'Tausret's heir is real,' said Aya. 'And I know the city in which he lives.'

Chapter Eleven

He could not hold her gaze any more, so he started walking. He had been fooling himself about her. He had tried to make her into a mosquito, when in truth she remained a dangerous crocodile. He knew that she would no longer bite him with her teeth, but there were other ways for her to threaten him.

For example, right now, when he should have been thinking about the secret she had just divulged—a secret that could raze a kingdom—all he could think of was how close her lips had been to his.

'There is a living member of the Rameses line?' he asked cautiously.

She nodded.

'Male or female?'

'He is the heir, must he not be male?'

'If the heir were female, we could avoid a war.'

'You refer to a marriage of alliance?'

'The legitimacy of Setnakht's own heir would be unassailable if he were married to the daughter of Tausret.'

'I had never thought of that,' Aya admitted. 'Probably because the heir is male.'

And that, of course, was the problem. Intef ran his

hand through his hair and tried to think. Now instead of two men vying for the empty throne, there were likely to be three. The war would never end.

He speeded up his pace. 'Is that the errand, then? You wish for me to help you find the heir?'

'Before the High Priest does,' said Aya.

The young man would have to be destroyed, and fast, lest he raise an army. 'Do you know where this divine son is to be found?' he asked.

'I know more than the High Priest does.'

'And do you know what he looks like?'

'I know enough,' she said. 'He has a distinguishing tattoo.'

Intef asked nothing further. He did not wish to arouse her suspicions. If he could not extract the information from her himself, Setnakht surely would. Either way, it seemed that the most valuable treasure in Tausret's tomb was not made of silver or gold, but of flesh and bone.

'I forgive you,' Intef said.

'You what?'

'I accept your apology.' He could no longer even look at her. It was likely that Setnakht would kill the heir just as the High Priest wished to do. 'Let us begin again.'

'You will help me find the heir and spirit him to safety?' she asked, skipping to keep up with him.

'I will,' Intef lied. He hated himself. More death. More blood on his hands. He quickened his pace, as if he could simply outrun his guilt. Now he had lied to her not once, but twice.

'Careful!' Aya cried.

He felt his skull smash against brick. Pain pulsed through his head. He reached out for the wall, but could not find it. He swayed, then felt Aya's hands encircle his chest, bracing him.

'You hit your head!'

She held him steady as his senses returned. How had he forgotten about the seal to the false chamber? He had smashed into it with the full force of his stride and now a lump was forming on the top of his forehead. A terrible, deceitful lump.

'Intef, are you all right?' Aya was reaching for his head, but he stepped out of her grasp.

'It is just a bump.' There was no time for any of this. He turned and braced his chisel against the brick and landed his first blow.

'Shall I go fetch some water?' she asked.

He shook his head. 'There will be water in the false chamber when we reach it.'

Tap, tap, tap.

'But do you not wish to rest? I can search for a salve to help soothe your swollen head.'

'There is no time for rest,' he said.

Tap, tap, tap.

'Of course there is time. We were resting all morning.'

'You were resting,' he clarified. 'I was trying to get you to move.'

'That is a half-truth,' she protested. 'You were as immersed in our discussions as I was.'

'Yes, and this is what happens when we become immersed in our discussions.' He pointed to the bump on his head.

She shot him an imperious look, then lifted her hand once more and gently touched his forehead.

'Ouch.'

'I fear you are not fine,' she said.

Well, perhaps not, but it had nothing to do with his injury.

'There is an abrasion beside the bump,' she said. 'It is bleeding.'

'It will stop.'

'Let me help you.'

'The only help I require from you is for you to aid in chiselling our escape tunnel. Until then, if you could kindly cease speaking.'

'I am merely trying to be friendly,' she said.

'I fear that if we stand here talking any longer, our efforts at friendliness will be our demise.'

He watched the blood of frustration rise to her cheeks. She opened her mouth in exasperation and he caught sight of the small gap between her teeth. 'You are impossible!' she barked.

He shook his head, turned away. Better to be impossible than friendly.

'Aya, I am fine.'

He was not fine. She held the torch aloft, watching him work. The lump on his head continued to grow, but he would not stop to rest.

'Intef, will you not cease your chiselling just for a moment?' she asked, but he was so focused on his work that he did not seem to hear her.

'Intef!' Aya shouted and finally he stopped. He gazed at her in wonder, as if he had forgotten she was there. 'Are you sure you are all right?' she asked, glancing at his injury. Something was amiss. It was not just his sudden urgency to chisel. He had forgiven her too quickly. In one moment he had been condemning her, in the next, promising his help.

The man was as changeable as the wind.

'This morning you were full of jests,' she said. 'Now

you chisel as if the god of chaos himself were chasing you.'

He shook his head. 'I must take care not to lose sight of my duty.'

'To your family?'

'To get us out of this godforsaken tomb!' he shouted. He ceased his tapping and turned to her, his black eyes flaming. 'Listen to me now, for in this I do not jest: the air inside this tomb will soon turn sour. It will draw demons from the Underworld and we shall perish among them.'

'But we are breathing fine,' said Aya.

He sighed, annoyed. 'There is a finite amount of air inside every underground chamber just as there is a finite amount of water inside a pool. The larger the chamber, the greater the amount of air—and time.'

'But we have nine days, no?'

'Nine days for one person working—and breathing—alone, but we are two.'

He plunged his fingers into the knot of his belt, producing a small object she could not see. He lifted his sandaled foot and pressed it against the wall.

'Pay attention now, for our lives depend on it.' Holding the object between his finger and thumb, he rubbed it against the leather strap of his sandal until a single scratch mark appeared. 'Today is day one. In about twelve hours, when we grow naturally sleepy, we can assume it is night,' he explained. 'When we awake from that sleep, it will be day two, and we will make another mark.'

He pretended to scratch a second mark on his sandal and she got a better view of the object he held. It was the arrowhead.

* * *

He checked her expression for understanding, but she would not meet his gaze. She was staring at the arrowhead in his palm as if she had been struck by it.

He closed his hand around it. 'You have nothing to fear.'

But it was not fear blooming in her expression, it was heat. A crimson blush was creeping up her neck, as if she was remembering the last time she had seen the arrowhead. As if she was recalling their unlikely kiss.

Was it possible that she had felt it, too? That strange tenderness when their lips met? That unexpected want? He had assumed that her desire had been feigned, that she had only kissed him in order to manoeuvre her kicking leg into a more damaging position. Now he wondered if it was not as simple as that.

She seemed fascinated by the painted wall closest to her view. She turned away from him, flashing her torch up and down the columns of hieroglyphs.

'Tausret passed unexpectedly,' she remarked, keeping her gaze fixed on the wall. 'That is why only the ceiling and east wing of her burial chamber are decorated. She managed to finish this corridor, however.'

'I see,' said Intef, pretending interest.

'The paintings and the text in this sacred hall are from the *Amduat*—the book of what is in the Underworld,' she added. Her blush was taking its time in retreat. He wondered at her tumult of emotions. In the course of the hour, she had displayed shades of anger, derision, desire, sorrow and now, apparently, abashment.

He had the urge to take each of her passing sentiments and stuff them into one of the empty amphorae, to be consumed on days he wished to remember what it was like to feel. Which were most days, in truth.

'When I return to restore the tomb,' she was saying, 'I shall add more scenes like these to the main chamber. Pharaoh would like that.'

The more he knew her, the more he comprehended her essential goodness. Beneath the impulsive, sharp-witted courtier was a woman who would do anything to ensure the well-being of her Mistress, even if it meant sacrificing her own freedom. She would indeed have made a good soldier. It occurred to him that in many ways she already was.

But she was an enemy soldier, alas. There was no room for his desire for her. If he acted upon it, it would make him far more loathsome than he already was, for in four short days, he would be pillaging her Pharaoh's tomb, then delivering her to General Setnakht.

Mission accomplished. Duty done. Good woman, betrayed. The thought made him want to run into another wall.

She turned to face him, her torch illuminating both their faces. Now it was his turn to flush. It was as if she had intuited his thoughts. Her blue eyes shone black in the flickering torchlight and glittered like magic stones. Her lips beckoned and accused all at once.

'I have told you my secret, now you must tell me yours,' she said.

'My secret?' he repeated dumbly.

Which one? The secret that he was no mere thief, but a highly organised plunderer with help on the way? The secret that the treasure they extracted could help prevent the next war? The secret that part of that treasure was Aya herself?

In his wildest visions, he told her everything. She

listened without judgement and comprehended his motivations. Then she took his hand in hers and somehow forgave him.

'What is it?' she urged. 'What are you hiding?'

'I—' he began to tell her. He wanted to tell her, but the walls seemed so close. Too close. Crushing.

He stepped out of the torchlight and the moment passed. He sighed, feeling his good sense return. This was where he belonged—in the shadows. He was the man behind the next usurper—the criminal who would help Setnakht steal the throne. She had not been wrong about him. He *was* a dirty thief.

She touched his arm. 'You can tell me,' she whispered.

Damn him to the Devourer of Souls, he wanted to kiss her again.

But who would she be kissing? He was not the man she believed him to be, but a man who had been chiselled and sculpted by lies. He was a man who, in only four days, would betray her utterly.

'Talk to me, Intef,' she urged. 'We are friends, yes?'

Chapter Twelve

No, they were not friends.

That was what his eyes had told her. They were sharp eyes, like well-honed blades, and they deftly severed the invisible rope she had foolishly imagined strewn between them.

What a stupid question to ask him. 'We are friends, yes?' As if they could somehow erase the world of difference between them.

No, he had said with his eyes and inside the dark corridor his meaning had been as bright as day. *No*, he would not tell her his secret. *No*, they should not give in to this inexplicable lust. *No*, she could not trust him. They had become allies only by necessity. They could never, ever be more.

Good. Thank the gods for his good judgement, for in her mourning she had apparently grown weak and lost her own. The only feeling they should be allowing inside their hearts was the simple will to survive.

She watched him cross to the middle of the false chamber in four long strides, but she remained standing at its threshold, feeling foolish.

She had no idea why she had responded so unusually to the sight of the arrowhead. Seeing him pull it from beneath his belt should have inspired anger or even fear, certainly not the warm desire that had crept beneath her skin.

That kiss. She had tried to forget it—had tucked it away inside her heart with the other memories of things she could not explain. She wondered how she could have ever kissed him at all. More importantly, she wondered how she could ever have enjoyed it.

She loathed the memory of his hot breath, abhorred the thought of his gentle touch, scorned the vision of that small tremble she had perceived in his lips, as if he had been nervous and wished to please her.

She was the only person in the world who could protect Tausret from an afterlife of privation, yet she had enjoyed a kiss from the man who would make that privation manifest.

She should not have been kissing, but praying. During the past twelve hours, her beloved Pharaoh had been navigating the labyrinthine marshes and fiery lakes of the Underworld. She had been fighting the giant serpent and merging with the sun god and making the long journey back to the horizon.

Or so Aya hoped. Trapped inside the tomb, she could not know for certain if Tausret had succeeded in her journey. All she knew was that she had been negligent in her duty to her Pharaoh. She could not allow it to happen again.

'Forgive me, Pharaoh,' she whispered and felt the tiniest of breezes tousle her hair. Her heart skipped. 'Pharaoh?'

'Are you coming?' called Intef, giving her a fright.

'Just a moment,' she called back.

She gulped the strange air moving near the ceiling,

imagining it to be Tausret's own breath. 'I am here,' she whispered. 'I will not forsake you.' Then she crossed to the middle of the false chamber.

Although slightly smaller than the main chamber—only ten paces wide and twelve long—the false chamber loomed larger to Intef somehow.

Its eight noble pillars—four on each side of the room—held up a steep, barrel-vaulted ceiling whose painted stars glowed with an otherworldly light.

Two vibrant wall-sized murals graced each end of the space. Their beauty gave him pause. On the far wall, he saw the outline of the final brick seal.

'Your Pharaoh was clever,' he said. 'No tomb robber would ever think to search beyond this false chamber. It seems even truer than the main chamber somehow.'

He watched her approach the hut-sized burial container at the room's centre. She gazed at its gilded walls. 'And yet it is truly false,' she said.

He stepped behind her and breathed over her shoulder. Even in the low light, he could see her skin rising beneath his breath.

'There is a sarcophagus inside this shrine,' she informed him, 'but nobody is in it.'

He tilted his head slightly and breathed in her scent. How was it possible she could smell so good? He imagined himself bending to kiss her neck.

She turned to face him and his heart skipped. Gods, those eyes. They were watching him again, causing his thoughts to scatter.

'I have heard of false doors and hidden pits,' he said stupidly, 'but never an entire false chamber. It is a brilliant ruse.'

'Yet it was never meant as one,' she said. His eyes

slid to the base of her throat. She frowned and stepped away from him.

'Then why was it constructed at all?' he asked, pretending interest in the walls.

'I invite you to guess,' she said.

They were still standing far too close to each other. He could not allow her to drive him from his mission yet again. 'We have little time for puzzles,' he said and started across the chamber.

'Those sound like the words of a man who fears he cannot solve them,' she said, hoping the statement would reach its mark.

He stopped in his tracks. 'There is no one better than I am at solving puzzles.'

'Then guess.'

He continued to the other side of the chamber and paused before a pillar, studying an image of the deified Pharaoh Seti. 'This was originally Tausret's chamber and the main chamber was for her husband Seti,' he pronounced.

'Alas, no,' said Aya. 'The main chamber was carved only after Seti passed on.'

She motioned to the chamber's most splendid painting: a netherworld chimera with a ram's head and an eagle's body, whose massive blue wings stretched almost the entire width of the wall.

'That is from the Book of Caverns,' Aya explained. 'The great being is the sun god in his most elaborate form. Is it not a lovely rendering?'

'It is,' Intef said, but he was looking at her, not the mural. 'You seem to know much about the sacred books.'

'Tausret saw to my education herself.'

'You joined her court when you were young?'

'Three years old.'

'And your parents?'

Aya shrugged, then directed his attention to the mural. 'Do you see the images above the great being? They are the three other incarnations of the sun god: the sun disc itself, a scarab beetle and a child.'

'You know nothing of your origins?'

'Tausret told me that my father was a Libyan warrior. He died the same year Tausret's father Merneptah assumed the double crown. Come, let me show you the other mural.'

She turned on her heel and walked closer to the mural at the opposite end of the chamber. In it, Osiris's supine figure stretched across the top of the image in the dignified pose of death. 'I remember seeing the sketches for that image when Pharaoh was still planning the tomb,' Aya remarked in wonder. She heard his footfalls behind her.

Her gaze slid down to the bottom of the mural where an image of Osiris's standing figure and fully erect member caught her eye.

'That is from the Book of the Earth,' Aya said. 'An invocation of the power of resurrection.'

She turned to find Intef smiling wryly. 'I can see how such an image could inspire the wife of a pharaoh.'

'Was that a jest?' Aya asked with a small grin.

Intef grinned back smugly. 'It was the answer to your puzzle.'

Aya frowned.

'This was the original burial chamber for Tausret,' said Intef, 'but it was meant for a chief wife. When Tausret became Pharaoh, she decided to dig deeper.'

Aya bowed her head. 'I did not think you would arrive at the truth so quickly.'

'Then you underestimate my cleverness.'

'I believe that was Tausret's problem,' said Aya. 'She underestimated her own cleverness.'

'Now it is I who does not follow.'

'All her life Tausret was told that women begat kings, they did not become kings. After she was named regent, she remained in the shadows, letting Bay counsel Seti's heir, Siptah. She believed the boy needed a man to guide him.'

'A man indeed,' huffed Intef.

'Pharaoh did not yet understand her divinity, or her power. She only became Pharaoh in order to right Bay's wrongs and help save the people from drought. She was officially Pharaoh for only a few years, but she saved many lives. She was Egypt's greatest champion.'

Aya prepared herself for a cutting remark, but none came. 'And it seems that you are hers,' Intef said. 'Come.'

They crossed to the final sealed entrance—a wall of bricks separating the false chamber from the long entryway, which had been filled in with earth. Intef placed his chisel between the bricks and in minutes the wall was destroyed.

He plunged his arms into the wall of backfill and began heaving it in volumes on to the floor of the false chamber. Aya held out the torch and closed her eyes.

Forgive us, Pharaoh.

When she opened them again, Intef was standing before her, his muscular stomach heaving. 'The ceiling of the corridor is not as high as that of the chamber itself,' he said. He pointed up at the chamber's domed ceiling, then lowered his gaze to hers. 'We must begin our chiselling at the highest possible point.'

Aya shook her head. *Not the domed ceiling.*

'We cannot.'

'But this is a false chamber only,' argued Intef. 'Pharaoh's spirit will not return here.'

Aya gazed up at the lovely domed ceiling, replete with stars. 'This chamber represents a part of Tausret's life, her history. We must leave it as it is.'

'We will save hours, perhaps even a whole day,' he argued. 'I do not think you understand the haste we must make.'

'I understand—but to despoil this chamber would be like carving a hole inside my own heart.' She dropped to her knees and assumed the position of entreaty. 'Please, Intef, keep the sacred chamber whole. I promise you that I will do everything I can to help us make up the time.'

He was shaking his head. 'It could mean our deaths, do you understand?' But he turned from the chamber, stormed up the ramp and wedged his chisel in the corridor's low ceiling.

'I will never cease to thank you for this,' she called meekly.

'Five days,' he growled, then landed his first blow.

Chapter Thirteen

Her gratitude was like a burst of rain. In the many hours since he had landed his first blow to the corridor ceiling, she had arranged the back wall of the false chamber for their living quarters, acquired and prepared a washbasin, and discovered, among other things, two bed mats, three oil lamps and a cache of fresh figs.

He knew all this because she had announced her accomplishments to him as she had completed them, along with a steady stream of thoughts on a variety of topics, including the hazards of the Underworld, the threat of the Sea Peoples and techniques for preparing perfume.

Her chatter was cheerful and seemed to speed the passage of time—so much so that when her talking ceased, the false chamber seemed quite gloomy.

'Aya?' Intef called from atop the mound of dirt. No response. It had been several hours since he had heard her soft voice.

He ceased chiselling and descended the growing mound of rubble that was his perch. He had made an arm's length of progress through the limestone so far, and the hole in the ceiling through which they would escape had begun to take shape.

His fingers were aching badly. He had practised his masonry skills for a full cycle of the moon in anticipation of this mission, but with less than five days to chisel out, he feared his conditioning would not be enough. He could do no more today.

He had an urge to make water and resolved to find some discreet part of the corridor between the two chambers. As he crossed the false chamber he lifted his torch and took stock of the changes Aya had made.

She had done her best to sweep the spilled dirt off the tiles, and had arranged a small sitting area to one side of the false shrine. A jug of water and a serving of cheese and bread stood ready to be consumed and she had decorated the table with a blue glass vase full of figs.

She had nestled the bed mats in the sunken area between the pillars—one in each corner. They lay many paces apart—a welcome configuration. Everything depended on his ability to get as much chiselling done as he could. He did not need her beauty or nearness distracting him in the night.

He stepped into the corridor, thinking he might find her there, but the hall was empty. He noticed two small doorways on either side of him and remembered Hepu's description of the unfinished chambers. He flashed his torch into one of the doorways and gasped.

Four full-sized chariots made of solid gold stood side by side, as if preparing to roll off to war. They had been wedged between the walls of the first unfinished chamber along with piles of weapons—exquisitely carved bows and arrows, jewel-encrusted javelins, and every manner of gold, silver and copper blade, polished to a high shine.

At the back of the unfinished chamber, which was nearly as wide as the false chamber and half as long,

Intef noticed a shelving structure that stretched to the ceiling. Several hundred palm-sized figurines stood in neat rows on each of its half-dozen shelves. They were *ushabtis*—the ever-present denizens of Egyptian tombs—servants of the afterlife.

Intef had seen thousands of *ushabtis* in his life. The markets of Thebes were famous for them: tiny men and women who carried baskets in their arms and spells on their backs. *I am here when thou callest*, their inscriptions read, always willing to till a field or set a table in service of the deceased.

But the *ushabtis* that occupied this chamber had a decidedly different mission. Each wore the same spare uniform: a simple loincloth, thick sandals and a triangular leather cap. Each stood at attention, his hands behind his back, a leather shield resting at his side, awaiting command. These were soldiers.

Intef lifted a soldier from the shelf and felt his chest squeeze as he remembered the last time he had seen his mother alive...

'Intef! You have come home!' his mother shrieked. Tears poured down her face. 'I did not think I would ever see you again.'

She dropped her cane and opened her arms, and Intef rushed into her embrace. 'Of course I came,' he said, feeling a rush of love so powerful that he ached. She was a small woman and in the past he would have lifted her off the ground and whirled her around him, but he noticed that her lower leg had been wrapped in linen.

'You are injured.'

'Did the messenger say nothing of it?'

'Only that I was needed urgently at home. Mother, are you unwell?'

He reached down to inspect the cloth, but she swatted his hand away. 'It is nothing to worry about—just a ruse to get you to visit your poor old mother.' She reached up and took his face in her hands. 'It has been too long, my beautiful boy.'

'Only four years.'

'Only four years?' She moved one of his curls from his eyes. 'Setnakht's other soldiers come home every harvest.'

Setnakht's other soldiers were not deadly assassins.

'You know I have been busy,' said Intef. 'Setnakht is very close now to seizing the double crown and uniting Egypt for good.'

She frowned. 'Each time I see you, you are more like your father.'

'I shall take that as a compliment,' he said. Guilt pulsed through him. If it had not been for Intef's selfishness, his father would have been taking care of his mother right then.

'Come inside, Intef. Let me pour you a cup of beer.'

Intef watched with alarm as his mother lifted her cane and hobbled into the small mudbrick hut where Intef had been raised. 'Mother, you are not well.'

'I am well enough,' she said. 'I miss your father, though. I will join him in the afterlife soon.'

'Pah,' said Intef. 'You are still a young woman!'

Intef's mother laughed.

He wandered over to their family's small shrine—a shallow concavity that his father had carved into the wall long ago. It had once held a statue of Bastet, the feline goddess of the home, but since his father's passing his mother had replaced the statue with a finely carved *ushabti* of a soldier—a memory of his father.

Intef kissed his fingers, then touched them to the figurine's head. He should have dropped to his knees and made a proper prayer, but his lips were trembling and he did not wish to burden his mother with the heaviness in his heart.

'Sit down,' his mother said, pointing to the three stools and small table where the three had always taken their meals. There were dangerous memories everywhere he looked. In one corner of the hut, his father's fishing pole remained propped against the wall. In another lay the two wooden swords that he had once used to spar with Intef.

Intef accepted the cup from his mother's scythe-calloused hands and guzzled it down in a single draught. 'Do you have anything stronger?' he asked. 'Mead? Wine?'

'There may be a little mead left from the Festival of Osiris,' his mother said, rising to inspect a cluster of amphorae. 'Wine is too expensive.' She lifted an amphora and tilted its contents into Intef's cup.

'You will be able to afford as much wine as you like now,' said Intef. He plunked a bag full of silver *deben* on the table.

'What is that?'

'Booty from these last years of raids. It is yours now, Mother. We can get you a good doctor and you will not have to lift a scythe ever again.'

His mother blinked back a tear, but it did not appear to be one of joy. 'Is that why you think I called you home?' she asked. 'To ask for *deben*?'

'Of course not. But I have been wanting to give you—'

'I do not need *deben*, Intef. I need my son.'

Intef took his mother's hand and pulled her close. Love flooded into his heart. He hated this feeling. It was one of the reasons he had stayed away. The longer he stayed, the more he would feel it and the more difficult it would be to leave.

'How long can you stay?' she asked hopefully.

'As long as you need,' he lied. He squeezed her hand. He would stay as long as his heart could take. Usually it was less than a week.

'I have missed you, Intef,' she said. 'All these years.'

'And I have missed you.' *More than you will ever know.* 'But you understand I must do my duty.'

'Your father would be proud of you. You must know that. You are a man of principal just as he was. Of honour.' She cringed in pain as she walked to the table and took her seat at one of the stools.

Intef felt a lump in his throat. If his father were alive, surely he would be proud. But he was not alive and that was Intef's fault.

He did not know if he could even stay another night.

But it did not matter, for the next morning his mother was cold in her bed, dead and gone. And whatever remained of Intef's heart was gone, too.

His torch flickered with a rush of air. He turned to discover Aya standing in the doorway to the unfinished chamber.

'Intef, are you all right?'

'I am fine. Fine.'

'What are you doing?' she asked.

He blinked and looked around. 'Just…remembering.'

She watched as Intef returned the *ushabti* he held to the shelf. Sadness surrounded him like a fog, but she resisted the compulsion to console him. *Not friends*, she reminded herself. Still, there was too much silence.

'You have been chiselling for many hours,' she remarked. 'You must be tired.'

'I am,' he said. 'I fear I can do no more today.'

'In that case I must take my turn,' she said. 'May I show you something first?'

They crossed the hallway to the opposite unfinished chamber. 'This and the other unfinished chamber were supposed to comprise the second burial chamber,' Aya explained. 'But the workers came across cracks in the ceiling and were forced to stop.' She motioned to a large crack in the ceiling. 'Pharaoh said that it was the gods trying to tell her to dig deeper.'

Intef cast his gaze about the small room, which was divided into two smaller, rectangular-shaped rooms—one visible and the other hidden by a thick wall. In the visible room, shelves full of perfumes and oils lined the walls, their valuable glass and alabaster containers exuding powerful scents.

She directed his attention to the back of the room where she had spaced two empty amphorae. She had poured a large pile of black earth between them and propped a tall copper shovel against the wall. His eyes grew large with recognition.

'It's our—'

'I know what it is,' he said, though he could hardly believe it.

'What is the matter?'

'It is just…you surprise me.' It had been so long since he had felt anything at all—it was hard to recognise the strange delight.

'You are not pleased?' she asked. 'We needed somewhere to—'

'It is not that I am not pleased. I simply would never

have guessed that an advisor to a pharaoh would be willing to arrange such a thing.'

'Why? Because it is dirty? Believe me, I have performed much dirtier work than fashioning a toilet.'

He turned to her, wondering what kind of work she meant. But she ignored his silent query. 'I remembered the existence of the cache of earth just today,' she said. 'Pharaoh included it in her tomb to help ensure an abundant harvest. I will replace it, of course. After we escape.'

He studied the makeshift assemblage of equipment, which included a wash basin and even a pile of cut-up rags. She watched Intef eagerly.

'I am impressed,' he said. It was the solution to a problem that had been making his bladder ache for hours.

She glanced at his pose and he realised he was standing with his legs crossed, hunching like an old man. A small laugh escaped her and it cheered him instantly.

He decided to play dumb. 'What? What is it?'

'Just look at you,' she said.

He made a show of looking down at his own stooped posture. 'It does appear that I need to use the newly constructed facilities,' he remarked.

'Indeed, it does appear that way.' She placed her hand over her mouth and he found himself longing to see her special smile.

'Did I tell you how grateful to you I am?' he asked again.

'You really did,' she said.

'Gratitude has filled my heart to overflowing!' he gushed.

Suddenly her laughter morphed into a glorious, gap-toothed grin. 'Intef, you look like a pilgrim arriving at

the Abydos temple! I must insist that you avail yourself
of the facilities this instant!'

He bent over further, continuing to peer up at her. 'I
certainly will,' he said. 'As soon as possible.'

'Intef, go!'

Chapter Fourteen

When he returned from the latrine, he was whistling cheerfully. The sadness that had surrounded him seemed to have evaporated and the careless, arrogant tomb raider swaggered to her side.

'I should take my turn now,' she told him, peering into the false chamber.

He returned a wicked frown. 'In the latrine?'

She tossed him a scowl and they crossed the false chamber and ascended the ramp of earth. Ducking her head beneath the ceiling, she noticed a large hole. Beneath it he had dug out a concavity in the dirt.

He squatted just outside the concavity at a small stretch of wall just below the ceiling. 'The most important principle in stone work is patience,' he said. 'Funnel your energy into small, rhythmic movements. Let the tools do the work.'

He took up his hammer and chisel and began to tap on the wall. She should have been watching his technique, but she was distracted by the large sculpted muscles of his back and shoulders, which twitched and flexed with each tap.

He was a strong, powerful man and she knew that

she was blessed to have him here. Even if she could have freed herself from her bonds, she would not have been able to escape the tomb alone. She could not even make her own fire, by the gods, and she would have had to fashion her own tools. Without him, she simply would have perished.

She owed him a great debt.

And she would pay it. She would furnish him with enough gold to ensure his family's comfort for the rest of their lives. It did not matter that she would have to spend the rest of her own life working to replace those riches. Life was life and he had restored hers. In a very real sense, he was her Osiris.

'It is not necessary to work hard, you see,' he was saying. He tapped out a small, square portion of stone and demonstrated it to her. 'Now you try.'

She positioned herself in the place where he had crouched and tried to mimic his movements. After what seemed like an endless number of blows, a small shard of stone fell from the wall.

'Well done!' he said. 'Now let us try it inside the tunnel.' He placed the lamp on the ground in the concavity beneath the hole, then ducked his head and stepped in after it. He reached out his hand.

'Come,' he urged. 'I promise not to bite.'

Without taking his hand, Aya followed him into the small space. To her amazement, it was large enough to accommodate both their bodies standing upright, with their heads poking up into the tunnel he had chiselled so far.

'You have made great progress already,' she praised. She was just a hand's width from his chest and the soft glow of the lamp below them illuminated the fascinating curves of his muscles. She tried not to stare at him, though he was once again occupying her entire field of vision.

Worse, she found her heart had begun to beat so intensely that she could actually perceive its movement beneath her skin. He was peering down at her curiously, as if he had noticed it, too. She needed to distract his attention.

'Your chiselling is excellent,' she remarked, as if she were an expert. 'I can only aspire to such efficiency.'

He smiled and handed her the tools. 'There is no reason to be nervous.'

'I am not nervous.' She placed the chisel against the rock above them and gave it a few thumps with her hammer, quickly realising that chiselling overhead was much more difficult than chiselling on a vertical wall.

She paused and breathed in, catching a whiff of his scent. When he had collapsed atop her the day before, she had faced an assault of lavender so rich and potent that it had reminded her of nothing so much as the royal harem laundries.

She inhaled him now, her senses exciting to a savoury mixture of sweat and dust and musk. She breathed in his scent again, for one breath did not seem to be enough. Neither did a second, nor a third.

She could hardly even concentrate on her chiselling! He did not look like a magician, but it seemed as if he had conspired with the god of magic to anoint himself with some beguiling perfume.

She landed another blow, then filled her chest with air and held it. 'What are you doing?' he asked.

'Holding my breath,' she peeped.

'Why in Great Egypt are you doing that?'

'It…helps my technique.'

A shard fell and Aya squatted to the ground to inspect it, gulping the unadulterated air near the floor. 'It is much larger than I expected,' she remarked. It was an ill-considered choice of words, especially given her current and rather unfortunate proximity to the holiest part of him.

'Larger is not necessarily better,' he said, adding, 'when it comes to chiselled stone.' She could almost envision his jackal's grin.

She returned her attention to the shard. She would not allow his crass humour to unnerve her. She remained crouching at his feet, feigning fascination with the cut stone until even she grew bored with it.

There was nothing to do but return to standing.

As if reading her heart, he opened his hand to her. 'Come, let us practise chiselling a bit more,' he said.

She gazed at his large, calloused digits. She could see each bump and bend, could imagine the long hours they had spent working to save their lives.

She did not understand the feeling spreading through her body. Perhaps it was a kind of fear. That would certainly explain why her senses seemed to have sharpened. Though in truth they always sharpened when he was near.

Perhaps she was like an antelope—a creature of nervous awareness. She certainly noticed every change in his expression, every inflection of his voice, every variation in his movement. And that cursed scent!

If she was the antelope, then perhaps he was the lion whose attack she was always trying to avoid. Perhaps that was the reason for her visceral experience of him. She had to be aware of him: she was protecting herself from attack.

But he had had many chances to harm her already and had seized none of them. Further, he had made it very clear that he had no interest in her at all. If anything, it was she who was stalking him.

But that idea made even less sense. No one was stalking anyone. And that strange quickening of her heart whenever he was near was not fear. It was simply her desire to escape the tomb. So why was she still crouching on the floor at his feet?

'You delay, Aya,' he said, moving his open hand into her sight line. 'Have we tired you out already?'

'Of course not!' she huffed.

She placed her hand in his and set out on the perilous journey of returning to standing. As she moved upwards, she passed the pillars of his lower legs, then the thick, bulging dunes of his thighs.

Finally she arrived at the dangerous terrain of his loincloth, which had assumed the shape of a sacred pyramid and seemed to be growing outwards by the moment. Her heart throbbed as she successfully moved past the obstacle and arrived at the undulating hills of his stomach.

She was not out of danger, however, for as she moved ever upwards, her own breast seemed to graze against the tented loincloth that she thought she had successfully left behind.

The fleeting sensation caused a small but debilitating tremor to rumble through her body and she jerked backwards, hitting her back against the wall. Still, she soldiered on, her eyes scaling the muscular plateaus of his chest and nearly tripping on the small dark beacon of one of his nipples.

Finally, she returned to standing and gazed into his eyes. They had not been this close to each other since he had lifted her chin in the corridor and told her *no*.

'Really, though,' he said in puzzlement, 'how does holding your breath help you chisel?'

She did not answer. Instead she resumed chiselling with new energy, scolding herself for acting so foolishly. Several more shards went tumbling to the ground.

'How am I doing?' she asked.

'Try to let the tools do more of the work. Not too hard, not so soft. Calm and deliberate, like the wood-tapper bird.'

Calm and deliberate indeed. She could practically hear the sweat accumulating on her brow.

'It gets rather hot up here near the ceiling, does it not?' she asked.

'It does.'

She continued tapping. 'It must be difficult without a lamp,' she observed.

'Not really.'

It was like speaking to the wall itself. She did not know why she felt the need to make small talk. They had been co-existing for hours without having to fill the silence with stupidities. Besides, she needed to preserve her energy. Her arms were beginning to burn.

'Chiselling is hard work, is it not?' she asked.

'It is.'

Finally she lowered her tools. 'May I take a short rest?'

'Of course,' he said.

He was gazing down at her with an odd grin and she felt as if there were a bird fluttering its wings inside her stomach. She could not tell if he found her pathetic or charming or totally hopeless.

If the latter, she was certainly not improving her image by resting after less than a quarter of an hour's work. Still, her arms were throbbing mightily. Perhaps that was the reason for his grin. He found her comically weak.

She glanced about for some object upon which to comment, but she was standing too close to his body to be able to view much else. His arms were like muscular branches compared with her slender reeds.

And there it was again, lurking all around her—his lusty scent.

He was still grinning at her. It was as if he understood the battle taking place within her and found it amusing. He ran his hands down her dusty arms. 'How do your arms feel?'

Better now that you are doing that.

'They burn a little,' she said. Her heart pounded.

He moved his hands up and down her arms several times, as if to remedy the burning. But he only transferred the burning from her arms to the place between her thighs.

'Please do not do that,' she said. 'I mean—that does not seem to remedy the burning.'

He removed his hands from her arms as if they were ablaze. He had vowed not to think about her, was trying not to even look at her, yet here he was, rubbing her arms. What was he thinking?

But that was the problem. He was not thinking. He was letting his lust overrule his good judgement. He was acting a fool.

'Why are you grinning at me?' she asked. 'Do you find me funny?'

'Not at all,' he said. It was not that he found her funny. He found her irresistible. The way she twisted her lips into a knot with each careful blow. How she hovered near the ground, as if searching for her courage amid the rubble. Her cursed nearness. It was all he could do to keep himself from swallowing her whole.

'Then why are you smiling?' she asked.

'I am not smiling,' he said, affecting a frown.

'Why *were* you smiling?'

'It is just…the situation.'

'What is funny about the situation?' she asked with relentlessness.

'Nothing, really,' he said.

She shook her head. 'It really bothers me when you are not truthful.'

'You do seem rather…bothered,' he observed. At least that was the truth. Her face was growing redder by the moment.

'I *am* bothered,' she said and scowled. '*You* bother me! You are hiding something from me and I do not know what it is.'

'It is normal to panic in such a small space. Let us—'

'I am not panicking!'

'Shh…' he said, then did something completely wrongheaded. He wrapped his arms around her and pulled her against him.

It felt so good—as if she had been enveloped in the wings of Osiris himself. When was the last time she had been embraced? She was not close with anyone at court and Tausret had never been physically demonstrative in her affections.

Perhaps that was why Aya did not attempt to free herself now.

This is a novelty, she told herself as she lay her head against his chest, *a curiosity, that is all*.

But that was not all. It was as if her heart were sighing. His strong arms seemed to be giving shelter to all the rebellious, wrongheaded and imperfect parts of herself. It was as if he had given her a place where she could hide. A kind of cave.

Time slowed and she was enveloped by the simple feeling of his being pressing against hers. She inhaled his scent, delighted in the feeling of his hands touching her skin, counted the beats of his heart.

For many moments, it was enough. But gradually she began to imagine all the other ways she wished to touch him.

There were so many things she might do. She could reach up and touch his chest, for example. There it was, just below her eye level, begging to be caressed. She could trace the bones of his shoulders. They were so strong and prominent, like gates to a fortress.

She could stand on her toes and press her lips to his and hope that he kissed her back. She sensed that he would, though she could not be sure. She had never felt this way before. Her whole body seemed to throb with yearning.

She noticed that the rate of his breaths had increased despite his having done no chiselling at all. Surely he was feeling it, too—this strange desire that had sprouted between them once again like a weed.

She glanced downwards. Perhaps not a weed, but a tall, lusty obelisk beneath a curtain of cloth. There it was, like the answer to a question she did not even know she had asked. Either he was feeling the same yearning, or he had been blessed by the god of resurrection himself.

What would happen if she simply took that part of him in hand? The very thought made her blood go rushing once again into her cheeks. It was rushing other places, too.

Though she had never done such a thing herself, she had seen such acts at festivals. In addition, the women of royal court made a study of the pleasures of the flesh and spoke of them openly.

Now, standing so close to Intef, she wondered why she had not watched and listened more closely. Normal women were expected to enjoy the various expressions of desire, for they were a natural and essential part of life.

But she was not a normal woman; she was an advisor to a pharaoh. And she was currently labouring to escape that Pharaoh's sacred tomb. She should not even be thinking of Intef in such ways, let alone resting against his chest. She could not forget her duty.

'I fear I do not have the strength for sustained chiselling,' she said. With all the strength she had left in her, she lifted her head off his chest.

'Do not worry so much about your duty,' he said thickly.

Were they still discussing her chiselling?

Not friends, she reminded herself, lest she become confused once again.

'I think I can chisel on my own now,' she said, then took a deep breath and stepped out of the tunnel. 'Your instruction is greatly appreciated.' She scooted backwards atop the pile to give him enough room to pass.

He blinked, then seemed to snap to attention. 'Of course,' he said. He stepped out from beneath the tunnel and moved past her, careful not to brush against her in the tight space. Time seemed to resume its normal passing, as if the two had just awoken from the same lusty vision.

'Now go to bed,' she said with mock sternness, 'for the good of Egypt.'

'For the good of Egypt,' he said with a small salute, then padded down the ramp into the dark.

Chapter Fifteen

That night Intef had fallen asleep to the rhythmic sounds of metal against stone. When he awoke, the chiselling had ceased. He wondered if it was morning yet, then heard Aya thrashing in her sleep. He lit his torch and crossed to her bed mat. She was moving her limbs beneath her bed sheet as if she were trying to push away some invisible demon.

He observed her for a long time, telling himself that he was trying to determine whether or not to wake her. In truth, he was trying to determine whether or not he could manage to be near her for four more days.

It had been a mistake to accompany her into the cramped space of the tunnel. It would have been enough to have demonstrated his chiselling technique once on the wall and then left her on her own, yet he had insisted on squeezing next to her inside the emergent tunnel.

His body's response to hers had been difficult to control. In only a short time, he had become rather helpless with desire. He had pretended to embrace her in response to her impending panic. In truth, it was in order to soothe his own irrepressible lust.

If only he could have reminded himself that in three

days Aya would be gazing upon him not with lust, but with loathing.

Just thinking about it caused a heavy dread to overtake him. He wanted Aya to think well of him. It seemed the most important thing in the world. But how could she ever approve of him after she learned what he was going to do?

There was no solution to the problem that did not involve a betrayal of his own duty. Thus he could do nothing other than to purge her presence from his heart. In order to do that, he needed to stay as far away from her as he could. After he handed her to General Setnakht, he would need to find a way to forget her completely.

He wished he could smash something. He strode out of the false chamber and flashed his torch down the long hall. The images from the Underworld seemed to come alive beneath the low flame. He caught sight of an elegant woman in a fitted red sheath holding a looped ankh cross in her grip. Atop her head was a sun disc cradled by a crown of horns. She was Hathor, the goddess of love and beauty.

Aya. She was all he could think about and he did not understand why. It was as if in the quiet darkness of the tomb, something had been resurrected inside him: a latent yearning that was triggered every time he saw her face or heard her voice or even said her name.

Aya.

In his youth he had certainly known his share of women. Before he had joined the army, he had peacocked around the sprawling marketplaces of Thebes with the other young men. He had inherited his father's good looks, along with a healthy young man's lust, and had happily feathered many a nest.

But that had been before Intef had chosen Nebetta and then failed to save his own father's life.

There had been no women after that—only the war that Amenmesse slowly lost to Seti and the needless deaths of thousands of Egyptians, many of whom had perished beneath Intef's own arrows.

How could he enjoy the pleasures of a woman when he was killing other Egyptians? How could he even consider the joys of life when his homeland was being torn apart?

Now his youth was behind him and nothing had changed. Above the ground, armies were assembling for battle and the war for the double crown raged on.

And yet—Aya.

He needed to distract himself, but where could he go? There was only one part of the tomb he had not yet seen.

He stepped into the second unfinished chamber and was greeted with the familiar layout of their makeshift latrine. Instead of moving into that room, he took a hard right, passing a thick wall. He turned the corner again, flashing his torch on the walls and expecting to discover more bottles of perfume.

Instead he looked out over a strange wooden world.

It was a great horde of furniture. There were gold-plated chairs and quilted couches and silver-embossed tables with golden lions' feet. There were bronze beds with jewel-encrusted headrests and feather-stuffed pillows. But there was something unusual about this gilded cache. Everything in it was small.

At the centre of the room, the pale glitter of electrum caught Intef's eye. It was the shiny triangular headboard of what appeared to be a cage. Stepping closer, Intef realised he was looking at a child's cradle. It had been so richly embellished with gold and jewels that

he hardly noticed its most miraculous characteristic. It was made of wood.

A wooden cradle! By Anubis, this was a rich find indeed. In the Black Land, wood was worth its weight in gold and children's cradles were usually made of reeds.

Intef reached out to the cradle and gave it a push. It creaked as it rocked and he could almost imagine the child sleeping peacefully inside it.

Beside the table was a box full of toys—balls and blocks and small wooden figures carved into the shapes of animals. At last he understood the nature of the cache. This was the furniture that belonged to Tausret's only son. It was the prince's playroom.

Intef squatted to study the cradle. Its legs had been wedged into two perfectly bent pieces of wood that rocked effortlessly along the floor. Intef wondered if its craftsman had been a weapons maker, for it appeared that he had used the same wood-bending technique that was used in the production of bows.

Holding his torch, he gently tipped the cradle backwards to get a better look. On the underside of the rocker he noticed a small bronze engraving.

For the granddaughter of
Pharaoh Merneptah
Born in the first year of his reign
Made by Hemaka
Chief Craftsman to Pharaoh

Intef reread the second hieroglyph. Incredibly, the craftsman had mistakenly etched the symbol for granddaughter instead of grandson—a grave error. If it had been detected, the cradle would never have been allowed inside the tomb.

Intef swept his torch around the room one last time. The figure of a life-size stuffed doll caught his eye. It was sitting in one of the smaller chairs and seemed to be watching him closely. He moved to inspect it.

The first thing he noticed was the doll's hair. It was long and dark and appeared to have been crafted from a horse's mane. Small bunches of the hair had been painstakingly sewn into her pillowy head, then gathered at the base of her neck and tied with a bow.

It was the kind of toy that would have belonged to a girl, not a boy.

The doll's features had been just as carefully fashioned. Her lips were a smiling bud of henna-dyed thread and her nose was a shiny round of brown leather.

The doll's eyes were her finest, and also strangest, feature. They were made of two almond-shaped stones of lapis lazuli. They had been sewn into place with black thread, making them appear as if they had been kohled. The colour of the stones was remarkable: a deep midnight blue shot with gold. Thin lines of black paint defined the circles of the eyes, but instead of a black dot in each eye's centre, there was a triangle.

A triangle inside a circle. Where had he seen that shape before?

Intef was inspecting the doll for any marks of ownership when a scream of fear split the silence.

'Stop! Guards!'

Aya knew she was being visited by another memory, yet she could not seem to extract herself from its hold on her sleeping mind...

She was lying on her bed outside Tausret's private chamber, trying to fall asleep. The full moon had just moved into view—framed by the palace courtyard. Aya

stared up at the milky white orb without seeing it, for her mind was focused as it always was on the day ahead.

There had been so much to do in the five years since Pharaoh Seti had died and left Siptah—the son of a harem wife—as his heir. The boy was fifteen years old but still too sickly to rule and so Aya's mistress, Chief Wife Tausret, continued to function as regent in the boy's stead.

There were audiences to be held and decisions to be reached and appearances to be made, all of which Aya, as Tausret's servant and advisor, was required to attend. It seemed that the King of every nation on earth wished to solicit Egypt's aid, for the terrifying Sea Peoples were once again on the march.

Aya closed her eyes and she could hear the crickets in the courtyard singing their relentless song. Suddenly, the crickets ceased.

She opened her eyes and felt her heart jump into her throat. A man was standing over her. He wore a voluminous white tunic over a bulging belly and carried a small copper lamp between his thumbs.

He stroked his long beard. 'Hello, Aya,' he whispered.

'Chancellor Bay?'

Aya stood up from her bed mat to greet him. 'What is the matter, my lord?'

She feared there had been a robbery. It was the only explanation for his appearance in Tausret's wing of the palace so late at night. Either that, or someone had died. 'Do you need to speak to Regent Tausret?' Aya asked. 'Wait here and I will wake her.'

Aya made a move towards the entrance to Tausret's chamber, but Bay held her by the arm. 'You stay right here with me,' he growled and it was then she noticed his strange grin.

She glanced at the guards standing at the entrance to Tausret's chamber. One was gripping his sword, the other his bow. They were watching closely, frozen as two ibis birds.

Bay squeezed his hands into his waist belt and produced two gold ingots. He held them out to the guards as if offering samples of cheese.

'It appears you have a choice,' Bay said, approaching them. He glanced towards the edge of the pond where a pair of his own guards hovered in the shadows. 'Or you can drop your weapons, accept these ingots, and spend the rest of your lives in beer and bread.'

The guards released their weapons, accepted the ingots and scurried out of the courtyard like geese before the storm.

'Stop!' Aya shouted after them. 'Guards!'

Bay pressed his hand to her mouth. 'Shush now, Little Cow,' he hissed. He tossed her down on to the bed mat and stretched out beside her. 'I am here to tell you that you are going to be my wife.'

Aya could smell the stench of wine on his breath and see the glitter of madness in his eyes. 'I am going to get you with child—a little heir of my own. And I shall rule this land for the rest of my days.' The lamp's yellow light danced wickedly beneath his chin. 'Just think of it—a Syrian scribe as Pharaoh of Egypt!'

'You are not in your right mind, Lord Bay,' she said carefully. 'Come, let us find some water to splash on your face.' She tried to sit up, but he gripped her wrists, pushing her back on to the mat.

Terror shot through her. She fought to keep her calm. 'Unhand me, Bay.'

'That is no way to speak to your new husband, Little Cow.'

She attempted to roll away, but he simply rolled atop her, paralysing her body with the weight of his own. 'Get off of me!' she shouted.

'You are so cruel to me, Wife!' He pressed his hips against hers and she could feel his engorged desire rub against her leg.

She fought to keep her calm. She needed to dissuade him. 'Lord Bay, I am but a slave. I serve Regent Tausret alone.'

'You are no slave,' he said. 'And Tausret is a weak and ineffectual regent.'

He pressed his hips harder against Aya's, forcing her legs apart. 'She panders to foreigners and calls it diplomacy.' He tunnelled his hands beneath her tunic. 'She squanders our tax revenues in gifts to the poor. She cannot even produce a proper heir. Ah, there we are.' He pushed his finger into Aya's womanhood. 'How many sons has she lost? Four? Five?'

'Three,' called a voice from behind them. Tausret was standing in the doorway of her chamber in her blue nightdress. She held out a dagger. 'Release her, Bay. Now.'

Bay rose to his feet, laughing. 'You are a cowardly woman. You cannot even hold that dagger properly.' He walked towards Tausret's trembling figure. 'Do you not see that even your own guards have abandoned you?'

Bay plucked the dagger from Tausret's hands and pointed it at her chin. 'Go back to bed, old woman,' he said, 'lest I decide to rid Egypt of you myself.' He tossed the dagger aside and shoved Tausret to the ground.

'Come now, Wife,' he said, turning back to Aya. 'This will only hurt for a moment.'

But Aya was no longer lying on the ground. She had seized one of the guards' abandoned bows and arrows and was taking her aim. She released the arrow, but it flew beneath Bay's arm and landed on the floor.

'Little Cow?' he said, turning to see her readying her second arrow. 'How dare you?' He was rushing towards Aya. She was shaking so badly that when she released the deadly projectile it only wobbled to the ground. His hands encircled her throat.

Wrath flamed in his eyes as he began to squeeze the life out of her. Her head seemed to fill with air. He was lifting her off the ground. She had nearly given in to death when she saw the arrow shoot through the side of his throat.

'How cowardly is that?' said a voice.

Tausret.

A hand was gripping her shoulder.

'Aya, wake up!'

Aya opened her eyes. 'I am awake.' She gulped the air.

'You were having another vision.' His voice was thick with concern.

She touched her throat. 'My arrows…would not reach their target.'

His hand remained on her shoulder and she prayed he would keep it there. She knew he was not her friend. She knew she could not trust his intentions. She knew there was something he was concealing from her. But at the moment it felt as if he was the only thing keeping her tethered to the world.

'What target?' he asked.

She placed her hand atop his and let out a sob.

'It is all right,' he whispered. 'Nothing can harm you. I am here.'

He said nothing more, but she felt his presence around her like a cloak. She had been haunted by her memory of Bay's death for years, but only now, with Intef's hand atop her shoulder, did she feel safe speaking his name aloud.

'The target was Chancellor Bay,' she said at last.

She saw Intef mask his surprise.

'He tried to rape me,' she said. 'He said that he was going to make me his wife. He said that he would get me with his son and heir. I tried to fight, but my arrows would not stop him. He almost choked the life from me. It was Pharaoh Tausret who finally killed him. She saved my life.'

Intef was shaking his head in confusion. 'But the young Pharaoh Siptah killed Bay, not Tausret.'

'The High Priest circulated that lie,' said Aya. 'He killed Siptah himself.'

Intef looked pained. 'I thought Tausret killed Siptah.'

'The High Priest made up that lie, as well. He wanted to discredit Tausret in the eyes of the people. He sent out the news to all the temples and they disseminated it throughout the two lands. It is unfortunate that most citizens believe whatever they hear—especially when it comes from a priest.'

Aya watched Intef run his fingers through his hair in the way he always did when he was frustrated. 'What is the matter?' she asked.

'It pains me to think of you being groped by that

vile man.' He stood and began to pace. 'And then he
choked you?' She could see his jaw clenching as he
walked back and forth, shaking his head as if trying to
rid himself of a demon.

'He was not successful.'

'You almost died!'

'But I did not. Tausret's arrow pierced his throat.'

'He wished to marry you?'

'That is what he said. What is the matter?'

'To think of you married to such a beast—' His voice
broke. He took a breath, shook his head several times
more. 'It pains me.'

'I would have escaped him,' said Aya.

'Not before he damaged your soul.'

'You underestimate my cleverness,' she said, echoing
his words. He stopped in his tracks and gazed at her.

'You find me funny?' she asked.

'Not at all—why?'

'You are grinning again.' She could not read his
thoughts, though she wished to more than ever.

He returned his expression to a frown and went back
to pacing. She could practically see him studying the
events she had recounted, trying to make sense of them.

'I mean no offence,' he said, 'but why would an ambitious man such as Bay wish to marry a servant? If he
wanted an heir, would he not wish to marry a woman
of rank?'

It was an innocent question, yet it felt like a punch
to her stomach. As Tausret's advisor, Aya had always
seen herself as a woman of rank. But Intef was right.
She did not have a name or any family. She was half
Libyan, by the gods. There was no reason for any noble
man to take her to wife.

'He was very drunk that night,' she said, her stomach sinking further still. Was it possible that in addition to terrifying her, Bay had also been mocking her?

She did not wish to think about it any longer. 'I fear I have wasted precious time sitting here,' she said, rising to her feet. 'Tell me, where are the hammer and chisel?'

Chapter Sixteen

Aya climbed into the tunnel and went to work, but after what must have been no more than a few hours, she could not continue. She staggered down the ramp of earth with her lamp and took her seat at its base.

Intef had not yet even fallen asleep. 'What are you doing there?' he called from his bed mat.

'Just resting,' Aya said. 'I will take up the chisel again soon.'

'You should stop for the night,' he said. 'Chiselling is hard work.'

'For a woman,' she added. 'That is what you wish to say, is it not?' Intef rose from his mat, crossed the chamber and sat down next to her. 'Well, you are wrong,' she continued. 'It is of no consequence that I am a woman.'

'Of course it is,' he said. 'Women are weaker than men. That is a fact.'

'Only some women.'

'Flex your arm muscle,' he said. She lifted her arm and he encircled it with his hand. 'Go ahead,' he said. 'Flex.'

'I am flexing,' she cried. She heard him chuckle. 'Beast!'

'Now feel this,' he said. He took her hand and placed it on his own arm. His muscle bulged inside her palm, sending a strange flutter of excitement through her. She stretched her fingers wide, but still she could not encompass it.

'I will allow that you are slightly stronger than I,' she said.

He laughed. 'Slightly stronger? I am a lion to your lamb!'

'It is not your strength that I question, it is your logic,' Aya explained. 'I am an inferior chiseller only because I am untrained—not because I am a woman.'

He appeared to consider her argument. 'Well, I suppose I must concede.'

'You concede?'

'You make a good point,' he said.

But you are supposed to be an unreasonable brute!

'My own mother was quite strong,' he added. 'She once captured a crocodile in her arms and tossed it back into the river!'

Aya laughed, then paused. 'That was before your family fell into poverty, yes?'

'Yes. Before my father died.'

She had reminded him of his sad history and now hardly knew what to say. She noticed that she had not yet taken her hand off his arm. She gave it one last squeeze and the two fell silent.

Finally, Aya spoke. 'I know I should rest, but I do not feel tired.'

'Nor do I,' he said. 'Though you are an exhausting woman.' There was a smile in his voice.

'And you are an exasperating man,' she replied warmly.

'We will be fortunate if we get out of here without

killing each other first.' His eyes lingered where he had touched her arm. It felt almost as if he were touching it again.

'I am afraid that we have already tried that once,' noted Aya.

'And failed miserably, bless the gods.'

'I suppose my dearth of muscles has served us in that regard, as well.' She rubbed her arm in the place where he had touched it.

Intef's eyes acquired a sudden glint. 'It is unfortunate that your underdevelopment is not limited to your muscles,' he said.

'Excuse me?'

'I mean that your arms are not the only part of you that lack training.'

The man lived to exasperate her! 'You seem to have analysed my strengths and weaknesses in great detail,' she said.

'I am a soldier.' He leaned back and his eyes slid up and down her torso assessingly. 'It is what I do to my enemy.'

'What other part of me lacks training, then?' His eyes slid over her bare shoulders, following the straps of her sheath to the bumps of her breasts.

He blinked once and returned his attention to her face. 'Your aim.'

She cocked her head in confusion.

'You are haunted by memories of demons that you cannot hit,' he said. 'Perhaps if you could improve your aim while you are awake, they will not bother you in your sleep.'

'I cannot control what I do in my sleep,' she said.

'Have you ever tried?'

'Of course not.' The very idea struck her as absurd.

'Then how do you know?' He raised one of his lux-
uriant brows and she felt her resistance crumbling. 'If
I am to help you protect the heir, then I must insist that
you have at least some practice with the bow.'

'You seem to have gathered up many good reasons to
send arrows flying inside this sacred house,' she replied.

'Not flying,' said Intef. 'Hitting their target.'

He stood and lifted the lamp and its low light flickered in his eyes. 'Let me help you slay your demons,'
he said, and reached out his hand.

She could not help herself—she took it.

Intef selected a small bow and a quiver of arrows
from the weapons room and handed it to Aya. 'Make
yourself familiar with this,' he told her. 'Grip the wood.
Test the strings. Practise manoeuvring it. You may even
wish to give it a name.'

'A name?'

'Something to elicit the favour of the gods.'

He strode down the corridor and into the main chamber, aware of the swift passage of time. He should have
been getting the rest he needed, not preparing for target practice.

But right then, helping Aya had suddenly seemed
more important than any other concern. In three short
days, he was going to deliver her to the twin lions of
General Setnakht and his son. The least he could do
was show her how to roar.

Arriving in the main chamber, he searched the storage rooms. Target practice was best with some sort of
human-shaped figure and Intef thought of the doll he
had discovered inside the unfinished chamber.

It was an enigma he could not seem to purge from
his mind. Why would a boy child ever be given such a

toy? And then there was the problem of the cradle and its mysterious plaque. Royal craftsmen were among the best trained of elite workers. How could a royal craftsman mistake the hieroglyphic for grandson?

'For the granddaughter of Pharaoh Merneptah' the plaque had read. If the heir was a woman, the contest for the double crown would be altogether different. Whoever wedded the heiress first would win.

There would be no bloodshed at all in that case, for Rameses would be marrying into divinity. His legitimacy would be unassailable. His dynasty would be secure, Egypt would be unified and nobody would have to die.

Intef was so lost in his thoughts that he practically stumbled upon a long wooden bed frame standing upright in one of the storage chambers. Its base was made of several long slats of wood—a fine target.

He set the bed standing on its end at the entrance to the main chamber and found the coal brazier he had discovered the first night. Blackening his fingers with soot, he traced a small circle at the centre of the bed's wooden base.

He strode down the corridor and returned to Aya's side. 'Have you familiarised yourself with the bow?'

'I have.'

'And how do you find it?'

'It is as any other.'

'When your training is complete, it will be as a third arm.'

She gave him a doubting smile. 'You are quite sure of yourself, are you not?'

'You have no idea,' he said gravely.

How easy it was to make her blush. The colour

seemed to travel as quickly up her neck as the lust travelled down into his depths.

'Do you see that long plank of wood at the end of the hall?' he asked.

'I do.'

'Can you send your arrow to the centre of the circle I drew?'

'I can.'

'Well?'

She lifted an arrow from the quiver, placed its nock on the string, then drew and let fly.

The weakly shot arrow wobbled through the air before shooting downwards and ricocheting off the floor.

Aya was shaking her head. 'Perhaps this is a bad idea.'

'Nonsense,' he replied. 'It was your first try. Try again.'

She pulled another arrow, set it and drew it back. 'Hold it there,' he said. He reached around her from behind, his naked chest muscles pressing against her bare shoulders.

It was not the only place their bodies touched. He could not tell what was more unfortunate, that his desire had found a resting place in the small of her back or that his thighs were pressing hard against the soft contours of her buttocks.

He considered stepping away from her, but the bow had been pulled and she was waiting patiently for his counsel. He adjusted the position of her fingers and helped her pull back further on the string.

'Do you feel that?' he whispered in her ear.

'Um…yes,' she breathed. He sensed her shudder.

'What is it?' He made the mistake of breathing in her scent. His desire stiffened against her back.

'What is what?'

'What is it that you feel?'

She seemed to search for the right word. 'Effort.'

He felt the same. It was a huge effort not to toss the bow aside and pull her to the floor.

The gods are cruel, he thought.

He slowly stepped away from her.

'Hold your stance,' he said. 'Now look at the target with your cleverest eye. Imagine it is an enemy. Think of someone in particular.'

'All right.'

'Now tell me who it is.'

'It is the High Priest.'

'Why is he your enemy?'

'He wants to kill the heir.'

'And you are not going to let him, are you?'

Aya shook her head. 'When can I release it?'

'When you feel your heart is true.'

She instantly released the arrow. It went flying down the corridor, missing the bed frame entirely.

'A spectacular miss,' he remarked with a grin.

'It slipped from my grasp!' She wiped her hands on her sheath. 'It is so hot in here.'

'It must be daytime in the world above,' he remarked and watched in wonderment as she propped the bow against her leg and produced a cloth from beneath her belt. She patted her brow, then wiped down her sweat-glazed arms in long, elegant strokes.

'Does it not seem stuffier than yesterday?' she asked. She lifted her hair off her neck and fanned herself, and he noticed an unnatural mark on her skin.

'You have a tattoo.' He pointed to a small mark he had spotted at the back of her neck, just below her hairline.

'What?'

He stared at the mark. It was a tattoo for certain. 'A triangle inside a circle,' he said. 'Does that mean anything to you?'

He saw a flash of awareness traverse her expression. 'Nothing,' she said, though he noticed her swallow hard.

'Were you not aware you had a tattoo?' he asked. He had seen the shape before, quite recently. But where? He tried to get a better look at it, but she swayed away from him.

'I had no idea,' she said. She placed her hand over the mark briefly, then let her hair down. 'It must be from my infancy. Tattoos are important in the Libyan tradition.'

'Do you not wish to see it?' he prodded. 'I can draw it for you. Or trace it against your skin.'

'It is not necessary,' she clipped. She tucked her cloth inside her belt and lifted her bow. 'Shall we resume?'

Puzzled, he handed her an arrow. She nocked it quickly and let it fly. It landed even further from the target than the first.

'You are distracted,' he said.

'I am not distracted,' she protested. 'On the contrary, I have never wanted anything more than to hit that cursed circle.'

'That is why you are not hitting it.'

She shook her head and sent another arrow tumbling to the floor. He needed to get her mind off the tattoo.

'You must first clear your thoughts. Then you must focus on the truth inside your heart.'

'Perhaps the gods do not wish me to wield a bow,' she said.

'Perhaps the gods are bored and wish to entertain themselves,' he said, then added, 'Cursed bastards.'

He waited for her exasperation to surface. Five, four, three, two...

'You dare to curse the gods inside a house of—'

'Do you wish to sleep soundly?' he interrupted.

'I do.'

'Do you wish to defend yourself against enemies yet to come?'

'I do.'

'Then lift the bow.'

She did as he commanded.

'Your position is terrible. Square your feet. Lift your shoulders.' She did as she was told, but her posture lacked conviction. He stood behind her once again.

'Now tell me the reason you are living,' he breathed into her ear. She was so close. He could smell her. He could sense her beating heart.

'I do not understand,' she said.

'Why did the gods keep you alive, by Seth?'

'To protect Pharaoh's house.'

'Why else?'

'To protect the heir,' she replied.

'And who is it that would like to see you dead?'

'The High Priest.'

'Now tell yourself where you are going to put that arrow.'

'Right in the middle of the—'

'Cease!' Intef interrupted. 'Do not say it aloud. An archer never says where she is going to put her arrow—she just puts it there!'

He lifted an arrow from the quiver and positioned it for her. 'You must not allow anyone else to determine your fate,' he whispered. 'Ever again. Now aim and, when you feel certain of this truth, let fly.'

And that was what she did.

Chapter Seventeen

The following nights were free of visions. Aya slept long, chiselled hard and lived to shoot arrows.

Several times, she caught herself rubbing the back of her neck, wondering about the tattoo Intef claimed to have seen there. What a strange coincidence that she would have the same tattoo as Tausret's heir—though surely there was some logical reason for it. Perhaps it was a mark bestowed upon every young person who entered into Pharaoh's service.

Once while Intef was chiselling, Aya wandered into the main chamber and rifled through Tausret's jewellery boxes, searching for something she could use as a mirror. She stopped herself when she saw Tausret's precious pectorals and bracelets all in a tangle.

She said extra prayers that day, begging Pharaoh for forgiveness. In every other way, she had been trying to conduct herself with the utmost reverence. Indeed, when she was not chiselling, she was praying at Pharaoh's shrine, or reciting purifying spells, or doing ritual cleansings of all the chambers.

Still, no prayer could make it cooler or improve the quality of the air inside the tomb and, as the hours passed, her breaths were less satisfying somehow, as if she were not breathing air, but malevolent spirits.

The darkness had begun to bother her, as well. She knew that the chambers in which they dwelled were large, but when she blew out the wick of her lamp they seemed to close in all around her.

Archery was the only thing that seemed to comfort her. As soon as she had understood the essential role of her own heart in the act, her arrow had flown true.

Each day she improved, and by the third day—or was it the fourth?—she was able to land the arrow practically wherever she liked.

It was as if her archery were improving in direct proportion to the decrease in the quality of the air.

That evening, after Intef could chisel no more, she challenged him to a contest. 'There can be only one person with the title of best archer in Egypt,' she pronounced, trying to lift his spirits. 'And I fear that person is no longer you.'

'A jest!' exclaimed Intef. 'It seems that your sense of humour has improved along with your aim.'

'So you accept?' He shot a glance across the chamber to the tunnel. 'Even if I started chiselling right now, I would still be tired in only four hours or so. We will not lose any time.'

She did not wait for him to refuse her. Instead she pulled three footrests from Pharaoh's furniture stash and set them out along the corridor along with three flickering lamps.

'You dare to despoil more of Pharaoh's sacred furniture?' Intef asked.

'I dare to despoil the reputation of the best archer in the land.'

She offered Intef his bow and a quiver full of arrows. 'Very well, then,' he said with a grin. 'I will go first. Prepare to be humbled.' He took his place beside her and raised his bow.

'Pharaoh Tausret was an able archer, you know,' remarked Aya. 'She rode out against the invading Shekelesh tribe in the second year of her reign and defeated them.'

Intef shook his head. 'I did not know that,' he remarked. 'But I do know that you are trying to distract me.' He inhaled sharply, then shot his arrow. It landed at the centre of the first footrest. 'If only Tausret had been a man,' he said.

Aya raised her bow and waited for her anger to pass. If only Tausret had been a man? But Aya knew what he was about. 'You are going to have to do better than that to distract me.' She steadied her heart and let her arrow fly and landed it a finger's width from his.

'Well done,' he said. In a single motion, he lifted his bow, set his arrow and sent it to the centre of the second footrest. 'Your woman Pharaoh would be proud.'

Woman Pharaoh? She would not let him draw her fire. 'My *Pharaoh* would certainly be proud,' Aya said coolly. She waited until her mind was clear and her heart true, then released her arrow. Once again, it landed just next to his.

'Indeed she would be proud,' he said, sending her an admiring nod. 'Women do not often excel in wielding weapons.'

He drew back his bow and released his arrow for the final time, landing it just to the right of the centre of the third footrest.

'They certainly do not,' Aya agreed, 'for men such as you fear being bested by them.'

She raised her bow and in an instant his arrow had fallen to the ground and her arrow stuck in its place.

He stared at her in wonder. 'Apparently I have just experienced that particular outcome.'

'And how do you feel?' asked Aya, setting down her bow.

'Proud.' She searched his eyes for mockery, or some hint of a jest, but found only a kind of softness that she had not seen in them before. 'It appears that you have a gift,' he said.

'If a woman can shoot an arrow, then why can a woman not be pharaoh?' she asked.

He sighed. 'A woman can certainly be pharaoh—just not Tausret.'

'Why not Tausret?' Aya asked.

'She was a weak and ineffectual ruler. She bankrupted the country and failed to produce an heir. She was unskilled in diplomacy and could not keep Egypt united.'

'Who told you that?'

'Who tells all the histories? The holy priests, of course.'

'And you believe those stories?'

'I am the son of farmers from Thebes. Of course I do.'

'Intef, may I tell you a story of my own?'

He watched her lift one of the lamps and motion to him to follow her, and soon he was sitting atop the pile of earth beneath their growing tunnel while she ducked inside it and began to chisel. 'Can you hear me?' she asked.

'Quite well,' he said. He gazed at her sandals and

the small, intelligent feet that donned them. 'You may begin your story.'

'This is a true story,' Aya said, beginning to tap at the rock. 'About how Tausret died.'

'Did you not say that she died on the birthing blocks?'

'Yes, but I wish to tell you how she got there. I believe the High Priest hoped this story would end with me.'

Intrigued, Intef leaned back against the wall next to the tunnel. 'Go on, then.'

Aya tapped softly as she spoke. 'It was almost a year ago, already the second year of the drought. I was standing beside Pharaoh's throne in the reception hall of the palace, receiving a delegation from the kingdom of the Hittites. There must have been two hundred men filing into the hall and I remember how their robes swished across the marble floor as they walked.'

'Two hundred Hittites?' said Intef. 'An extravagant invitation for Pharaoh to extend in the middle of a drought.'

'But they were not invited,' said Aya. 'They had arrived in Pi-Rameses without notice. Their capital Hattusa had been sacked by a confederation of the Sea Peoples. They were on a mission, searching for allies.'

'It is the first I have heard of the sack of Hattusa,' he remarked. 'Go on.'

'As the bearded noblemen assembled before the throne,' Aya continued, 'a ripple of alarm seemed to pass through their ranks. I watched several men notice Tausret and frown, though I could not determine what they found wrong with her.

'As all Pharaohs, she wore the heavy double crown of the Lord of the Two Lands and in her hands held the symbolic shepherd's guiding crook and goading flail.

She was in every way the leader of her flock, but the Hittite noblemen continued to whisper and stare, and Pharaoh asked me what I thought was the matter.'

'And what did you tell her?'

'I told her I thought it was perhaps her lack of a pharaonic beard.'

Intef laughed. 'And a man to wear that beard!'

'The great Pharaoh Hatshepsut wore a beard. And she was very much a woman.'

'I suppose you are right in that,' Intef conceded. Although Hatshepsut had been erased from history by her successor, her legend lived on among the women of Egypt. 'Go on.'

'A tall man in a henna-coloured robe stepped forward. He prostrated himself before the throne and made the customary obeisance. Then he motioned to a group of servants who presented Pharaoh with twenty amphorae of the finest Hittite wine, fifty pairs of shoes from the weavers of Keftiu and ten golden necklaces strung with pearls.'

'A fine collection of gifts,' said Intef.

'Not for Tausret,' replied Aya. 'She did not care about filling her own closets with riches.'

'Really? I was always told she was a selfish, greedy kind of woman.'

'Not at all!' said Aya. 'She told the ambassador to bestow his generous gifts on some other worthy ally, that her only interest was in securing grain for her people.'

'Did the ambassador not take offence?' asked Intef.

'No, for that was when the crowd of men split apart and in their cleft appeared a middle-aged man in a bejewelled leather skull cap and a lavish white robe,' Aya said.

'The King of the Hittites?' asked Intef.

'So it was,' said Aya. 'King Suppiluliuma the Second. He sank to the floor before Tausret just like his ambassador had done. When she bade him rise, he recounted the woeful tale of the sack of Hattusa, the great capital of the Hittites, and he asked for the aid of Egyptian troops.

'"We will give you men to stand against the Sea Peoples," Tausret replied, "but in return you must bring us grain—at least two hundred thousand barrels."

'The King's eyes grew wide. "Your Majesty," he said, "it is enough grain to feed a nation."

'"It is what I require," said Tausret.

'Without turning, King Suppiluliuma lifted his arm. "Leave us," he said and every member of the delegation except the ambassador exited the hall.'

Intef laughed with delight. 'A dramatic exodus! How I would have loved to have seen it.'

'It was as I describe,' said Aya. 'When everyone had departed I remember the King swept his fingers through his long beard and told Tausret that he could procure the grain she needed, but that he would require something more than just troops in exchange for it. Tausret asked him how much gold and silver he would like. He told her he was not looking for riches.'

'Do not tell me he refused Egyptian gold?' exclaimed Intef.

'He did indeed,' replied Aya. 'For he said that he had no heir upon whom to bestow such wealth. Then he mentioned the threat of General Setnakht in the south and how Tausret, too, was in dire need of an heir. I wonder if you can guess what he asked next?'

The answer came to Intef instantly, though he could hardly believe it. 'King Suppiluliuma asked Tausret to lie with him?'

'When you are not being rude, you are quite astute,' Aya teased.

Intef could not help himself—he bent his head beneath the tunnel and gazed up at Aya's standing figure, the dust falling down around her like rain. 'And did she agree to lie with him?'

'*Ack!* What are you doing there?' And there it was— that gorgeous, gap-toothed grin. He felt a strange rush of delight.

'You look rather lovely for a filthy stone mason,' he said.

'Return to your seat, young man!' she scolded.

'Ah! So now I am young.'

He returned to his place and heard the sounds of her chiselling resume. 'Well? Did she agree to lie with him or not?'

'She did not reply right away,' Aya continued. 'I remember that she stood up from her throne and began to pace. I watched the tall, weighty crown rock back and forth upon her head.

'"Lie with me and get me a child," King Suppiluliuma urged her, "and in return I will get you your grain. When our son is born, he shall bind our countries as allies. My name will not be lost. Nor will yours," he said.

'And I remember that Tausret's lips had twisted into a frown. It was the thing she feared most, you see—to bear another child. She had borne three sons as Pharaoh Seti's Chief Wife and none had survived his first year. She asked me for my advice.'

'And what did you tell her?' Intef asked.

'I told her to refuse him,' Aya said, 'but I was not convincing enough in my arguments. She kept talking about how many people would be saved by so much grain. At length she stepped down the dais and took the King's hand. "For the good of Egypt," Tausret said. And the rest is history.'

Intef sat in silence, listening to Aya's chiselling. 'You have helped me see the truth about Tausret,' said Intef. 'I am grateful.'

'People should not believe everything they hear from priests.'

'The priests of Thebes always said that women should not be pharaohs. But perhaps women make the best pharaohs of all,' Intef mused.

'If a woman is a good pharaoh, it is not because she is a woman,' said Aya. 'It is because of who she is.'

Intef frowned. He had not expected such an answer, yet he perceived the wisdom in it. 'It is *ma'at*. Justice. That is what you seek for Tausret,' Intef said.

'I have never thought of it that way,' said Aya. She stepped out of the tunnel and sat beside him. Sweat poured down her dusty arms in long stripes. 'Right now what I seek is strength, for it seems to have left me.'

He stared at the hammer and chisel she had dropped in the dirt. His hands ached just to look at them. 'I fear that my strength has also abandoned me for the night,' said Intef. 'If night it is.'

He glanced at his sandals. According to the marks, they had been labouring for four days. Had it really only been four? It seemed like more than that. Perhaps five or even six.

'The air grows sour,' said Aya. 'We are running out of time.'

'Nonsense,' said Intef, but his tone lacked conviction. The heat inside the small space was nearly unbearable and the air itself seemed dangerously thin.

'I find myself in need of one of your jests,' she whispered.

'Just one?' he said.

'Intef, I fear we are going to die. You cannot chisel any longer, nor can I. The air—'

'Shh…' he said. Her breaths were too short. He touched her arm. 'What is our greatest tool inside this tomb?'

'The chisel, of course.'

'Not the chisel.'

'The hammer, then.'

'Not the hammer.'

'What then, Intef?'

'It is calm. A wise man told me that once.'

'How can we be calm? We chisel so much and never reach the sky.'

'We will reach it.'

'And if we do not?' asked Aya.

Then it has been my life's privilege to know you.

'I fear that I have failed you,' she said, 'that we have run out of time, that—'

'You have not failed me, Aya. On the contrary.' The top of her head was just a hand's width away. Impulsively, he bent and kissed it, foolishly allowing his lips to linger in her hair.

She stiffened at his touch. 'Do you not fear a deadly kick from your enemy?' she asked, but there was humour in her voice.

'No, but I am worried that my enemy may soon become too filthy to recognise.'

She laughed. 'I am made of sweat and ceiling dust.'

'Then I love sweat and ceiling dust,' he said. The word lingered in the air around them like a strange spirit. Love.

'It is so hot, Intef,' she said, breaking the spell. She lifted the sweat-glazed hair off of her neck and fanned herself with her hands. She closed her eyes. And there it was once again—that unusual tattoo beneath her hairline: a triangle inside a circle.

She must have sensed him staring, for her eyes flashed open and he was struck with their piercing blueness. He turned away, remembering at once where he had seen the shape of her tattoo before. It had been painted on the eyes of the doll he had discovered inside the unfinished chamber. The doll's eyes had also been blue.

'Aya, how many years ago did Pharaoh Merneptah begin his reign?' he asked. 'The priests say that four and twenty years have passed.'

'The priests are correct in that,' said Aya. 'He was crowned the year I was born.'

A strange knowing was emerging at the edges of his mind. 'There is a cradle in the unfinished chamber that was constructed that same year,' Intef said. 'Have you seen the cradle?'

'I have,' Aya said. 'It is a beautiful object—acacia wood, no?'

'There is a plaque hidden beneath its base. It names the granddaughter of Pharaoh Merneptah—born in the first year of Merneptah's reign.'

'Granddaughter?' said Aya. 'It must be a mistake.'

'Perhaps it is one of the babies Tausret lost,' Intef offered casually.

'They were all sons—I saw them myself,' said Aya.

'What about the heir? Did Tausret ever say for certain that her living heir was a son?'

Aya paused, thinking. 'No, I suppose not.'

'Can you think of a reason she might have wanted to keep the child's identity secret?'

'I believe Tausret did not wish for her child to share the same fate as she had.'

'What fate?'

'Tausret spent her life trying to produce an heir. She said she often felt like a brood mare. It did not seem to matter what was in her mind or her heart—only what was in her belly. I imagine that she did not wish for her one living child to share that same fate.'

'But such a child would only share that fate if she were female.'

Aya shook her head. 'We are running out of time, Intef.' She stepped back into the tunnel. 'I must continue my work.'

'Is there anything else you remember Tausret saying about the heir?' Intef said. He heard a frenzy of tapping. 'Anything that might help us in our search?'

He could barely hear her words over her blows. 'Just that he abides in Pi-Rameses...and that he has a distinguishing tattoo.'

Suddenly, all the puzzle pieces seemed to fall into place. Tausret had a daughter, Merneptah's secret granddaughter, who was a twenty-four-year-old woman with eyes as blue as a doll's and a distinguishing tattoo. She would have been a worthy marriage target for some ambitious official—someone like Chancellor Bay.

'Aya, it is you,' Intef said suddenly. 'Do you not see? You are the great-granddaughter of Rameses the Great Ancestor. *You* are the heir. You are Tausret's daughter.'

Chapter Eighteen

It was as she had feared: the sour air had begun to drive them both mad. It had started with her bizarre idea for an archery contest. They should have been chiselling, not shooting arrows! Then Intef had put forth some absurd theory that Aya was the heir to the double crown. Aya, in her weakened mental state, had been unable to contradict him.

Then, as she dozed on her bed mat that night, Aya found herself inside what she thought was another one of her memories.

Slowly she realised that it was not a memory at all, however. It was as if she were beholding some version of the future...

She was standing on a cliff looking out over a vast desert hardpan, searching for signs of movement below. Hours before, there had been a great battle. Hundreds had perished, but the losers had not yet come to collect their fallen.

Everywhere there was death. The air hummed with the buzz of flies. Somewhere in the distance, a pack of jackals had already gone to work.

Aya spotted movement near the middle of the plain:

a man in a long white kilt and leather breast guard. He was lying on the ground, his hands and wrists tied, as if someone had taken him captive and then changed his mind and left him to die.

Though he was far away, Aya could see the tattoo on the back of his neck: a triangle inside a circle. He was no mere man—he was the heir to the double crown—Tausret's son. She started down the steep cliff.

She did not get far before she stumbled. The rocks were unstable, the path steep and treacherous. She had to go slowly, lest she fall to her own death. She kept her eyes on her footfalls, not daring to look up.

Finally, she arrived at a large flat rock about halfway down the cliff and paused atop it. She caught sight of a moving chariot on the plain below. It was borne by a single white horse and a man in a white hooded robe. She recognised his long beard and corpulent figure even from the distance. It was Chancellor Bay.

He was careening across the flat plain at great speed. He lifted his whip high in the air and cracked it above his horse. He was heading towards the heir.

Aya had to get to the young man before Bay did, for she knew the chancellor would kill him if he could. But Bay's chariot was moving faster than her unstable legs could take her and she knew she would not reach him in time.

In that instant Bay's white hood flew off his face. He looked up at the cliffs and in the strange space of the vision Aya could hear his words. 'What are you doing, Little Cow?'

'I am stopping you,' she whispered.

She found the centre of her heart and let the arrow fly. Snap went the first string from the horse's harness.

It coiled in the air like a snake. The chariot veered to the side while she loaded another arrow and let it fly.

Snap went the second string of the harness. The horse ran free, leaving the chariot teetering across the plain, raising a great cloud of dust. Bay tumbled to the ground just twenty paces from where the heir lay writhing.

Aya watched in horror as Bay calmly returned to standing. Incredibly, it appeared he was not harmed. It was then Aya noticed his leopard skin pelt and adornments of the priesthood.

The man was no longer Chancellor Bay at all, but the High Priest. He drew a sword from the sheath around his waist and walked calmly towards the young man.

'Do not touch him!' she shouted.

She launched another arrow and pierced one side of the priest's voluminous robe, pinning it to the ground. She followed it with another arrow that pierced the other side.

The priest stopped in his tracks, pinned. He looked to his sides, puzzled by the two arrows that kept him in place. He tried to move forward, but he was stuck. He looked up at Aya and hissed.

Then he disappeared—replaced by a long white snake with shiny white scales. Apep. The beast wriggled out from beneath the High Priest's robe and slithered towards the heir. Aya had one arrow left. She cleared her mind and took her aim.

The arrow landed right in the middle of the snake's head, skewering it to the ground. Aya yelped for joy. She had done it. The heir to the Horus throne was safe! For once in her life, Aya had done Pharaoh proud. She had done her duty.

She made her way down the cliff and rushed to the

young man's side. He was still lying on his stomach, his face buried in the dirt.

'I slew your enemies,' she said. 'I have come to release you from your bonds.'

She gently rolled him to his side, then on to his back. He blinked up at her and the sky seemed to be reflected in the colour of his eyes: a deep, uncanny blue.

And then she realised that she was not looking into a man's face, but a woman's. It was her own face. She was looking at herself.

Aya awoke and stared into the darkness. What had she just seen? The tomb was hot, she could barely breathe. Where was Intef? She had to tell him about her vision.

'Intef?' Arriving at the foot of his bed mat, she crouched down and reached for him, but discovered only a slack bed sheet.

The false chamber was eerily quiet. She crossed to the ramp and climbed up it. 'Intef, are you here?'

There was no response. A feeling of dread spread over her. She felt along the ceiling to the lip of the tunnel, crouched down and reached out once again. 'Intef?'

She felt the hardness of the tip of the chisel beneath her fingers. She pulled the instrument towards her, but it would not come free. She moved her fingers down the cold metal, arriving at the shaft and feeling Intef's own fingers wrapped around it. They were as cold as the metal itself.

'Intef!' she shrieked.

No. This could not be happening. She moved her hands over Intef's body, pressing and probing and praying he would respond. Nothing. She held her hand over his mouth, trying to determine if he still made breath.

She could feel a small movement of air coming from his nose. Blessed Isis!

'Intef, wake up!' she shouted. She pushed against his limp body and was rewarded with a low moan.

Aya's heart raced. He was alive! But what was wrong? Had he fallen and hit his head? She needed to get him out of this cramped, dusty space. 'Come, Intef,' she said. She tugged at his arm. No response.

She was going to have to move him, but how? She retrieved his bed sheet and rolled him on to it, then tugged it with all her might down the pile dirt. Finger by finger, hand by hand, she pulled him down the ramp until he was lying atop the tiles of the false chamber.

She needed to see if he was injured. She needed light! She crossed to the sitting area and felt for where Intef kept the striking stones. She fumbled desperately among the objects, finally seizing upon the stones.

This was going to be difficult. She had never made fire herself. She had always allowed Intef to do it. She groped about for the bit of rope he always used to set the flame. There it was, thank the gods, and also the lamp.

Now she had everything she needed to make light except the actual ability to do it. She tried to picture Intef striking the stones. He always seemed very focused on the task, as if he were willing the sparks to appear.

She made a preliminary strike. Nothing.

'Great Amun-Ra, deliver me strength,' she implored. She struck the stones together as hard as she could, but still no sparks flew. She tried again, then again. She lifted the striking stone as high as she could, then smashed it down upon her own thumb.

'Ow!' she howled. She could feel the blood oozing out of the wound. She thrust her thumb into her mouth and sucked, trying to stop the bleeding.

She needed to calm herself, but she could not seem to catch her breath. Her efforts had made her dizzy. She stood and braced herself against a pillar. Each time she inhaled, she felt a slight stinging in her lungs.

'The air inside this tomb will not last for ever,' she remembered Intef saying. *'Soon it will turn sour. It will draw demons from the Underworld...'*

'And we shall perish among them,' Aya whispered.

The knowledge of her fate hit her all at once and she froze. The air had turned sour. It was full of demons. Curse the gods—she and Intef had run out of time.

'No!' Aya raged. This was her fault. If only she had allowed Intef to begin his tunnel in the high vaulted ceiling of the false chamber, he would have arrived at the surface by now. She had been too worried about despoiling the beautiful ceiling and now he was lying beneath it as a result.

And soon she would be, too.

She buried her face in her hands. Not now—not after all these days, not after everything that had happened. She did not want to die, but her dizziness was getting worse. Soon she would be like Intef. Alive, but sleeping. Feeling nothing. Eventually, even that nothing would slip away.

A quick, merciful death.

She no longer accepted Osiris's will. 'Where are you, Pharaoh?' she sobbed. 'Is this not your house of eternity? Are you not a god yourself? Help me!'

Aya felt her way along the walls towards the doorway. She would visit the main chamber. She would visit her beloved Pharaoh. It was the only thing she could think of to do. There she could speak her pleas directly to Pharaoh's *ka*, for Pharaoh was the only one who could help her now.

She arrived at the doorway and turned into the corridor. If she were being truthful, it was not the main chamber where she felt closest to Tausret, it was just here in the hallway at the junction of the two unfinished chambers, where the crack in the ceiling was most pronounced.

She had felt Pharaoh's breath here once, she could have sworn it. 'Tausret? Powerful One? Mistress?' She paused and breathed in.

Her heart leapt. There it was again. A small movement of air, as if Tausret's spirit hovered close.

'Is that you?' Aya stood as still as she could. Slowly, her dizziness abated. 'Forgive me, Beloved Tausret.'

The air seemed to speak in Pharaoh's voice. *'There is nothing to forgive.'*

'I do not wish to die.'

'Then live, Aya. Live!'

Aya took one last breath, then crossed the false chamber and rushed back up the ramp. Finding Intef's tools where he had left them, she climbed up the footrests inside the tunnel. She braced herself atop the final footrest and began to tap.

Not too hard, not too soft. Tap, tap, tap.

She breathed and tapped, breathed and tapped, trying to stay calm, just as Intef had advised, until once again her world was spinning. She made her way down the footrests and went to visit Pharaoh.

'Powerful One, give me strength,' she begged, standing in the corridor and breathing deeply. Slowly, her dizziness diminished and she crossed the chamber, stopping to place her hand over Intef's nostrils. A small, warm wind flowed out of them. Aya tipped her head to the painted stars. 'Please, keep him alive!'

Tap, tap, tap. She worked for as long as she could,

but soon became dizzy again. She returned to speak with Pharaoh, breathed and gathered her strength, then crossed back to the ramp and resumed her chiselling.

She did not know how many times she repeated this dance. Ten? Twenty? She had no sense of time. Were hours passing, or days? She did not know if the surface was near or far. All she knew was that she had to keep going.

Tap, tap, tap.

Her limbs started to fail her. The trip from the tunnel to the corridor began to feel like the journey of a hundred leagues. Once when she began to grow dizzy, she fell from the footrests. Another time, when she moved to descend the ramp, she collapsed upon the dirt. She breathed in the dust and found that she could not even cough.

She returned to her post. She needed to speak to Pharaoh, but she could no longer remember why. She imagined herself dashing down the ramp and making her way to the corridor. She pictured herself praying to Pharaoh and breathing in her strength. She saw herself bend to Intef and check his breath. There it was still—a tiny thread of breath. All was well. In her vision, she returned to her post. And there she was, working away. *Tap, tap, tap.*

The world was spinning now and her lids had become too heavy to keep open. She closed her eyes and delivered one last blow to the chisel. And in that tiny sliver of time, she beheld the beginning of her own end.

It was light. A tiny shaft of it—pouring down from above. The darkness was no longer complete.

She had finally passed into the Underworld. There was no other explanation for the sudden, blinding brightness. It was what the Underworld was, after all. Ra's nighttime sanctuary. The land of the midnight sun.

She inhaled the air—another of the Underworld's luxuries. She drank it like beer, letting it fill up her lungs. It was nearly the end. Soon she would begin her journey to the Hall of Judgement where Anubis would weigh her heart and find it too heavy by far. He would wait for Thoth, the god of scribes, to record the results and then Osiris would bow his head in disappointment and the Devourer of Souls would come for her.

She opened her eyes, expecting to take her first glimpse of that beautiful afterlife that she would travel through, but that would never be her home. Instead she saw a shaft of light shining down from above. She inhaled and discovered the air to have become sweeter. It was pouring in with the light, filling her with energy.

She lifted her chisel and landed another series of blows. Another small chunk of the ceiling fell away, allowing more light. More air. More strength.

She began chiselling in earnest, her heart full of suspicion. Surely this was some trick of death. At any moment, the ceiling above her would disappear and she would lift her head to behold a verdant land of swollen rivers and fertile fields and eternal souls: the land of the Underworld.

The ceiling was disappearing before her blows. Its stony chunks were falling like an avalanche. Her head had stopped throbbing and the world had ceased to spin. The opening was now big enough to fit through. She took another long, fortifying breath, then lifted her head above the surface.

There was no river in sight. She seemed to be in a small valley between hills, but there was not a single green plant growing upon their sloping grounds, nor any eternal soul anywhere.

There was noise, however—the soft twitter of invisible birds. Looking closer, she caught sight of them flitting among the boulders all around her, twittering and chattering and whistling their cheerful songs.

If life had a sound, this was surely it: birdsong. A cacophony of soft notes filling the air.

Chirp, chirp. Twitter, twitter. Caw, caw.

The music was so glorious that she paused to listen and did not immediately notice the sky.

The sky! There it was all around her—a miracle! It was pink. No—yellow. No, it was orange with a tinge of white. It was changing, growing more beautiful by the moment. It was...dawn.

If life had an aura, it was this: the quality of dawn. The sun god's arms were reaching out from beneath the horizon. His light was fragile, but each minute growing stronger, larger.

She felt her spirit growing larger, too. The birds were no longer chirping, they were cheering. Somehow she had done it. Like the sun god himself, she had come forth at dawn. She had made it to the surface. She had fulfilled her promise to Tausret—had refused to die and had been reborn.

She breathed in the fragrant morning air and her eyes filled with tears. They landed on her lips and she tasted them—salt, dust—the taste of life.

Intef.

She rushed to the false chamber and found the place where Intef lay. She splayed her hand before his nostrils and said a small prayer, willing him to be alive.

And if he was not? Her stomach took a plunge. If he was not alive, then the tomb would remain intact...but it would not matter. A gauzy curtain of grief would cloud her vision. She would search for the heir, but be unable to find him or protect him. She would be lost for ever.

The gods would not dare take him from her. They had given him to her as a gift, after all. He was the answer to her prayers. He was the man who had severed her bonds and rescued her from oblivion.

He had shown her how to laugh, how to trust and how to begin to forgive herself. He had steadied her aim and taught her how to slay her demons. He had shown her what it meant to feel the lightness of desire inside her heart.

He had called her beautiful and made her believe it.

He had made his mark on her spirit, had chiselled his name into her hardened heart. Even if their paths were meant to diverge, she did not wish to live in the world without knowing he was in it.

And yet there was no more breath in him. She crouched low and bent her ear to his mouth. Closing her other ear with her hand, she lay completely still and concentrated hard.

There it was! The tiniest of exhales, like the flap of a butterfly's wing. Thank the gods! He was still alive.

Her strength had returned with the fresh air, but would his? The new air was flowing into the chamber. It just needed to be encouraged. She pulled the sheath off of her back and began to fan him with it.

She had always tried to maintain her modesty around Intef. Now she was standing above him in nothing more than her loincloth! But it did not matter. Nothing mattered but to bring him back to life.

She crouched close to his mouth and listened for his breaths once again. They were coming more quickly now—she was sure of it. She fanned her tunic over him several more times, then dashed back up into the tunnel.

She needed to let in as much air as she could. She hacked away at the ceiling, and soon the opening was as large as the tunnel itself.

She rushed back and crouched at Intef's side, fanning the air as she went. The light from above cascaded down the ramp and on to Intef's naked chest.

But it was not moving.

If only she could open his mouth, perhaps she could return his breath to him. What she needed was an adze—that axe-like instrument that priests used to prepare mummies for the afterlife. She felt certain that if she had an adze, she could say the sacred spell and touch the instrument to his lips and he would be restored.

She did not have an adze, so her own humble chisel would have to do. She touched it to his mouth and began the spell: 'May his mouth be opened. May his mouth be unclosed by Shu with this iron knife... I am the goddess Sekhet and I sit upon my place in the great wind of heaven.'

She paused to see if the spell was working, but there was no movement at all. What cruel trick of the gods was this? That she would live and he would die? It could not be; she would not let it be. 'Hail, you who tows along the boat of Ra,' she called up to the ceiling, continuing the spell. 'The stays of your sails and of your rudder are taut in the wind as you sail up the Pool of Fire. Behold you gather together the charm from every place where it is...'

She stood and waved her sheath over him, fanning so furiously that she seemed to whip the air into a storm. 'Drink,' she urged him. 'Drink the air.'

She bent and placed her lips on his and breathed into him. She watched his chest fill with air, then released his lips and saw him exhale. She repeated the motion, filling him with her breath. Over and over she breathed into him, until she felt as if she had given all of her breath away.

Then—a miracle. He coughed and gulped the air. Her heart leapt as she perceived a slight tremble in his lips. No, it was more than a tremble—his lips were moving, twisting into a mischievous grin. 'Good morning,' he said. He opened his eyes and grinned.

'Intef!' She collapsed to the floor beside him in a fit of sobs. 'You returned to me.'

'Well, of course I did,' he said, as if he had just returned from a stroll. He sat up and smiled down at her. 'I seem to have indulged in a particularly deep sleep.'

'The demons invaded your lungs,' Aya explained. 'You were barely breathing.'

His expression sobered. 'I felt them there. And I felt it when you expelled them.'

She lifted her head and gazed into his eyes. 'You are crying.'

'Dust in my eyes,' he said, 'though I am rather happy to see you.'

'I was so afraid I had lost you.'

'You saved me,' he said. 'Do you know what that means?'

'That we must make an offering to Osiris?' she asked.

He bowed his head. 'That I must serve and protect you for ever.'

Chapter Nineteen

She laughed at him, but in his heart he was gravely serious. How could he give her up to General Setnakht? It did not matter that she was the heir to the double crown, or that revealing her identity could prevent a war. What did a man's duty matter at all if he could not protect the ones who mattered most?

'You saved my life,' he said.

'I believe it was you who saved mine,' she said. 'You worked yourself to near death on that tunnel.'

'But you were the one who finished it. You saved us both.' He pulled himself to his feet and summoned a grin. 'You must be thirsty after all of that.'

He crossed to his bed mat and reached for an amphora of beer and two cups. He spied a loaf of bread and placed it under his arm, then gathered up his bed mat, as well.

He paused, his thoughts scattering. It appeared as if he were preparing for a picnic, yet somewhere in the world above, the troops of two armies were gathering and would soon be killing one another—Egyptian against Egyptian.

And he was the only man in the world with the ability to stop them.

But in order to stop them, he had to betray the person he cared for most.

He was fooling himself again. It was more than just care he felt for Aya. She was the woman who had captivated him. She had ignited his desire and overwhelmed his thoughts. She had taught him history, bested him with her bow and then challenged him with her own wits. She had resurrected him in every sense of the word. She was the woman that he...

He laughed helplessly.

'What is so funny?' she called from behind the shrine.

What was so funny? That every time he looked into her eyes, a feeling of love rushed into his heart.

'Well?'

'You are clearly the superior chiseller,' he offered.

'Well, of course I am,' she retorted.

How dare he betray this woman? There should have never been any question in his heart: he needed to keep her as far from General Setnakht as possible. He needed to get her out of this House of Eternity as soon as he could.

Why was there not more time? Just days before, he had been huddled inside his wooden prison practically begging the minutes to pass. Now he was begging them to stand still.

He peered down at his sandal. He could discern five small marks representing five days of chiselling. He was certain more days had passed—possibly six or seven.

Still, his partners had not planned to arrive until the ninth day, which meant that there were a few more hours that he could spend listening to her voice and breathing in her scent and fixing her image in his mind—just a little more time to figure out exactly how he was going to break her heart.

He crossed to her sleeping area and retrieved her bed mat, then returned to the middle of the chamber where he lay both mats down next to the false shrine. Without a word, she sat down upon her mat and rested her back against the wall of the shrine.

He shot her a look and she returned a guilty grin. 'Why not rest against it? There is no one inside it after all…as far as I know, at least.' She winked at him.

He poured her a cup of beer and watched her carefully. 'You have changed, I think.'

She chuckled softly. 'Perhaps I have been inspired.'

'By digging through the tunnel?'

'By managing to keep you alive.'

'How did you do it, Aya?'

'Pharaoh helped me,' said Aya. 'She gave me her breath and I gave it to you.'

'You were brilliant.'

'On the contrary, I was mad. So were you. The malevolent spirits confused our thoughts. You kept raving about how I was the heir to the Horus throne. Imagine that!'

Her laughter hit him like a stone. But of course she did not believe him. Would he have believed her if she had told him that he was the divine descendant of a living god? He would not belabour the point. Besides, what truly mattered was that they had survived. He raised his cup. 'In that case, to madness!'

'To madness!' she echoed and the two lifted their cups and drank.

The bittersweet liquid slaked her thirst, but when she looked up from her cup, she nearly spat. Her sheath!

She had been talking to Intef all this time without noticing her own nudity. Worse, he seemed to notice her bare breasts the moment she did, causing a heavy blush to flood into her cheeks.

'I feel as if I have just waded into a pool of lotus flowers,' he said, then laughed. She watched him swallow more beer—though he did a rather terrible job of it—and politely look away.

She reached for her sheath and pulled it over her, feeling an inexplicable embarrassment. There was nothing to be ashamed of, after all. Egyptian women bared their breasts often, for they were one of the loveliest features of a woman's form.

Still, Aya rarely displayed her breasts in such a way. The advisor to a pharaoh did not have time to indulge in such flights of vanity.

Now it seemed that her vanity had run away with her thoughts. To what had he compared her breasts? A pool of lotus flowers? What a ridiculous comparison! Surely he had been mocking her. Still, the idea sent a strange warmth through her.

'Intef, are you all right? You seem to be choking.'

'It is nothing,' he said. 'Just…the beer. It is so… lovely.'

She had never heard beer described as lovely. Then again, she had never enjoyed a cup of beer with a man she had recently brought back from the dead.

'It is nice to rest here in the daylight,' she commented, tearing off a chunk of bread and chewing it thoughtfully. The light itself felt like a kind of food. It poured down from the tunnel in a luminous stripe, making her heart feel light.

A memory rushed in. 'Oh, Intef, I nearly forgot to tell you the news!'

'What news?' he asked her.

'I defeated my demons! In my vision last night I stopped them one by one.'

'Really? How did you do it?'

She sat up on her knees beside him and pretended to raise a bow. He nearly gasped. The breasts that he had been so skilfully avoiding up until now reared up into his direct line of sight.

She pulled back her string and readied her invisible arrow.

Her pose was magnificent. She looked like some divine huntress kneeling there, her head high, her stomach taut, the swooping curve of her back like a bow itself.

'Is that Bay you are aiming for?' he asked, hoping she would take a long time spotting her imaginary target.

'It is Bay on a chariot riding faster than time,' she said.

She sighted a target somewhere across the chamber and trained her invisible arrow on it.

'Remember to breathe,' he told her, though he might have been speaking to himself. She took a deep breath and he watched her breasts rise and fall before him. 'Now let go,' he muttered.

She let her imaginary arrow fly. He exhaled.

'Can you guess where it went?' she asked Intef. He already knew: it had landed inside his very heart. 'Well?' she asked.

'Did it slice right through Bay's wicked beard?'

She was shaking her head delightedly. 'I severed the reins of his horse. I sent his chariot to the ground.'

'Well done!' Intef praised. He was paralysed by her loveliness. He could have watched her for days. Months. Years.

'Oh, but I am not done.'

And the gods are great and terrible, he thought.

She loaded another imaginary arrow.

'And where is that one going?' he asked.

She cut him the sternest of looks. 'An archer never says.' She retrained her eyes on her invisible prize and breathed in.

She was heartbreakingly beautiful. It was not just the red in her cheeks or the gap in her teeth or the way her black hair hung down her neck like a feathery headdress.

It was the new certainty in her gaze—the unmistakable boldness that seemed to have emerged with her success with the bow...and now the chisel. He could feel the power radiating off her like heat. It made him feel weak, at her command.

She released her next invisible arrow, then another. 'And those arrows—where do you think they went?' she asked.

'Through the heart of Bay himself?'

'Nay, for in my vision Bay was no longer Bay—he became the High Priest. I sent my arrows into each side of his robe.' She flashed the haughty grin of a conqueror and his stomach took a lusty plunge. 'I pinned him to the ground.'

'Congratulations!' he said. 'You overcame your captors!'

As for Intef, he could not seem to overcome his desire to seal her grin with his own lips.

'But then the High Priest became the Serpent himself and I had only one arrow left.' She filled her chest with air and pulled her imaginary bow taut. Then she did something utterly ruthless. She puckered her lips and kissed the air, as if blowing the Serpent of Chaos a goodbye kiss. 'I sent that arrow right through the serpent's head.'

He gazed up at her, unable to speak as she released her final arrow. Who was this fiery goddess standing before him? What had happened to the woman who had failed her Pharaoh, who regretted everything she said and did, who feared she could not chisel well enough to do her duty?

'It is all thanks to the Goodly Thief,' she said. She held up her invisible bow.

'You named your bow the Goodly Thief?'

'Do you not like the name?'

He laughed. 'I am honoured.' He could not stand to look at her any more, lest he combust with longing. 'Come, sit next to me,' he said. 'Let us rest a while.'

She glanced across the chamber. 'I think I shall go bathe myself first. Saving your life was rather dirty business.'

He tried to conceal his chagrin. 'Of course.'

When she returned, she seemed to gleam in the low light. She handed him several wet cloths. 'You are welcome,' she said, her eyes scrutinising his filthy limbs.

He laughed and stood, wiping down his limbs and watching the cloths become dark with dirt.

'There is so much to do now, is there not?' she mused. 'I have been thinking about how we might find the heir.'

'Ah,' he said, stepping to the other side of the shrine to discreetly cleanse the rest of him.

'I know you will be returning to your family first,' she said. 'I have decided to take refuge in Pharaoh's mortuary temple until you are able to join me. I will be safe there and I can begin our plans to find the heir.'

Intef said nothing in response. He returned to his mat and forced a grin.

'Is there something the matter?' she asked.

'Nothing.' *Our plans*, she had said. Curses.

'I suppose we must decide when to make our escape,' she said. 'Tonight?'

'Too soon,' he blurted. He lay back. 'We should remain here tonight and tomorrow and recover our strength. I am still very tired, I fear.'

That was a lie. He was not tired at all. He had never been more awake.

Chapter Twenty

'I am also tired,' she said, lying down by his side. 'So much chiselling...' She gathered his bed sheet around her and in moments she was asleep.

He understood at once that this was how it would always be. He wanted her, but he could never have her.

At best, his desire for her was an inconvenience. At worst, it was a trick of the gods. Or perhaps it was a trick of the tomb itself, which seemed to teem with demons and illusions.

He could never have her. Whatever they had forged together was made of glass. Even if he could spare her the pain of witnessing the tomb pillaged, he would still be the man responsible for doing it. It was an unforgivable offence. No matter what happened, the glass was going to break.

Besides, she was already elsewhere. She was thinking about their escape, beyond that where she would go and how she would find and protect the heir and beyond that how she would undo the damage to Tausret's tomb. None of it involved him.

She was a kind of rainbow—so close to him, but totally beyond reach.

And that was well, for rainbows were dangerous illusions. He did not want to indulge in their beauty. He did not want any part of them. They kept people smiling and bathed in colour, even when the world was falling apart.

Intef remembered the last time he had seen Nebetta.

He had been standing on the western bank of the river at his favourite fishing hole, watching a fish writhe and twist on the line.

'I knew I would find you here!' Nebetta had said. 'Will you not join me at the Min feast?'

'Is it the Min Festival already?' Intef had asked, though he had been listening to the sound of beating drums across the water all afternoon.

'The ferry is leaving soon,' she'd said. She'd held out her hand to him. 'Join me, Intef. Let us return to the land of the living and dance and be merry. Do you not hear the lovely sistrums and the trumpets calling?'

'They sound like dying donkeys.'

She'd laughed heartily, as if he had meant the comment as a jest. The silken black strands of her hair had swept across her lovely face and she'd threaded them out of the way with unconscious grace.

I do not deserve her, he'd thought.

She'd sniffed the air. 'They have sacrificed four bulls. Can you not smell them roasting?'

'I smell nothing.'

'Come, Intef,' she'd begged. 'Do you not wish to dance with me?'

His fish had given a wild flop, then seemed to freeze.

'Go, Nebetta. Enjoy yourself. You will have your pick of men to dance with. As you can see, I am busy.'

She'd stepped backwards, as if he had just given her a shove.

'Come, Intef,' she'd said, but with less enthusiasm. 'Do you not like my new dress?'

He had studied her closely. She'd worn a clean white sheath that had been perfectly fitted to her slim figure. A thick pectoral made of colourful glass beads had lain heavy on her chest and a matching belt had brought colour to her lovely waist. Around her shoulders she'd worn a fine, gauzy shawl that must have cost a dozen barrels of wheat in trade.

'You look as if you have raided the closet of the old Priestess of Isis,' he'd said.

She had cringed. He'd hated hurting her, but it had been the only way to make her understand. *He was not going to dance with her. Not ever.*

'Do you not like how I have painted my face?' she'd asked.

He'd gazed at her mystical eyes, which had been kohled and then powdered with glorious green.

'I see you have been deep in the malachite pot.'

Her breaths had been short. 'I thought you liked the colour green against my skin.'

'You know that I have joined the rebel army, Nebetta. I am a soldier now. I cannot go off dancing with you. I must do my duty.'

'Every man in Thebes is in the rebel army. They are all at the feast.'

'Not every man.' His stomach had turned, as it always did when he thought of his father's death.

She'd stared out across the river. 'You must let him go, Intef.'

'I cannot,' he had whispered.

'You *will* not,' Nebetta had replied.

A breeze had come up and tousled her hair, but she had not attempted to correct it. She'd only stared off across the river while a single tear made a green malachite path down her colourless cheek.

He'd cut the fishing line with his knife. His fish had lain motionless on the ground, but he had not attempted to retrieve it.

'I am sorry, Nebetta.'

Nebetta's ferry boat had sounded its bell, but it had been Intef who had silently walked away...

He had been walking ever since.

Intef gazed down at Aya's slumbering form. She had rolled on to her stomach and her arms had stretched out on to the floor. It was as if she were embracing the tiles, protecting her Pharaoh. Even in her sleep, it seemed, she would not cease to do her duty.

What a good woman she was. How loyal and true was her heart. He knew that heart could not belong to him, or anyone else. It belonged to Pharaoh Tausret alone.

And thank the gods for that, for he had never wanted her heart. Love was only pain and he did not wish to suffer any more. He had done his duty as best he could, had kept her at a distance. And that was well, for soon he would give her to Setnakht.

He had no choice.

He braced himself against the shrine as a wave of nausea hit him. Setnakht would marry her to his son Rameses and she would become a royal brood mare, just as Tausret had been. Her life would no longer be her own. It would be no life at all.

But was that not the fate of all living souls? What did life mean if one could not serve some useful purpose? She had sacrificed her life up until now in the service of Tausret and was obviously proud of that fact. Who was he to decide what she would or would not wish?

What mattered were the thousands of lives that would be saved by her marriage—both living Egyptians and Egyptians yet to be.

No life was worth more than any other. Not even the life of the woman he...

He quickly slid down on the bed mat beside her and turned on his side, facing away from her. He seemed to be seeing things more clearly now, with so much daylight pouring in. There was no future for them, nor could there ever be. If Intef did not do his duty and give Aya to Setnakht, men would die. There was no more to think about.

He closed his eyes and, finally, went to sleep.

She awoke to the sound of his gentle snores. He was lying on his side, facing her. She could tell because she could feel the wind of his breath in her hair. It occurred to her that it was the first time she had ever slept beside a man. It was not an unpleasant sensation, though it was rather difficult avoiding the desire to nuzzle up against his chest.

She wondered what other pleasures lay unexplored between them. She feared there were many and also that she would never know them. She sensed their association was quickly coming to an end.

She had always sensed that he was hiding something from her and now felt certain she knew what it was: he was not going to help her find the heir. It was the only explanation for his misguided obsession that *she* was the heir. It was a lie he told himself in order to retain his own honour, for he planned to save his family and then return to the army where he belonged.

Strangely, she did not blame him. He was a good man, an honourable man, and it made sense that he would wish to return to his duty. It also meant that after this night she would never see him again.

The thought made her feel unexpectedly bleak. In her life at court, she had known many men. To a very few, she had even been attractive. She could count on one hand the number of times she had been propositioned by such men, though she had always refused them. She had never trusted their intentions, nor did she feel anything for them at all. In her mind, they were just alternative versions of Bay.

Now all she could imagine was Intef's touch, his kiss, his arms around her, and how much she wished to feel those things one last time before their time together was through.

When he opened his eyes again, all was dark. The cool night air was pouring in from the tunnel and he gulped it into his lungs. He felt full of energy and lay restless upon his bed mat, wondering what he could do to occupy himself.

The storerooms certainly needed tidying, as did the hall. They would need to bring the latrine to the surface—a task that he would insist on doing himself—and return all the furniture to the storage rooms. There really was much to be done.

He was pulling himself off the bed mat when he heard her sigh.

'Intef, are you awake?' He could not see her, but it sounded as if she was lying on her back.

'I am awake, but I did not believe you to be.'

'I have been awake for some time,' she said.

'It seems that we have become creatures of the night.'

'My thoughts will not cease.'

'Nor will mine. There is much to think about,' he said.

'And so little time.'

He moved to rise once again. 'I am going to begin organising the corridor now and—'

She placed her hand upon his arm. 'That is not what I mean.' Her voice was thick. 'Will you not lie beside me for a while?'

Confused, he lay back down beside her, noticing that she did not take her hand off his arm. 'Tomorrow at this time, we will be sneaking out of the valley,' she observed.

He laughed. 'Or running for our lives.'

'Are the Medjay guards as dangerous as they say?'

'Worse,' said Intef.

Aya gasped. 'If they catch us…'

Intef touched her hand. 'We will have our bows.'

'And each other.' She lifted her hand and entwined her fingers with his. 'You have taught me so much, but I feel as if there is much more you can teach me.'

His heart thumped. 'What is it that you wish to learn?'

She pulled his hand to her mouth and kissed it. 'Everything.'

He felt as if he had just been pushed over a cliff. Her lips were so soft on his hand. 'What do you mean, Aya?'

'I wish to wander the marshes with you,' she said. 'Will you take me to them? Will you show me the way?'

Intef placed his free hand over his mouth to test his breath. He needed to be sure he was not dreaming. 'Aya, do you understand what you are asking?'

'I understand. I only ask that you do not sow your seed. I cannot risk it.'

'But…the tomb…your Pharaoh…'

'I do not believe Tausret would be troubled,' she said.

'Apologies. I do not understand. I thought—'

'Intef, I wish to live. Just once, before I return to my duty. Last night I thought you had died and...' She paused, squeezing his hand.

His heart thrummed, filling with some unrecognisable emotion.

'I will confess that Pharaoh did not want me to return to my duty at all,' she said.

Intef nearly choked. 'What?'

'She made me promise once. After her death, she wished for me to live, to be free.'

'Why did you never tell me that?' asked Intef. They were the words a mother said to a daughter, further proof of Aya's identity.

'She said those words without knowing the future. How could she have guessed that her heir and her very afterlife would be threatened, and me the only one that could save them both?'

'But you must keep that promise, Aya, you must live. You must—'

'If I did not do right by Pharaoh, than what is my life worth at all? You feel the same about your family, no?'

Intef could not argue. 'You are a good woman.'

The very best.

'And you are a good man,' Aya said. 'I see that now. And here we are, both of us with the duties that await us,' she said. 'But we have this night—our last night together. I do not expect you to help me protect the heir. You have given me the ability to do that on my own. And I know you do not wish to be friends. But I have this...longing for you that I do not understand. I am only asking that we—'

'Shh...' he said. 'No more talking.' He could not listen to another word, lest his body die by a thousand quakes. In a single motion, he sat up and straddled her. It was the same position he had assumed their first night in the tomb. He leaned down and pressed his lips to hers, half-expecting to discover an arrow in her mouth.

Instead he found a soft, wet garden of lust.

It was as if she had taken their kiss from that first night and let it build inside her like a storm. She kissed him with enough passion to split the sky. She arched her body against his and he felt lightning shoot through his limbs. She swept her tongue through his mouth and he felt thunder in his bones.

'For one so inexperienced, you are rather good at this,' he said.

'I have had the best of instructors.'

He pulled her lower lip into his mouth and sucked it. He was rewarded with her soft intake of breath. He pulled up her sheath and helped her lift it over her head, and there were her wondrous breasts—he could look at them all he liked.

And so he did. He gazed at the two small shapely mounds, like a drinking man gazing at two fine glasses of wine. He wanted to drink her in, all of her, and promised himself not to spill a drop.

He wrapped his lips around her nipple and heard her moan as his tongue caressed and teased. He moved to her other nipple, squeezing her flesh in his hands. 'Oh gods, what are you doing?' she said lustily.

'I am going to make you melt,' he said.

Desire pulsed through him. He fumbled with the knot of her loincloth, aware he was moving far too fast. He could not help himself.

He sent a silent prayer of thanks to Hathor, then pulled the garment free. She lay atop his bed sheet completely naked now and, because he could not see her, he determined that he was going to learn her body by kissing every part of it, leaving the best for last.

It would not be easy. His desire was already fully erect. It yearned to reach her paradise. But this was only her third time. It was also quite possibly her last time. He wished to make it unforgettable.

He began his important work at her feet. He massaged her soles with his hand, then kissed each of her toes one by one. He kissed slowly up the insides of her calves, then placed two long, soft kisses in the crooks of her knees.

'That is lovely,' she said.

Encouraged, he kissed up to the tops of her thighs and up and down both her arms. She was beginning to relax. He kissed her hands—sucking each finger—then went on to her shoulders, where he kissed just along the delicate bones.

He felt as if he were worshipping a goddess. He silently begged for her good favour as he kissed her holy throat, then kissed up and down her sacred neck.

'Oh, Intef,' the goddess breathed and he moved on to her ear and breathed his lust into it like a secret.

He kissed slowly down her chest—small, thoughtful kisses, for he did not want to rush. He was doing more than simply learning her body, he was attempting to chisel it into his mind. He wanted to remember it for ever.

He kissed all over her hips, letting his mouth hover over her desire so she might feel his breath on it. He heard her breaths becoming heavier.

He moved his head between her knees and began to kiss her inner thigh. One kiss, two kisses. Up he went, closer and closer to her desire.

Her legs squeezed together, trapping his head. She

laughed nervously. 'What are you about, my dear soldier?'

'The more you can relax, the more pleasure you will feel. But you must trust me. Can you trust me, Aya?'

She nodded. 'Just please...go slowly.'

He smiled. 'I will go so slowly that you will be begging me to go faster.'

Chapter Twenty-One

She doubted he could fulfil such a promise. Still, if the act of coupling with Intef made her feel anything like his kisses had been making her feel, then perhaps she would become a beggar.

She knew what came next, of course. Of all the people of the world—the Egyptians, Libyans, Nubians and Asiatics—it was the Egyptians who were the most open about it. And why should they not be? It was natural— like breathing or eating. It just happened that Aya had been too busy all these years to take very many bites.

Now she hurriedly tried to recall the things she knew. She had engaged in the pleasures of the flesh several times, so why did she not understand what he was doing now?

As he began kissing slowly up her thigh, she started to have a clue. They were not just kisses he was placing on her skin, but tiny fires. They smouldered and sparked, causing other fires to break out in other places, until she began to feel as if her whole body was burning.

And yet he was kissing her so very slowly! Maddeningly so. But did she really wish for him to speed up? No. Yes. Gods, she did not know what she wanted.

Meanwhile, he was moving relentlessly up her inner thigh. He seemed to be telling a story whose conclusion would soon be reached.

Was this a story she wished to hear? Did it have a happy ending? She was tensing again. Perhaps this was a bad idea. She really did not expect this particular part of it, though of course she had experienced the other thing at least twice. Blessed Hathor, what had she got herself into?

'Relax, my goddess,' he said. 'Let me take you. Let yourself feel how much I want you.'

He plunged his head back between her thighs and continued to kiss. And then he was there. Right there. Kissing between her legs. Kissing her.

She opened her mouth to speak, but nothing came out. She squeezed the sheets in her fists and felt a rush of pain that was pleasure, that was torture, that was also ecstasy.

And then she felt his tongue—hot and wet and moving inside of her. Touching her. Tasting her. She sat up in alarm. 'Surrender to me, Aya. Let me give you pleasure.'

She lay back and opened her legs just a little bit more. 'Yes,' he said. 'That is it.'

Perhaps she gasped. Maybe she moaned. She could have cried out. She did not know, for her awareness had collapsed into the exact size and shape of a man's tongue.

Cursed Seth, this felt wondrous. Why had the women at court never gossiped about this particular…pleasure? Why had they said nothing of the terrible ecstasy, the mind-numbing bliss? Not a word! Though perhaps Aya had just not been listening.

Oh, sweet river. She was all mixed up and growing

warmer and warmer by the moment. Evil man. With each sweep of his tongue he seemed to be coaxing her yearning. She began to move her hips, trying to encourage him in his pursuit.

'Yes, that is it, Aya,' he said, but he seemed to be slowing. She was moving her hips, but his tongue was no longer moving with them.

'Yes, Intef,' she said, trying to encourage him, but he was no longer giving her what he had just taught her to want.

He withdrew his tongue and hovered over her. He was retreating from her, even as her whole body seemed to be crying out.

'Please, Intef,' she gasped.

He moved away from her. She could no longer feel him touching her.

His voice came out of the darkness. 'What do you want, Aya?' he asked in a low, dangerous voice.

'I want you,' she said. She felt ragged, desperate. She needed to feel him again. Soon.

'I will give you what you want, but first you must say the words.'

'I beg you.'

She could practically see his triumphant grin. He moved over her and she felt his legs straddle her hips once again. He lay atop her with all his weight and in the crush of him she could feel his desire pressing against her stomach.

Its presence seemed to infect her with a kind of fever. She felt ill with the want of him. So this was what she had been missing all these years. A man's desire and a desirous man to go with it.

There was no light, yet she was delirious with visions

of him—an enemy, a lover, a dangerous god hovering over her, ready to take his fill.

She wanted him to take it. She wanted it so badly that she felt if he did not do it soon she might burn up beneath him.

He braced himself on his arms and pulled back his hips.

'Yes,' she said.

'Yes?'

'Yes, please,' she added. 'I beg you.' She could hear the soft tumble of fabric as he removed his kilt. He hovered astride her. She could feel the tip of him brushing up against her. He reached his finger down and gently stroked her, making her shudder. 'You are so wet,' he breathed.

'Is that good?' she asked.

'What do you think?'

'I think—' she began saying, then felt his lips upon hers once again.

'Do not think,' he breathed into her mouth.

He was lying heavily atop her, kissing her, when she felt the tip of him push into her just a little. She startled, but the weight of his body prevented her from moving much. He pulled out of her. 'What is the name of your bow?' he asked her.

She laughed. 'You already know the name.'

'Indulge me,' he said.

'The Goodly Thief.'

'Tell me how you ready your Goodly Thief for its delicate work.'

She smiled and felt her limbs relax. 'Well, first I select an arrow from the quiver.'

'And then?'

'I place the arrow on the nock.'

'Yes?'

'Then I make sure that the tip of the arrow is lying properly on the bow rest.' His desire hovered just outside her entrance, poised.

'Go on,' he said. 'What next?'

'Then I check the angle of my body and move my bow into position,' she said. He raised himself up and braced himself on his arms above her.

'And then?'

Her desire had begun to throb. 'I know what you are about, cunning man,' she said.

'Do you really?' he asked, and in that moment he pushed himself inside of her and she was full of him.

He was overcome with sensation. 'Blessed are the gods,' he murmured. This woman. This woman, this woman, this woman. Pangs of lust catapulted through his body. It was all he could do to speak her name. 'Aya...'

'Intef...'

'Are you all right?'

'Yes,' Aya said, gasping. 'I am...quite well.'

He bent to reassure her with a kiss and was met with something greater than reassurance. Passion seemed to pour out of her.

'Ah, my love,' he said. 'Where have you been all these years?'

He began to move inside her, as slowly as he could. This was only her third time, he recalled, though he felt rather new to the situation himself. He had never wanted a woman as much as he wanted Aya.

He could hardly believe his feelings were real. After his father had died, the only lust he had felt was for revenge. Over time, that lust had turned to stone and, lately, that stone had eroded into dust. He had felt so low for so long, he hardly knew what real happiness was. Now, buried beneath the earth, he felt as if he were flying.

'Aya...' he breathed. He began to move inside her. Her soft, warm depths enveloped him and, with each successive thrust, he felt simultaneously closer to her and also closer to the moon. He wove his hands with hers and watched her beneath him. He wanted to remember this moment for ever.

It could not last. He was too aroused. His body yearned for release. He was moving faster, gathering his rhythm. He needed to bring her with him, but he was already far above her, pumping his wings.

'Oh, Aya, forgive me,' he cried. She felt so good and it had been so long. He could not wait for her. He could only squeeze her hands tightly and pull himself out of her as he reached the hot vent of air and began to soar.

His body quaked. His stomach lurched. His mind split in two. There was no darkness, nor was there any light. There was only air—perfect, buoyant air—ferrying him into bliss.

He spilled himself on her stomach, then collapsed beside her. For many moments, he could not feel the floor. 'Aya, I am sorry,' he uttered at last. 'That was not how it was supposed to be.'

'But it was wonderful,' she said, and there was enough wonder evident in her voice for him to believe her. And yet he knew she had no idea.

'I did not go slowly enough. I did not give you your pleasure.' He wiped her stomach with the bottom corner of the sheet.

'You did give me pleasure,' she said. 'It was all pleasure.'

'You do not understand. I did not do my duty.'

She giggled. 'My pleasure is your duty?'

'You have no idea how I can make you feel, Aya,' Intef said. 'How I will make you feel!'

'You have already made me feel so much pleasure,' she said, but he could hear the yawn in her voice. She reached for her loincloth and he heard her tie it back into place. 'Gratitude,' she said. She rolled over and kissed him on the cheek. 'For showing me the marshes.'

It was as if she had just thanked him for pointing out a good fishing hole. He ran his hands through his hair. No, no, no: this was all wrong. He was not done yet; he had hardly just begun. He reached to pull her atop him, but she was nuzzling herself inside the crook of his arm and in moments she was asleep.

He spent the next several hours making all sorts of vows. He would correct this injustice and soon. He would give her pleasure unlike anything she had ever experienced. He would show her the moon, then give her the stars on a platter.

So consumed he was with this new purpose that he did not even notice himself falling asleep.

The next time he opened his eyes, the chamber was filled with light.

Morning. He should have been glad for it, but he only wished it would go away. He had wrapped his arms around Aya in the night and her backside was pressing into his hips. Somehow their legs had become entangled. He could not decide which limb belonged to whom—and he did not want to decide. Not ever.

He needed to visit the latrine, but he ignored the urge. He squeezed her closer. He needed another night—that was his first thought. His second thought was that he needed many other nights. His third thought was that the gods were cruel and that the moment he left her side it would all be over.

He closed his eyes and breathed in the scent of her hair. It was a mix of dust and hibiscus oil and her own special musk. He felt certain that he had never smelled anything quite so appealing.

He wanted to taste her, so he lifted her hair and placed his lips at the base of her neck. Pulling away, he noticed her tattoo. The mark was quite small—a circle no bigger than his thumb and, inside the small circle, a triangle.

He kissed the tattoo, for it was the last time he was going to ever think about it again. She was the heir to the Horus throne, but nobody would ever know, for he would tell no one.

He had finally decided: he would not give her up. He would complete his mission for General Setnakht and hope it would be enough to prevent war. But Aya's life was her own, just as her own mother said it was, and she deserved to live it. He had no right to stop her.

Carefully, he disentangled himself from her and padded into the smaller unfinished chamber to use the latrine. He had grown so accustomed to the dark over the course of their entombment that it no longer felt like the dark at all to him, but instead a kind of alternate world.

It was the place of fragrant lavender and bittersweet beer and Aya's soft voice in the air. It was the strange abode in which he had chiselled through walls and touched invisible limbs and discovered the deepest pleasure he had ever known.

The darkness was beautiful, but it was not without its dangers. He had lost himself so thoroughly in it the night before that he had somehow left Aya behind. It was a regret he feared would haunt him the rest of his life.

There was no more time for thinking about such things, however. Intef's fellow tomb raiders could arrive as soon as that night and Intef needed to get Aya out of the tomb before they did.

As soon as the sun set he would escort her to Tausret's mortuary temple and then return to the tomb to meet his brothers and complete the mission. He could not allow her to witness the devastation that was about to ensue.

He was standing beside his fellow tomb raiders inside General Setnakht's war tent. It was the eve of Intef's entombment and the four had come to receive their final orders.

The General was distracted, however. He paced about the tent, lecturing his officers and shouting curses at the flies. At the corner of the tent, his son Rameses was puzzling over a large papyrus.

'I believe the High Priest will assemble his army here where the land is flat,' Rameses said, pointing at the papyrus. 'Thus he will be able to utilise his advantage of numbers.'

General Setnakht cringed. 'We will have no chance against him—not without mercenaries.' The General stepped before Intef. 'We need Tausret's gold, you understand, Beetle?'

'Yes, my lord,' said Intef, keeping his eyes on the floor.

General Setnakht turned to Intef's erstwhile partner at arms—the ill-mannered Theban called Ranofer. 'You are certainly well made,' observed Setnakht. 'With those arms, you should be able to extract at least four bags of gold.'

'When I am done with that tomb, my lord will be able to purchase the entire army of Kush!' shouted Ranofer.

Setnakht regarded the other two tomb raiders, a pair of lovers named Den and Huni. 'You two men are also quite well fed,' he observed, then turned to his son. 'Rameses, remind me why we selected such brutes?'

'The nested coffins, Father,' replied Rameses, still studying the map.

'Nested coffins?'

'Inside the sarcophagus. The men must be able to lift the lids to reach the golden mask.'

'Ah, yes, the death mask,' said Setnakht. He began pacing the room once again. 'I want you to take that cursed mask and everything else of value that you can, do you hear me, soldiers?'

'Yes, my lord,' the men said in unison.

'Every precious jewel and golden dagger, every silver goblet and electrum-encrusted plate. The more you take, the greater your rewards.'

Abandoning his map, Rameses crossed the tent and stood before them. 'You will bring back fantastic riches, we will win this war and my father will be Pharaoh.' *And I will be Pharaoh after him*, he seemed to say.

'And we shall erase the name Tausret wherever it appears,' added Setnakht. 'On every King's list and on every temple wall. Even inside her splendid tomb!'

Intef stepped from the unfinished chamber back into the corridor. Enough light was reaching the entryway for Intef to discern the colourful paintings adorning the walls and he caught sight of Tausret's humble cartouche.

It was not surprising that General Setnakht planned

to erase Tausret's name. Egypt's Pharaohs had been erasing one another's names and images for thousands of years. What surprised Intef was the anger that sparked inside him at the thought.

She does not deserve it.

When you erased a person's name, you erased part of their spirit and, without all its parts, the spirit could not go on.

He no longer believed Pharaoh Tausret deserved such a fate. How thoroughly he had misjudged the woman who had sacrificed herself for the good of Egypt. It scared him to think of how credulous he had been of the news he had received all these years. Erroneous news, as it turned out. Lies. He had given over his life to the southern rebellion and now wondered how much of it was based on things that simply were not true.

He realised all at once that this would be his last mission. He could not go on fighting for any more causes if he could not trust that the reasons for them were true. The only thing he seemed to have any faith in any more was Aya herself.

Chapter Twenty-Two

He crossed the chamber and saw that Aya was still asleep, so he climbed up the ramp and stepped up the footrests inside the tunnel to get a view of the world into which they would soon be escaping.

The Great and Majestic Necropolis of the Millions of Years of the Pharaoh: that was what they called the small cleft between hills on which he gazed. The name was larger than the valley itself! And yet scores of kings were buried here, along with enough gold to fill a hundred ships.

Intef turned around to admire the natural backdrop for the sacred valley: a tall peak in the poetical shape of a pyramid. It ensconced the unmarked tombs in its mystical shelter, concealing them from would-be thieves. The area was further safeguarded by a small army of guards—the legendary Medjay—two of whom were currently running down the valley towards a column of smoke.

Intef craned his neck to get a better view. There appeared to be a fire some way down the valley. He turned to discover two more guards only a few cubits away from where he stood. They, too, were making their way towards the blaze.

He ducked back into the tunnel, his heart beating. The guards had not seen him, but only because of the boulders all around the site of the hole. It was an incredible stroke of fortune that they had dug the tunnel where they did. Just a few cubits to either side, and it would have been exposed. They would have surely been discovered by now.

Thank the gods that Aya had insisted on digging the tunnel where they had.

He returned to the false chamber and Aya was finally stirring beneath the bed sheet. 'Good morning, Sister,' he said, following the customary greeting for a lover.

'Good morning, Brother.' She pulled down the sheet and flashed him a sleepy grin.

All at once he understood why men wrote poetry and built monuments. All those elaborate toilings on papyrus and stone were simply an effort to honour moments like these, when beauty appeared unbidden, making the world seem wondrous and alive and utterly worth living.

And soon he was going to have to say goodbye to it all. He was going to have to say goodbye to her.

'There is a fire down the valley.'

She sat up in alarm.

'It is quite far away—nothing to worry about. It may even help us. Perhaps there will be fewer guards when we leave at sunset.'

'Must we wait until sunset?'

An innocent question, but it needled his heart. Was she so eager to sever their bond? The answer was, yes, of course she was. She had always been.

'I doubt we will be ready before then,' he said. 'Besides, the cover of darkness will help protect us from detection.'

It was in that moment that the quality of the light inside the chamber shifted. It became darker, as if a cloud had just passed over the sun. He could no longer read her expression.

'What is it, Aya? What is the matter?'

'Intef, there is a man behind you.' She rose. 'A very large man.'

'It appears your help has arrived,' said a familiar voice. Intef turned to discover Ranofer, who was gazing at Aya and shaking his head.

'You naughty rogue, Intef! Where on earth did you find her?' Ranofer peered around the chamber, as if he might find his answer somewhere among the murals. He turned and called up the ramp, 'Come quickly, Brothers. You are not going to believe this!'

Another large man with a short, goat-like beard stumbled into the false chamber. 'What is this?' he said. 'Has our beetle found a bird?' He took a step towards Aya.

'Stay away from her, Den!' shouted Intef.

'All right, all right, Brother, calm yourself,' said Ranofer. He opened out his arms. 'By the gods, are you not happy to see us?'

The fourth member of their party came stumbling down the ramp, carrying a load of sacks. He noticed Aya, his eyes growing as big as plates.

'Say nothing, Huni,' warned Intef. 'There will be no more comments from any of you.'

Intef glanced behind him at Aya. She had gathered the bed sheet tightly around her nudity. Her face was as still as a stone.

'You were not supposed to arrive until the ninth day,' said Intef. 'At night.'

'Today is the ninth day,' remarked Den, stroking his beard. 'We are right on time.'

Intef shook his head. Where had the days gone? 'We made a little fire down the valley.' Ranofer displayed his ash-stained hands. 'A little distraction for the guards.'

Intef nodded. He should have guessed the reason for the smoke. Why had he not guessed?

'We bring news from above,' said Huni, setting down his sacks. 'The High Priest has amassed an army in the desert south of here. General Setnakht's army is gathering to face him. The winner of the battle will take the double crown.'

Intef felt a pang of hope. 'Does the General no longer require our services, then?'

The three men laughed. 'The mercenaries merely await their payment,' said Huni.

'How much payment?' asked Intef.

'There are hundreds of mercenaries,' said Ranofer. 'We must take as much treasure as we can carry. We must give them a reason to fight.'

Intef heard Aya gasp. She was stumbling backwards. She bumped against the wall of the false shrine. She looked as if she had just been hit by an arrow.

He rushed to her side and helped ease her down to the floor. She made no resistance, apparently too stunned to even push him away.

'Where in Great Egypt did you find her, Intef?' asked Ranofer.

'Do kings buried in these hills still keep their own harems?' jested Huni.

Intef tried to meet Aya's gaze, but she would not look

at him. She was gazing somewhere beyond all the men, her expression lifeless.

'Well, Intef, who is she?' Ranofer asked.

Intef willed himself to speak. 'She is… Sobek. Daughter of Ankhu,' he lied. 'She stumbled into the tunnel yesterday, lost and starving.'

Aya kept her gaze on the distant wall as Ranofer squatted to study her face. 'Where did you come from, my sweet?' he muttered. 'And how did you end up here?'

'She came from Aswan,' Intef said. 'She has a dying mother and four starving brothers there. Robbing a tomb is her last hope to save them.'

Intef felt vaguely ill. It was the very lie he had told Aya the day they had met.

'There is Libyan in her,' said Ranofer. 'Are we sure she has not been sent by an enemy tribe?'

'Her father was Libyan,' Intef answered. 'Her mother was Egyptian.'

'Why not let her speak for herself!' snapped Ranofer. He placed a strand of her hair behind her ear. 'Tell me about your owner, pretty Sobek,' he cooed.

Her lips were trembling. 'Deceased,' she whispered.

'Your family is starving, eh? But you look rather hale to me. Perhaps that is what you say to all your fellow tomb raiders?' He nudged Aya in the ribs.

'Do not touch her,' growled Intef. 'She is mine.'

The words seemed to shock Aya into waking and she turned to meet Intef's gaze. 'How could you?'

Ranofer returned to standing. 'Did you not tell her we were coming, Brother?'

She jumped to her feet and stepped away from the two men. There were tears in her eyes. 'I belong to no man! I am not yours and I never will be.'

'A spirited little heifer,' remarked Den. He glanced at her bare arms. 'She can certainly help us with the haul.'

Ranofer nodded thoughtfully. 'What do you think, Sobek? Will you help us bear the riches from this tomb? In return, you may have a share of them.' Ranofer held out his hand.

Take it, thought Intef. *Play the part.*

If Ranofer even suspected that Aya was a servant of the late Pharaoh, he would consider her a threat. At the very least, she would be bound and silenced.

'How much?' she asked. Intef exhaled.

'Enough to save that poor, ailing family you claim to have,' Ranofer said. 'If you do not wish to help us, however, you may leave now and hope the guards do not catch you.'

Aya accepted Ranofer's hand and shook it.

'A reasonable woman!' remarked Ranofer. He squatted to strike flint, then lit a torch. 'Come now, Intef,' he said. 'Lead us to the riches.'

Aya collapsed to the floor as Intef and the three men disappeared down the corridor. She lay upon the cool tiles, waiting for the tears to come. When none did, she sat up and looked around the chamber, blinking.

Everything around her seemed changed. The magnificent images of the gods that adorned the columns seemed smaller somehow, their colours less vivid. The splendid murals seemed to lack lustre in the hazy daylight.

She gazed up at the starry ceiling. Days ago, when Intef had first flashed his torchlight upon it, the stars had seemed otherworldly, as if they had been plucked from the very sky.

Now they appeared clumsy and false, as if they had been painted on haphazardly by a careless workman.

She smiled desolately, remembering the moment Intef had told her about his bereft family. The lie had been there all along, as obvious as the bumps of a crocodile, yet Aya had allowed his sparkling eyes and gallant grin to divert her attention from it.

It had been more than just his handsome face, however. There had also been his gentle nature and funny wit. There had been the compromises he had made for her and the way he had listened to her ideas and let them change his mind. In the small space of the tomb, he held much more power than she, yet he had given much of that power away. He had treated her as an equal.

It had surprised her how much she wanted him. It had surprised her even more that he had wanted her.

It was not simply the hunger they shared for one another. It was not the gentle way they pleased each other, or the music that seemed to play when their bodies intertwined. It was something else—something otherworldly, as if their union had been fated by the gods.

But it had all been a ruse.

She sat patiently, waiting for the tears to come. Nothing. The situation was too incredible to believe. How could a man who had worked so hard to help her have betrayed her so completely?

More importantly, how could she have allowed it to happen?

It was as if he had placed her beneath a kind of spell. He had impressed her with his good deeds and placed the smoke of lust beneath her nose and soon had her begging for his attentions.

She had been so thoroughly swept up in his magic that she had even convinced herself of his goodness.

Such an honourable man he is! she had told herself. *To risk so much to save his family!*

The Goodly Thief she had even named her bow. The Goodly Thief!

Ah, what a fool she had been.

There had been clues all along, after all. If he had really been such a respected archer in Tausret's army, she would have heard of him. The Sons of Ra—what kind of company was that? His self-proclaimed status as the kingdom's best archer did not mix with his savage criticism of its ruler.

And then there had been his keen interest in the identity of the heir. Of course he would be interested. General Setnakht would want the heir dead even more than the High Priest did.

She untangled herself from the bed sheet, but could not gather the energy to fetch her clothes. She gazed down at her naked body and laughed bitterly.

As if any man could ever want her—a hardened woman long past her prime, a cold Libyan crone with a strange face and soulless stare. She had wanted what she could not have instead of being satisfied with what she had always possessed: Pharaoh's love.

It was the only true thing in her life and it was enough. It was more than enough. It was more real than any sunrise and richer than any tomb. In her pursuit of life, she had forgotten her life's purpose. She would never err like that again.

She heard clanging somewhere near and quickly donned her sheath. The men were in the weapons room, carrying out their wicked work. Soon they would have all the golden daggers gathered. They would pile up the spears and pluck the jewels from the chariots' reins.

There was no way that Aya would be able to replace it all.

How could she stop them? She could not defeat the four large men on her own. Even armed with her bow, she would not be able to pin them to any surface. If she tried to injure them, she felt certain they would simply slit her throat.

There was one way to stop them. She gazed up at the shaft of light shining down from above. She could sneak away. Right then, she could escape out the tunnel and run down the valley to where the guards had gathered around the fire. 'Come with me!' she could tell them. 'You have been tricked!'

In no time, she could have Intef and his three co-conspirators standing beneath executioners' spears.

Pharaoh would be avenged and Aya redeemed.

And Intef would be dead.

Finally, the tears began to fall. She could not do it. He had lied to her, he had betrayed her body and soul, yet she could not bear the thought of his death. She hated him and she never wished to see him again, but she did not wish to live in a world without him.

It was like watching a pack of hyenas eviscerating a fresh carcass. Intef stood at the entrance to the first unfinished chamber watching his fellow tomb raiders begin their pillaging in earnest. They prowled about the room in a kind of frenzy, seizing upon the treasures and tossing them into piles.

'Look at this slingshot!' Huni remarked, gazing in wonder at the solid gold weapon. 'It looks as though it should be adorning some rich woman's hair!'

'Give me that,' said Den, grabbing the object and

shoving it beneath his kilt. 'I do far more hunting than you do.'

'Let us not forget our purpose, Brothers,' Intef uttered, though for the moment even he could not remember quite what that was.

Intef saw Ranofer admiring himself in a shining copper shield. 'It is so clear,' Ranofer said.

Intef gazed into the polished copper and drew a breath. The image of himself was the clearest he had ever seen, yet had somehow never been murkier.

What had happened to the handsome youth with the luminous eyes and hopeful grin? He was gone—replaced by this mirthless wrinkled man, whose lips stretched into a soulless frown.

Intef adjusted the angle of the shield, hoping to catch the sparkle in his eyes, but they remained dull and crooked, for they were the eyes of a thief and a liar. A man who betrayed the ones he cared about the most.

He handed the shield back to Ranofer. 'It will be worth dozens of *deben* melted down,' he said.

'Melted down? I plan to keep it,' Ranofer remarked.

Intef sat on the floor of the unfinished chamber, glad that Aya was nowhere near. When he had left her inside the false chamber, he feared he might never see her again. He had also prayed for it.

His stomach felt hollow, as if a hole had opened up inside it.

'A golden hilt, by the gods!' Den shouted.

Intef imagined Aya scrambling up the tunnel and out into the daylight. Which way would she run? Would she disappear into the hills, or would she run directly to the guards and tell them that they had been tricked?

'Look at this saddle,' remarked Huni. 'It is as red as the desert.'

If the latter, then the guards would soon be upon them and Intef and his fellow tomb raiders would have nothing to do but to await their own deaths.

'Ha!' Intef laughed and Den shot him a look.

'What is so funny?'

'Everything.'

'It is true, then,' mused Den. 'Nine days inside the tomb has driven you mad.'

'Five days, Den! Only five!' shouted Intef madly.

Den and Huni exchanged a look.

Intef laughed. Perhaps he was mad. He certainly could no longer count properly, nor did it seem was he in control of his fate. That was in Aya's hands and he prayed that she would have mercy. Still, he would accept whatever punishment she delivered, for she had been right about him from the beginning: he was a dirty, miserable thief.

The hole was growing larger. He needed to find something to fill it. 'I will return shortly,' he told his fellow thieves, grabbing his torch.

He headed for the main chamber and turned into the first storage room, searching for an amphora of beer. He lunged towards the shelves, stumbling on one of the chests.

His leg hit hard against the wood and he slammed down on to the ground. Pain ripped through him and he laughed bitterly.

Good. He wanted it to hurt. He touched the wound on his leg to discover it wet with blood. Even better. He wanted to bleed until all that was left of him was a heap of drained flesh.

He reached out and grabbed the closest amphora he could find. He ripped off the seal and took a long draught, only to discover he had opened the sacred wine. He closed his eyes. His betrayal of her could not be any worse. He could not be any more loathsome.

Yes, he could.

He tilted the amphora to his lips and drank until he could drink no more. He could feel the liquid spilling down his cheeks. Wine was much more potent than beer and thank the gods for that, for his mood was already improving.

Still, he could not seem to get her last words out of his mind. *'I am not yours and I never will be.'*

Well, what had he expected? He had not only betrayed her, he had done so to her face.

He took another long gulp of wine. If he had only kept better track of the days, he could have got her out of the tomb before the men had arrived.

Perhaps he had not wanted time to pass. Maybe he had wanted more hours with her and simply wished them into existence. Whatever the reason, he had been a fool. Now not only would they be parted, but she would loathe him for ever.

'I am not yours and I never will be.'

Chapter Twenty-Three

Aya heard the men's voices close. They were dragging a horde of weapons into the false chamber atop one of Pharaoh's larger bed sheets. The cache was so heavy that they had to pause several times to rest as they dragged it to the base of the ramp.

'What is the matter, Sobek?' asked Den. 'Did you not expect you would have to share?'

Aya wiped her tears. 'Not at all.'

Ranofer gave Aya a gentle pat on the head. 'You will not come away with everything you wished for, but we are not unreasonable men. If you carry your load, you will have your share. Come, see if you can lift this pile of daggers.'

Aya did not respond. It was one thing to witness the robbery of Pharaoh's tomb, it was another to aid in its plunder.

'I suppose you are right,' said Ranofer, chuckling. 'If we can hardly drag it down the hall, how could you possibly do it?'

The men departed, returning with another sheet filled with goods. Where was Intef? Aya dared not ask.

Soon all the most valuable contents of both unfinished chambers lay on sheets at the base of the ramp.

'We are going to need to fashion a litter for all this,' Huni observed.

'I think I saw a bed we can use for the rails,' said Den.

'Come, Sobek,' Ranofer said, motioning to her. 'Let us find a load that might be suitable for you.'

Arriving in the main chamber, the men began opening Pharaoh's garment chests one by one. 'Well, look here!' Ranofer exclaimed, holding up Tausret's finest beaded net dress. 'Is this not golden thread?'

He handed the garment to Aya and she remembered the last time Pharaoh had worn the dress. It had been at the last Festival of Min. Tausret had entered the open courtyard at nighttime and the torches made the delicate threads of the net sparkle as she walked, like sun glinting off a spider's golden web.

Aya clutched the dress to her chest, as if the memory itself depended on her preserving the garment.

'And look at this belt!' Ranofer exclaimed, holding up a carnelian-studded belt of the finest white leather. He draped it over Aya's hands.

He continued in that manner until all of Pharaoh's most expensive garments were hanging over Aya's arms. She bit her lip, willing herself not to cry.

'Come, I know the royal jewellery is somewhere near.' They crossed to another storage room and soon Ranofer and the others were rifling through several nested boxes. Aya looked away as the men lifted the golden beaded pectorals and elaborate rings and armbands from Pharaoh's most sacred stores. She felt the urge to vomit.

'What is wrong, Sobek?' asked Ranofer.

'I find myself in need of a drink,' replied Aya.

'As do I,' Den seconded.

The men packed up their newfound jewels and the four crossed to the sustenance room, nearly stumbling upon Intef, who lay against one of the crates. His eyes were closed, his legs splayed, and there was a large amphora settled on his stomach.

'Intef!' Aya shouted. He startled awake.

'Brothers! What are you doing here?' he slurred.

'You are drunk,' said Ranofer. 'Where is the wine?'

'There is no wine inside this tomb.'

Ranofer snatched the amphora from Intef's hands and pushed it up to his nose. 'This is wine!'

Intef's laugh was thin and metallic. 'You have discovered me, Brothers! It is just there on the bottom shelf.'

Aya watched in horror as the men unsealed the three separate containers of sacred wine and began to drink.

Intef looked away from her. It was as if he did not even know her, as if all that they had shared had been a fatuous vision that had disappeared with the daylight. Was this the true Intef, at last?

Of course it was and shame on Aya for ever believing otherwise. What she had not anticipated was the degree of his depravity. To think that all along he had known about the terrible plundering that was going to take place. Such elaborate lies he had told her! His bereft mother and dying brothers, his newfound admiration for Tausret, his promise to help her find the heir to the throne—all of it nonsense!

No wonder he was drinking.

'Drink up, men,' said Ranofer, 'for the most difficult task lies before us.' And so it was that four of Pharaoh's

six irreplaceable amphorae of wine were unceremoni-
ously drunk right before her eyes.

Yet the stolen wine and pilfered jewellery were small
indiscretions compared to what happened next. Had Aya
known the task to which Ranofer had been referring,
she might have seized her bow and arrows right then
and killed them all. As it was, she only watched with
suspicion as the men finished their bread and wine and
stepped back into the main chamber.

'Intef, bring your chisel,' Ranofer called and Intef
staggered to his feet and appeared with the other men
standing around Pharaoh's sacred shrine.

Aya caught Ranofer's gaze. 'You do not intend to
open the shrine?'

'Does a clam-digger not open the clam?' returned
Ranofer.

'But—' Aya took a breath. 'For what purpose?'

'You are not much of a tomb raider, are you, Sobek?'
Ranofer remarked. 'Watch now and learn.' Ranofer
wedged the chisel in the seam of the shrine and landed
a blow.

Soon the four men were peeling back the walls of the
shrine, revealing the inner shrine. 'And so it goes,' said
Ranofer. He chiselled through the second gilded box,
then the third, until finally they were staring at Pharaoh
Tausret's giant pink granite sarcophagus.

Aya might have screamed her rage to the heavens,
but she found she could not speak. She could hardly
even breathe.

'Do you see now why there are four of us, Sobek?'
asked Ranofer, as if he were a teacher giving a lesson
in letters. The men took their places around the lid of
the sarcophagus. 'All together now,' said Ranofer. 'One,
two, three.'

* * *

Intef and the other three men heaved. As they lifted the massive granite lid off of Tausret's sarcophagus, Intef braved a glance at Aya. She was standing near the entrance to the main chamber, as if any moment she might make her escape. A part of him hoped she would.

She seemed to be frozen in place, however. She was gazing at the granite lid that had been propped against the sarcophagus as if to better apprehend its features. They were roughly those of a woman's face.

Huni gazed down at the first of the nested coffins and Den clapped him on the shoulder. 'Do not look so worried, Brother. Remember that she was just a woman.'

'And what of her *ba*—her winged personality?' asked Huni.

'It flew out of this tomb the moment it smelled your stinking breath!'

The men laughed and gathered around the lid of the second coffin and Ranofer began the count. 'One, two—'

'What are you doing?' Aya interrupted.

Do not speak, thought Intef, willing her to stay silent.

'What does it look like we are doing?' Ranofer replied.

Intef could see that she had composed her expression carefully, but she was barely concealing the quiver in her lip. 'What value is there in exposing the mummy?' she asked.

The three men exchanged glances, as if sharing a private jest. 'Let us see if you can guess,' said Ranofer, 'as part of your education.'

The men lifted the gilded wooden lid and placed it on the ground, then lifted another lid of solid gold.

Ranofer held up his torch and the three men peered

down into the coffin that contained Tausret's mummy. Huni gasped. Den shook his head. 'It is lovelier than I imagined.'

Ranofer gestured to Aya. 'Come, Sobek, you must see this.'

Aya stood frozen in the doorway to the chamber. Intef could not tell if she was on the verge of tears or murder.

'You will never see anything more magnificent in all your life,' goaded Ranofer.

'Leave her be, Ranofer,' said Intef. 'Can you not see she fears Tausret's *ka*?'

The men stared down at the solid gold death mask staring back at them with jewel-encrusted eyes.

'I do not understand,' said Huni. 'I thought Sobek would be delighted to behold such a treasure. Do women not love such things?'

'You have hit upon the very problem,' mused Den. 'She is a woman and thus as inconstant as a cloud.'

'That she is a woman has nothing to do with it,' snapped Intef. He hardly recognised his own voice.

The men set the death mask on the floor and returned their attention to Tausret's unmasked mummy.

There she was. The Powerful One. Her cheeks were brown and sunken, her linen-wrapped limbs barely thicker than bones. Still, somehow, Intef could see her greatness.

Ranofer began probing beneath her wraps with his thick fingers. 'What are you doing?' asked Intef.

'Looking for amulets, of course,' he said. 'They can be quite valuable.'

Intef was feeling a powerful urge to consume more wine.

'Surely we have enough treasure now with all the jewellery,' he said, but Ranofer turned to Den and Huni.

'Will you not help me search, Brothers?' Soon Den and Huni had joined him. Intef gazed at the deceased woman, searching for some excuse to stop them from desecrating her completely.

It was then he spotted the scroll. It was lying inside Tausret's desiccated hand, as if she had been embalmed with it in her grip. Intef gently lifted it and began to read.

I, Tausret, Daughter of Merneptah and Takhat, Granddaughter of Rameses the Great Ancestor, do hereby swear before Thoth that my daughter, Aya, born of my flesh, is the last of the Rameses bloodline.

She bears the sacred mark upon her neck, drawn there by the High Priestess of Isis in her third year, and the records of her birth can be found in the Isis Temple at Pi-Rameses.

Let it be known that the blood of Rameses flows on.

At the bottom of the scroll was Tausret's royal cartouche in the form of a wax stamp along with a familiar symbol: a triangle inside a circle.

'What is it?' asked Den. He was gazing over Intef's shoulder. 'What does it say?'

'It is…a curse,' Intef lied. 'It is addressed to anyone who might open the coffin and harm the deceased.'

'Read it,' said Huni.

'Do not read it!' cried Den.

Intef rolled the scroll and placed it beneath his belt. 'Den is right,' he said. 'We should not read it.'

'We should destroy it!' cried Den.

'And risk unleashing the spirit of the curse?' Intef

shook his head. 'I will take it to a temple and have it neutralised by a priest. Now let us finish gathering our haul. We leave tonight.'

By the time the men had finished ransacking the main chamber, all of their bags were filled and they spent the rest of the afternoon in the false chamber constructing their litter.

As soon as they were settled in their work, Aya padded quietly back down the corridor. When she arrived at the threshold to the main chamber and saw Intef sitting beside the shrine, her heart skipped. A part of her wanted to rush into his arms.

The foolish part of her.

Without acknowledging him, she stepped before the open sarcophagus and gazed down at her beloved Pharaoh.

'I must move the lids back into place. I must return her to her rest.' She was trying her best to maintain her composure, though the sight of Tausret's unmasked face filled her with a despair so sharp she nearly choked.

'I know. I will help you do it.'

'I do not want any more of your help.' Still, she knew he would not leave until the burial was restored. He was obviously desperate to make himself feel better about what he had done.

She would not let him.

'You did not just betray me. You betrayed her!' He moved to stand, but she motioned him away. 'Stay away from her!'

He sank back down beside the sarcophagus. Here they were, alone together in the main chamber, just as they had been when they first met. Still enemies.

'Why, Intef?'

'General Setnakht requested the death mask. The men were merely following orders.'

'You know that is not what I mean.'

'Everything I do is for the good of Egypt,' he said.

She laughed bitterly and looked around the chamber. Several of the chests lay broken on the floor. Clothes were strewn about, along with several emptied amphorae and the splinters of the bed frame the men had violently disassembled.

'How can this be for the good of Egypt?' She really wanted to know. She prayed he could convince her, for just then she felt as though not only had Tausret's afterlife been destroyed, but that all her Pharaoh's efforts in this life had been, too.

'Tausret's treasure will pay for mercenaries in General Setnakht's army.'

'So your plunder will pay for more killing.'

She fought her tears, but they came anyway, falling on Tausret's resin-stained bandages, which had been tugged and loosened by Intef's careless partners.

'You could have stopped all this.'

Aya did her best to settle the cloths back into place. Without her death mask Tausret seemed so small and fragile. Even her elegant embroidered robe could not conceal her hollow ribcage and the wretched concavity of her stomach.

'I cannot stop anything now,' said Intef. 'The moment the tunnel was complete, the tomb was lost. You must understand this.'

'I thought you were an honourable man.'

'It is possible that the number of mercenaries we purchase will prevent a battle with the High Priest. It is why I am here.'

'To prevent a battle?'

'I am tired of fighting, Aya.'

'Then why have you spent all these years in Set-nakht's army?'

'I just want someone to prevail. I do not care who.'

Aya wiped her tears. 'Now it is I who no longer be-lieves your words,' she said, for if she did believe them, then she could not blame him. If he was speaking the truth, then the reasons for his actions were honourable. And she did not wish to believe him honourable—not right now.

'It is the only way to ensure a peaceful succession. I wanted to tell you. I—'

'Do you really think the High Priest will concede without a fight?' asked Aya.

'If General Setnakht can overwhelm him with the size of his army, then, yes. Everything depends on the mercenaries.'

She shook her head. 'You do not know the High Priest.'

Aya gazed down at Tausret, catching a glint of silver. There were two small silver objects wedged just behind her Pharaoh's leg. She reached down and touched the cool metal and sensed a memory hovering at the edges of her mind. They were a pair of silver gloves—too small for anyone but a child.

Where had she seen the gloves before?

She stepped back and studied Tausret's face one last time, then bent to kiss her cheek. 'I will not rest until your legacy is restored,' she whispered. She was going to say more, but she sensed Intef moving around the sarcophagus and looked up.

He was placing something inside Tausret's coffin. 'What are you doing?' she asked.

'Ah…'

Aya strode towards him and seized the object: a scroll with a broken wax seal. She opened it and began to read. "'I, Tausret, Daughter of Merneptah and Takhat, Granddaughter of Rameses the Great Ancestor…'"

When she'd finished, she felt the room begin to spin. She gripped the side of the sarcophagus.

'I am the heir,' she whispered. 'I am Tausret's daughter.'

She reached for one of the silver gloves. She remembered them now. Tausret had given them to her as a gift when she was young. They were decorations—not meant to be worn—but Aya had been too young to know it. She had pulled them from a shelf and had tried to wear them on her hands. Tausret had laughed and lifted Aya into the air, then hugged her with great affection.

Aya had tucked the memory away, for it had been rare for Tausret even to smile, let alone embrace anyone.

Like a mother would have embraced a daughter.

'Why did you seek to hide this from me?' Aya demanded.

'I tried to tell you, but you did not believe me.'

'But the scroll is proof!'

'Yes, and proof changes everything,' he said. He gave her a significant look and she slowly absorbed the meaning of his words.

It did change everything. Now there was irrefutable evidence of her birth. As Tausret's proven daughter, she had the Great Ancestor's blood running through her veins. She was part divine and could confer legitimacy upon whichever pretender she chose. She had just become a kingmaker.

Intef plucked the scroll from Aya's grasp and tucked it back into the coffin. 'Nobody needs to know.'

Aya's mind raced. 'If the heir were female, we could

avoid a war,' she echoed. 'You said that to me only days ago.'

'I was only speaking theoretically.'

'Do you not wish to avoid a war?' she asked. She placed the silver glove back into the coffin and pulled the scroll out again.

'It is not worth sacrificing your life. Did you not say that Tausret wished for you to live?' Intef asked.

Aya could hardly think. Outside, armies were gathering. She alone had the ability to stop them. 'Was Tausret foolish in her alliance with the King of the Hittites?' she asked Intef.

'I believe she was.'

'But many lives were saved through that alliance.'

'Except Tausret's own,' said Intef. He bowed his head. 'May she live on for ever in the Fields of Paradise.'

'There is no choice, Intef. It is my life or thousands of lives.'

He moved towards her, then seemed to stop himself. 'Please do not do this, Aya. Do not give away the rest of your life. You have served Great Egypt nobly. Now it is time to live.'

'If I married Setnakht's son, or even Setnakht himself, I would still be living.'

'You would become a royal brood mare, just like Tausret. Your mother kept you secret all her life just so she could avoid that fate for you.'

'And my mother worked her whole life trying to save Egyptian lives.'

He was shaking his head. 'This is all my fault. We should have escaped the night after you tunnelled through. I would have had you out of here sooner if we had not…' He paused.

'If we had not made love?' She smiled sadly. 'I know

you do not love me, Intef. You made that very clear. Nor do I love you.' She felt a pinch in her chest, as though she was betraying some piece of her heart. 'Though I respect your intentions, I cannot trust you and I know I will never be able to again. There is no need for you to protect me, or feel obliged to me any longer. We both seek what is best for the people of Egypt. I will give myself to Setnakht and his son Rameses and lives will be saved. There are many ways to honour Pharaoh's memory, but this is the best.'

Chapter Twenty-Four

They departed before moonrise. Aya went first and as she emerged from the tunnel she choked on the smoky air. Glancing around her, she could not see a single torch flickering anywhere along the ridges. She felt certain the guards had abandoned their posts. Ranofer's fire trick had worked.

They were fortunate it had, for it must have taken an hour for the men to lift all their treasures out of the tunnel. Aya watched in horror as they pushed up load after load, placing it all on the litter they had constructed with Tausret's own bed rails.

Aya gave no hint of the anger boiling inside her. To do so would have been to show weakness and she had vowed never to be weak again. She had made her decision and now she would carry it out.

They were a clumsy, lumbering group. The litter the men carried was so overburdened with Tausret's treasure that they had to stop every fifty paces just to rest. Aya welcomed the breaks herself, for she carried her own heavy object: the acacia wood cradle.

She would have preferred to have carried Pharaoh's death mask, but Ranofer would not allow it. It was the single most valuable item in all the horde and he placed it on the litter near him, for he wished to present it to his General himself.

Aya eyed the mask as she walked behind the men. Whatever happened, she had to return it. It was the most important component of Pharaoh's tomb. Without it, Tausret's winged *ba* would not recognise her body and would be unable to occupy it and take its rest. Eventually it would become lost for ever.

They walked throughout the night. By the time the sun god's light was painting the horizon in red and orange, they were standing atop a plateau, gazing down at a spectacle.

Two armies had assembled on the field below. On the eastern side of the field, an army of men and chariots stood in formation. There must have been ten thousand of them—row after perfect row of kilted, leather-clad soldiers, organised by weapon group.

At the head of the formation, Aya could see the royal banner of the Horus hawk flying high, followed by rows of archers, infantry and then chariots. Atop one of the chariot platforms she saw the white linen robe and leopardskin pelt of the High Priest of Amun.

On the western side of the field was an army of equal size, though much less organised. Its soldiers wore kilts and sandals, but few donned the leather chest guards and protective hats typical of soldiers of the double crown.

Nor were they separated in any discernible way: the spear throwers stood alongside the archers, who stood alongside the sword-bearers, while the chariots had gathered haphazardly around the periphery.

Towards the back half of the assemblage, the men

appeared rougher, somehow, and some carried unusual weapons. One man held a three-pronged spear, while another appeared to wield a terrifying scythe. At the very rear of the group, two men in long white kilts and leather chest guards sat atop twin white horses.

Aya looked back and forth between the two armies, trying to determine who held the advantage. They appeared to be equally matched, just as she had feared. There was only one way forward.

Holding fast to their heavy litter, Intef and the others stumbled down the plateau and headed for the rear flanks of the western army. As they made their final descent, the soldiers began to cheer, for their payment had arrived. Those who could survive the day would be compensated handsomely, compliments of Pharaoh Tausret.

Intef felt ill. It did not matter how much wealth they carried in their litter; it still would not make more mercenaries. The armies were simply too well matched. Soon it would be Egyptian against Egyptian in another bloody battle—perhaps the worst of the civil war. There was only one thing that could be done to avoid a fight, yet he prayed that Aya would not do it.

The soldiers cheered louder as the litter neared and Intef spotted a boy in the crowd. His sidelock of youth had not even been cut; it had instead been stuffed inside his small leather hat.

Intef glanced at Aya. She had spotted the boy, too, and her brow wrinkled with distress. She, too, knew there was a tragedy about to unfold. Half these men and boys were about to lose their lives so that one man or another could sit on the throne of Egypt.

He could see the solemn resolve spreading across Aya's face.

No, he thought.

He pictured her lying beneath Rameses's fleshy figure, night after cursed night. He saw her holding her pregnant belly and screaming in the birthing chair, then lying beneath Rameses once again. The cycle repeated year after terrible year. The very thought sent an agony through Intef's body more painful than any battle wound.

Please, Aya, he prayed. *Do not do it.*

The men set the litter down a good distance behind the last row of soldiers and Setnakht and Rameses rode out to meet them.

'Ah! There is my beetle!' said Setnakht fondly, greeting Intef. 'I see the ants have found you.'

'And a good deal of treasure as well, my lord,' said Ranofer.

Setnakht eyed the heavy litter greedily. 'Take it to my war tent and guard it there,' he commanded. 'We will retrieve it after we have brought the High Priest's army to its knees.'

The two Generals cajoled their horses around to return to their men.

'Wait!' called Aya. 'Do not go.'

Intef felt his heart collapse in his chest.

'What is it?' barked Setnakht. 'A woman? On a battlefield? Can you not see that we have a battle to fight?'

Aya shot Intef a look, then pulled the scroll from her sack. 'Not after you hear this.'

After that, time seemed to pass in flashes of awareness. 'I, Tausret Daughter of Merneptah,' Aya began reading out loud.

She was speaking loudly enough for the assembled

soldiers to hear her and when she finished reading the scroll it appeared that the entire army had turned to gape.

Intef could hardly watch as General Setnakht ceremoniously dismounted his horse and approached Aya. 'But you are obviously Libyan,' he said. He plucked the scroll from her grasp and read it closely, then took her face in his hands. 'Look at those eyes.'

'I believe that is part of the reason why my identity was concealed,' said Aya. She lifted her hair and the General peered at the tattoo on her neck.

Intef felt his heart lurch. For no reason at all, he wished to punch the General in the gut. Nobody should be looking at her tattoo like that save Intef himself.

'That is the same symbol that was on the scroll,' Setnakht remarked.

'That is not all,' Aya said. She directed him to the cradle that she had placed on the ground and lifted it so he could read the plaque. The General read over the hieroglyphics with great interest.

'How old are you, woman?' he asked Aya.

'Four and twenty years old,' she replied.

Setnakht peered up at the cloudless sky and shook his head in wonder. 'I dare say the gods are with us today and one in particular.'

He whispered a prayer to Horus, god of kings, then waved to a mounted spear thrower. The man galloped to Setnakht's side. 'Summon the High Priest to the middle of the field. We wish to apprise him of some new circumstances.' The soldier nodded and speeded off across the field.

'Come, Rameses,' Setnakht said, motioning to his son. 'There is someone I would like for you to meet.'

As Rameses turned his horse towards the group Intef

moved quickly to Aya's side. He gave her arm a tight squeeze. 'I understand what you feel you must do, but it does not have to be for ever. Marry him and stop the war, but leave him at the earliest chance. Run far away, Aya. Do not become this man's brood mare.' He pushed the arrowhead into her palm. 'Use your gift.'

Rameses dismounted and stepped before Aya, his small black eyes flashing, and Intef gave a short bow and stepped away.

Setnakht gestured grandly to Aya. 'Rameses, meet Aya, the great-grandchild of Rameses the Great Ancestor,' Setnakht was saying. 'Your new wife.'

Chapter Twenty-Five

'Wine!' Intef shouted. He could hardly make himself heard above the din. He was standing in the crowded courtyard of the Temple of Amun along with half of the population of Thebes.

He grabbed a passing servant by the arm. 'Get me more wine,' he demanded. He drained the contents of his cup and handed it to the man. 'Now!'

'Yes, my lord,' said the man, scurrying away.

Intef looked out over the jubilant crowd, which had spilled out of the temple courtyard and into the streets. Never before had there been such a gathering. Sun-baked farmers raised their cups alongside march-weary soldiers. Deadly Nubian mercenaries sang odes to chubby Theban babies. An infantry officer from the late Pharaoh's army sparred with an archer from Setnakht's ranks.

It would never have been possible until today. Not only had the battle been averted, but Egypt was united once again. There would be no more bloodshed, no more civil war, and the blood of Rameses the Great Ancestor would live on.

The servant returned to Intef with two cups of wine,

one of which Intef downed in a single gulp. He tossed the young man a gold *deben*—enough gold treasure to pay for a year's worth of bread. 'What are you waiting for?' barked Intef, holding up his empty cup. 'More.'

Now was not the time to lose himself in drink, yet Intef could not think of what else to do. His dream had finally come true: there would be no more fighting. He could meet his father in the afterlife and finally hold his head up. So why did he feel like the most odious creature on the face of the earth?

Two soldiers approached Intef, clanking their cups together. 'To the Hero of Thebes!' they shouted. Intef had to look twice. One man wore the pleated kilt and copper cuffs of an officer in the pharaonic army; the other wore the red armband and tattered rags of Setnakht's personal guard.

Intef forced a grin, then guzzled down another cup. Until this day, the only time he would have seen such men together was fighting one another on the battlefield.

But that very day, when Setnakht rode out to parlay with the High Priest, a miracle had taken place. The Priest had not only conceded the double crown to Setnakht, he had agreed to give over command of his army right then and there, as long as Setnakht promised to keep him in his position as High Priest of Amun.

General Setnakht had agreed and, when he had announced the news to both armies, he had added that every single man would receive a bonus in pay to celebrate the great news—that Egypt was finally united.

'Pharaoh Setnakht! Pharaoh Setnakht!' the men had shouted.

And it was that moment that Setnakht chose to introduce his son's betrothal. 'The divine blood of Rameses the Great Ancestor shall be united in marriage today!'

The High Priest had bound the couple's hands and said the holy words.

'And you are all invited to the feast!' Setnakht had shouted.

It was as if after a long drought the sky had opened up and the gods had deluged the people of Egypt with blessings. The cheering had been so loud that it had been heard all the way across the river in Thebes.

Now the two soldiers clapped Intef on the back. The story of Intef's heroics had already become legend. 'We heard that you discovered the Princess by listening to a crack in the rock,' said one soldier.

'And that you had to fight demons to free her,' said another.

'Ha-ha-ha,' Intef replied. 'Ho-ho-ho.'

He had no energy to correct them, nor could he bear to lie about his true purpose in the tomb, for the General had sworn him to secrecy.

Hence Intef merely bowed humbly before the soldiers' praise and drained his cup. Where was that cursed servant?

Another group of soldiers approached, followed by another, and Intef found himself repeating the routine until finally the entire courtyard began to spin.

'Long live the Hero of Thebes!' someone shouted and Intef was lifted into the air upon a tall man's shoulders. 'Praise for the mighty Beetle!' another shouted and he seemed to be floating above the crowd.

'The mighty Beetle!' they began to chant.

Intef wobbled atop the man's shoulders, trying to keep his balance. But when Intef opened his mouth to speak, the only thing that came forth was wine. It spewed out of his mouth like a fountain. The drunken crowd roared with laughter as Intef was set back on the ground and a battery of servants came to clean up the mess.

Getting his bearings, Intef found himself annoyingly sober once again. He spotted Ranofer surrounded by a bevy of women. His fellow tomb raider was motioning to Intef. 'Come here, you drunken fool!' he shouted. Intef ducked his head and tried to get lost in the crush of bodies.

He spied a platform along the western edge of the courtyard. A large crowd had gathered around it as if awaiting some official address. Next to the platform there was a doorway that appeared to open out to the river.

Keeping his head down, Intef headed towards the doorway. He had almost reached it when he heard a voice sing out atop the platform. 'Honourable Egyptians, I give you Prince Rameses the Third and his new wife, the Great-Granddaughter of Rameses the Great Ancestor.'

Intef's heart went into his throat and he studied the ground. They had not even said her name.

'Intef!' called a woman's voice. He looked up and there she was, stepping through the doorway.

'Aya!'

Following behind her, Rameses caught her by the waist. 'This way, Wife,' he said, forcibly turning her body towards the platform. He nodded at Intef, then whisked her up the stairs to the roar of the crowd.

'To the newlyweds!' shouted the announcer.

'To the newlyweds!' repeated the crowd, erupting into a cacophony of cheers.

Intef darted through the exit and put his hands over

his ears. He did not want to hear any more cheers. He had saved many lives that day, but two lives were ruined—hers...and his.

Aya gazed up at the high open windows of the royal bathrooms and imagined she was a bird. She looked down, pretending her feet were talons. The warm bath-water poured across her shoulders and she shook it off, as a bird might shake off its feathers.

Her two young body servants frowned, then began rubbing the soap into her skin. Soon her dust-caked flesh was covered in the mixture of oil and salts.

'Now the rinse, Princess,' said the elder of the young women and poured more warm water over her head. Aya watched the water trickle down through the drain in the bath chamber. It was as brown as mud.

'There was no time to bathe before the wedding,' Aya explained.

'Of course,' said the elder. 'It must have been a very long day for you, Princess.'

'What is your name?' asked Aya.

'I am Maya,' said the elder, then nodded to the younger.

'And I am Meryt,' said the younger, who was al-ready applying a new layer of oil and salts to Aya's skin. Maya took up her own handful of soap and started in on Aya's hair.

It felt strange to submit to the care of servants. In the past, Aya had always been the one to do the scrubbing.

Aya tried to relax and imagine herself alone, but the silence was too large. 'We were married on the battle-field, you see,' Aya said by way of filling it.

'So we heard, Princess,' said Maya. 'It must have been exciting!'

Aya smiled, but found she did not know how to respond. 'Before that Intef and I were many days inside Tausret's House of Eternity,' she said instead. 'The tunnel that we chiselled out was very long.'

The young women exchanged a look.

'What is it?' Aya asked. 'What is the matter?'

'It was our understanding that you were discovered in Seti's tomb, not Tausret's,' said Maya.

'And that you were alone,' said Meryt.

Aya stared at the clear-eyed young women. 'Apologies, I do not understand.'

'We were told that the hero Intef chiselled the tunnel from the outside in, not the other way around,' Meryt said.

'Ah,' said Aya. So the story had already been changed. It was not Tausret's tomb, but Seti's that would be remembered in the tale. And there would be no account of the pillaging that had taken place, despite Setnakht's sudden wealth and magnanimity. Tausret herself was central to the story, yet her role in it was already being quietly erased.

Worse, earlier that day when Aya had gently asked her new husband if he would dedicate some royal resources to restoring Tausret's tomb, he had flatly refused. 'I am going to move her into Bay's tomb,' he had explained. 'It is smaller and more appropriate for a woman.'

Aya's mouth had hung open. 'What will happen to her own tomb?' she had asked.

'Oh, it will belong to my father,' he had said and grinned. 'Is that not poetic?'

Tausret's fate was sealed, just as Hatshepsut's had been. The men who came after her would simply deny her existence. They would not only chisel her name off monuments, they would replace her in her very own tomb.

Aya suppressed a sob.

'It is normal to be confused, Princess,' Maya remarked. 'You have been through such an ordeal.'

'Soon you will be as good as new,' Meryt said cheerfully.

Aya smiled, her heart near to bursting with despair. No, she would never be as good as new. Tausret's tomb was desecrated, her afterlife destroyed, her memory to be erased, and there was no chance to save any of it, for Aya had just been married to the son of Tausret's enemy.

She had saved lives, but it seemed she had failed her beloved Pharaoh—her mother—once again. The servants could rinse her a thousand times: she would never again be clean.

'Do not weep, my lady. It is a joyous day,' said Meryt.

They rinsed Aya once again and soon Aya's skin was luminous with the sheen of expensive oils and redolent with sweet-smelling perfumes.

'Here is your bed gown,' said Maya, passing Aya a nearly translucent garment of fine linen. 'Is it not lovely?'

Aya stared at the gown without seeing it. Tausret's commanding voice resounded suddenly inside her heart: *Do not become some selfish man's brood mare.*

'Do you have something else? Something more modest?' asked Aya. The women exchanged another look. Maya departed, but when she returned, it was not a garment she carried, but a cup. 'It is the milk of poppy, Princess. It will help you through the night that is to come.'

'Gratitude,' Aya said, accepting the cup, but not yet taking a sip. She gazed down at her exposed breasts.

'May I bring my tunic with me anyway?' she asked. 'It will be a comfort to have it near.'

'Of course,' said the two women, speaking as one.

They led Aya across a hall and pulled back the beads of a sprawling chamber. 'Prince Rameses has requested that you wait for him on the bed,' Maya said, gesturing to a large mattress atop a wooden frame at the centre of the chamber.

Aya did as she was told, setting the milk of poppy on top of a table just beside the bed and her clothing in a discreet corner of the chamber.

A single torch smouldered on its perch near the bed, leaving the rest of the room in shadow. Aya waited atop the downy bed mattress in quiet despair. It felt as though she were sinking through the floor.

Any moment Rameses would come through the door and take his husbandly right. And he would do it again and again, without any precaution, until Aya was fat with the heir to the throne. Aya gazed at the cup of poppy milk sitting beside the bed.

Inside her heart, Tausret was nearly shouting now: *Do not become some selfish man's brood mare!*

Aya glanced about the sparsely decorated chamber. In a far corner, she spied a brazier and its poker, a fine copper wash basin and matching bedpan, along with numerous chests she assumed to be full of clothes.

Across the chamber there was a small sitting area that included several lounging couches atop a sprawling red carpet. A fine glass table stretched between the couches. It was the stage for a single, long-stemmed rose that had been placed inside an alabaster vase.

Beside the sitting area was a tall curtained window and Aya wandered towards it and stepped between the curtains.

She gazed out at a long, elegant colonnade that meandered past the palace walls and down towards the distant gardens. Where the colonnade disappeared around the bend, Aya spied the lovely river, shimmering beneath a blanket of moonlight. Two guards wandered down the colonnade, moving away from her towards the river. If she sneaked away right now, she might be able to evade their notice. She could dash across the grounds and slip into the river...

She was turning to retrieve her tunic when she heard the sound of laughter outside the door.

She scrambled back to the mattress just as Rameses swept into the chamber, followed by two women clad in little more than beads.

'Hello, Wife,' he said, shooting Aya a nod.

Chapter Twenty-Six

'Hello, Husband,' Aya said, watching the giggling women come tumbling into the room.

He gave one of the women a deep, lingering kiss and spanked the other on the backside. 'Go now, little kittens. I have work to do.'

The women departed and Rameses crossed the chamber. He held a jug in one hand and what appeared to be a woman's loincloth in the other. He tossed the loincloth aside. Standing before Aya in his long wine-stained kilt, he took a drink from the jug and let out a long burp.

'What is that look?' he asked. Rameses was a typical Theban with his sepia skin and glossy black hair. But his eyes were small and seemed to lack brightness. They were nothing like Intef's.

'What look?' replied Aya.

'You look as if you have just seen a demon.'

'I am merely...awestruck,' she said, 'by your well-muscled physique.' He was too drunk to recognise her insincerity.

'The women tell me I am in fine form,' he bragged, flexing his thick but rather un-muscled arms. He noticed the open window. 'Gods, did the chambermaids leave it open again?' He crossed to the window and lifted a long reed pole, gently pulling the curtains shut with it.

He returned to Aya, glancing at the cup on the table beside the bed. 'What is that?' he asked.

'It is milk of poppy,' Aya admitted. 'But I am sure it will not be needed.'

'Is milk of poppy not a medicine for pain?' he asked.

'It can be, but I was told it can also help a man with...' She glanced down at his loincloth.

His eyes flashed. 'No, it will certainly not be needed,' he said. He took another drink of wine and his eyes slid back to the cup. 'Though I admit I come to you in a rather...used condition.'

Aya might have been offended, or disgusted, but as she gazed up at the future Pharaoh of the greatest kingdom in all the world, she felt only a vague sense of pity—along with a strange premonition that it would be women—not war—that would be his end.

Just as Aya had hoped, he reached for the cup and took a long drink. Then he lay down next to her. 'Gods, your eyes are strange,' he told her.

'That is what they say,' she said. She turned her face away from him.

'Come now, I do not mind your face,' Rameses said, as if extending his generosity. 'Besides, it is what I put in your belly that matters.'

Aya forced a gamely grin. 'Still, I am not the prettiest woman in Thebes now, am I? Why do we not put out the torch? That way you can imagine a more beautiful woman beneath you.'

'Your cleverness seems to compensate for your strangeness,' said Rameses gently, as if he meant it as a compliment.

She reached for the torch and waved it out above them and soon they were lying together in total darkness.

He began to grope at her breasts. 'Excuse me, Husband, but do you mind if I have a cup of that wine you brought? I think it will help me relax.'

'Of course,' Rameses said. She heard him reach to the floor and lift the large jug, taking a long draught himself before handing it to Aya. While she drank, he continued to fondle her breasts.

'As soon as you can produce an heir, there will be no more need to lie together,' he remarked cheerfully. He gave her nipple a hard twist.

'Ow!' she cried.

'That is the spirit!'

Aya forced a soft giggle and pretended to drink, then returned the jug to his hands. 'Gratitude, Husband.'

She heard him take another long draught before sensing him stretch away from her to place the jug on the floor. Aya moved her hands over his exposed back and began to rub. 'Now let me help you relax,' she said.

He subsided beneath her touch almost instantly. 'Ah, that feels wonderful,' he said, letting out another long burp.

Aya rubbed and kneaded and probed until his rhythmic snore filled the chamber with its grunting music. She slipped from the bed, gathered up her clothes and crossed to the window.

Stepping between the curtains, she peered out into the moonscape and her heart skipped. Two guards who appeared to be deep in conversation were heading straight down the colonnade towards the palace. She retreated into the chamber, thankful they had not seen her.

Still, it seemed there were guards crawling everywhere and she had not a single weapon for her defence. She sat down beside the window, noticing the long reed pole that Rameses had used to shut the high curtains.

An idea surfaced. Aya grasped the pole and bent it backwards tentatively. It did not break. She searched through one of the chests of clothes and seized on a thin leather tie. She bent back the pole and tied the ends off, fashioning herself a bow.

Now all she needed was an arrow. The chamber was dark, but she tried to picture its contents. She recalled the rose inside the vase on the table and retrieved it, along with the arrow that she had tucked inside her dirty tunic. The arrow that Intef had given her.

Using the ragged thread of her tunic's hem, she tied the arrowhead on to the stem. She needed another arrow. She remembered the brazier poker she had seen in the corner and quickly retrieved it. Then she pulled her tunic over her head to cover herself. Holding her newly forged bow and two makeshift arrows, she slipped between the curtains.

'What are you doing, Wife?' called Rameses.

Her heart skipped. He could not have seen her, could he? Perhaps he had heard the swish of the curtains. 'I am just getting a breath of fresh air,' she replied.

'It is rather stuffy in here,' said Rameses. 'Why not open the curtains?'

Aya did her best to move the fabric back along its high pole, until a long beam of light from the rising moon shone into the chamber. She could see Rameses's profile. He was sitting up in bed. 'What have you there in your arms, Wife?' he asked, his voice thick with suspicion.

'It is a bow I have fashioned from the reed pole you used to draw back the curtains.'

'Clever woman,' said Rameses. 'So you mean to escape?'

'I do.'

'You know there is no chance for you? The moment you slip out that window, I will simply call the guards on you—or I will come after you myself.'

'No, you will not.'

Slowly he rose from the bed, and she raised her bow. 'What do you think you are doing there, Wife?'

'Come no closer,' Aya warned, 'or I will do what I must.' She stretched back the string of her bow and balanced the poker upon it.

'I had heard Tausret was a killer, though I did not expect it of her daughter.'

'My mother was not a killer, she was a giver of life. And I will give you your life if you let me go.'

'You are making a mistake,' he said, stepping towards her.

She quieted her mind and let her arrow fly. It landed on the front panel of his kilt, right between his legs, pinning him to the wall.

He gazed in drunken wonder at the arrow, then turned his attention to Aya, who was readying the stem. She set the projectile into place in her bow and aimed it at his heart.

'I am going to leave now and, whether you call the guards or not, I will escape.'

'Harlot! You are just as bad as your mother.'

'I am just as good as my mother,' said Aya. 'And I must warn you that if you do call the guards on me, your reign will be cursed.'

'Nonsense,' he said, but his smile was taut with fear.

'Would it help if I shot this arrow a little bit closer to Egypt's Mighty Bull?' She glanced at his loincloth and saw him swallow hard.

'Swear that you will not call the guards,' she said. 'Now!'

'I swear it!' he replied.

'Swear that when you are Pharaoh, you will put the people of Egypt first.'

'What?' he said, his expression pained. She drew back her bow. 'I swear it!' he said.

'Swear that you will surround yourself with honest men and will abide no corruption in your great house.'

'I swear it,' said Rameses.

'Swear that you will keep the grain coffers full and never let any Egyptian go hungry, whether citizen, captive, freedman or slave.'

'I swear it!' said Rameses.

'For whom do you swear it?'

'For citizen, captive, freedman or slave.'

'Libyan, Asiatic, Nubian or Egyptian! Say it!'

'Libyan, Asiatic, Nubian or Egyptian,' he repeated.

'This is Egypt and we are civilised,' said Aya. 'Now repeat after me: Long live Pharaoh Tausret, the Powerful One, Strong Bull, Beloved of Mut!'

Rameses's mouth twisted into a scowl. 'Say it!' cried Aya. She fixed her gaze on to his heart.

'Long live Pharaoh Tausret...' Rameses began repeating. By the time he was finished, Aya was gone.

Once again, Intef had become confused about the passage of time. They said that the nuptial festivities lasted four days, followed by seven days of feasting to celebrate the coronation of Pharaoh Setnakht. But it seemed to Intef that many more days had passed as he lay on the steps of the Temple of Isis, awaiting the next distribution of beer.

'Wake up!' shouted a familiar voice one morning before dawn. Intef felt a sandalled foot poke his back.

'Just one more hour, I beg you!' Intef said, thinking the man was one of the temple guards.

'In one more hour the hyenas will be coming for you,' said the voice. 'When you see the yellow of their eyes, you must not panic.'

Intef lifted his head. 'Hepu?' He rolled over to discover the old priest standing above him, the leopard skin of rank adorning his shoulders. He extended his hand to Intef, along with a generous grin.

'Hepu, is that a smile on your wrinkled old face?' asked Intef.

'Not at all,' said the priest. 'I am merely stretching my mouth.'

'What are you doing here?'

'Finding the Hero of Thebes. It appears that I have accomplished my first mission as High Priest of the Temple of Nekhbet.'

Intef glanced at the hollow-eyed leopard skull resting on the priest's left shoulder. 'Your kitty looks rather bored with that title already,' said Intef, stretching his arms.

'I see you have not changed,' said Hepu. 'And yet I am glad to see you. Come, Pharaoh Setnakht summons you.'

It was not long before Intef found himself in the audience chamber of the royal palace alongside his fellow tomb raiders, gazing up at their newly crowned Pharaoh.

'The four of you look worse than when you came out

of that godforsaken tomb,' Pharaoh remarked, laughing. 'What is that stain on your chest, Ranofer?'

'Blood, my lor—I mean, Your Majesty,' said Ranofer. 'The stain is from the blood of the sacred bull you so generously granted for sacrifice. I helped to butcher him myself. His testicles were particularly delicious.' Ranofer paused, seeming to remember himself. 'May Horus bless you, mighty Pharaoh! Life, prosperity, health!'

Pharaoh Setnakht smiled and shook his grey head. 'And you, Beetle! I have never seen a kilt so filthy! You look as though you could use a good soak in the river.'

'A good soak would be most welcome, Your Majesty,' said Intef with a bow.

A good long soak without the chance for air.

'But enough idle talk,' said Setnakht. 'Today is the first official day of my reign and I mean to begin it with honour.' He motioned to a scribe, who stepped forward and handed each of the men a rolled scroll stamped in wax.

'If it had not been for your deeds, thousands of Egyptian lives would have been lost. It is also likely that I would not be sitting on this fine throne.' Intef recognised the throne immediately. It was the very throne that had anchored Aya's rope inside Tausret's tomb. 'The scrolls you hold grant you the right to carve your own tomb wheresoever you may choose in this great Egypt of ours,' he said.

Pharaoh gestured to two servants carrying large, heavy sacks. They placed a single sack in front of each of the men.

'Each of those sacks contains four hundred *deben*— enough wealth to pay for the carving, adornment and provisioning of those tombs.'

Intef heard Den gasp. 'Pharaoh, this is most generous,' he remarked.

'I am humbled, Majesty,' said Huni.

'My own tomb...' mused Ranofer.

The old General's generosity was matched only by his cunning. Not only had he just ensured the four soldiers' afterlives, he had ensured their loyalty and discretion until their dying days.

Intef found himself speechless. He gazed down at the bag of gold in wonder. He had not expected such a boon. For the first time in many days, he felt his heart beat.

'Soldiers,' Pharaoh continued, 'there is no end to my gratitude for what you have done. Your labours have brought an end to the civil war that has plagued us these many years. North and South are finally united and beneath my rule. But tell me now: Is there anything more you want? Any other wish I could possibly grant?'

The men glanced at each other in confusion.

'Come, do not be shy. I vowed to reward you and this Pharaoh keeps his word.'

Slowly, Ranofer stepped forward. 'I would like a field, Your Majesty, to cultivate for bread and profit.'

'As would I,' said Den.

'Granted,' proclaimed Setnakht with a sweep of his hand. 'You each may choose a plot from the royal holdings.'

Huni stepped forward. 'I would request a herd of cattle to graze upon Den's weeds.' He cast Den a mischievous grin.

'You will have your herd.'

Pharaoh Setnakht turned to Intef. 'Beetle, what do you wish for?'

Intef's heart was pounding now. He felt newly alive with the idea blooming inside it. 'There is only one thing I wish for, Majesty,' said Intef, 'but it is quite a lot to ask.'

'Well, ask it, soldier, and let us see if we can restore the *ma'at* between us.'

'I wish for Pharaoh Tausret's death mask.'

Intef heard Ranofer gasp. Pharaoh Setnakht narrowed his eyes. 'That is a rather lot to ask. For what purpose?'

'It will be my greatest trophy,' replied Intef. At least that was partially true.

'It is an audacious request,' Setnakht remarked. He paused, then opened his arms and grinned. 'For an audacious act.' Setnakht whispered something to a servant and in moments the sacred object was being wheeled in on a cart.

'Keep it well,' Setnakht said.

Intef gave a deep bow. 'I am humbled,' he said, though he felt his spirit growing larger by the minute.

'Horus knows there will be plenty of gold when the rest of the tomb is cleared,' Setnakht commented.

'You will pillage the rest of the tomb?' asked Intef.

'Eventually,' said Setnakht. 'Rameses has suggested that the tomb belong to me.'

It was as Intef had feared. Tausret would be erased and right before Aya's eyes. Then in a small miracle Rameses himself swept into the chamber, followed by Aya.

'Ah! Speaking of Rameses,' said Setnakht, brightening. Rameses and Aya stepped up the dais and Aya stood behind him as he bent to kiss his father.

Intef studied her backside out of the corner of his eye, admiring how her lovely curves were accentuated by her fine linen gown. It appeared she had gained some weight after so many days of festivities and her skin seemed a bit darker, as if she had spent much time beneath the sun. Was it possible that her hair had grown that much?

'Apologies for our tardiness, Father,' said Rameses. 'We are so happy to be here to honour our four most intrepid soldiers.' Rameses turned to regard the soldiers and Aya turned with him.

Except that the woman was not Aya.

Had Intef finally gone mad? He glanced at the other men. They were staring at the woman with a subtle consternation of their own.

Rameses, however, was acting as though nothing was wrong. He descended the dais and stepped before Intef. 'Thank you, Hero of Thebes!' Rameses exclaimed. He kissed Intef on both cheeks, then moved on to Ranofer.

The woman who was not Aya stepped before Intef next. She looked very little like Aya with the exception of her eyes, which were as blue as the sky. 'When I was trapped in that tomb, I was helpless,' she said. 'You rescued me from my death.' Her words were unusually firm, as if she were not simply making an observation, but giving a command. Intef understood at once what it meant.

They were making a pact. This was the new Aya and it was important that the four tomb raiders agreed, for they were among a very few who knew otherwise.

She moved to seal the pact with a kiss on Intef's cheek.

'Is she all right?' Intef whispered in the woman's ear. 'Aya? Is she alive?'

The new Aya moved to kiss his other cheek. 'Yes,' she whispered in his ear, then stepped back. 'I thank you for all your good deeds, Hero of Thebes.'

For the first time in many years, Intef let hope fill his heart. 'You are most welcome... Princess.'

Chapter Twenty-Seven

Two years later
—west of Amarna, central Egypt

Intef peered down at the crumbling temple, searching for its caretaker. She was usually praying this time of day, but he had not yet seen her cross the temple's small courtyard to the inner sanctum where she went each morning to make her offerings.

He focused his attention on the small hut just down the valley. A column of smoke twisted up through an opening in the roof. That was where she was—still inside her hut, cooking.

The day before, he had watched her kill a gazelle from a position high in the cliffs. The beast had been bounding across the valley below at great speed, but her skill with the arrow was too sharp. The gazelle never even had a chance.

He hoped that he would not soon be sharing a similar fate.

He waited patiently, admiring how the sun god stretched his rays across the hilly landscape—giving here, withholding there. Some plants would wait until noon to receive his blessings.

For eighteen months, he had searched for her—first in Thebes, then north to the Delta, then through the Western Desert and everything in between. He had asked traders on their routes and priests in their holy sanctuaries. He had probed bustling markets and lingered at busy docks. A woman with eyes the colour of the sea? No one like that here.

The last place he would have guessed was Amarna—the abandoned city of the heretic King. But of course she would have come here. It was the one place in all of Egypt where religious lines could be crossed. Here, the sun god Aten was still worshipped in secret, far away from the Amun priests. It was a place of old gods and forgotten kings and quiet tolerance—the one place in Egypt where she could worship her Pharaoh in peace.

A woman with eyes the colour of the sea? Yes, there is one who lives in the hills outside of the village. We call her the Mad Woman of Amarna.

Soon Aya emerged from her hut, a vision in flowing white linen. She always dressed well when she went to the temple, though the rest of the time she donned a tunic so brown and ragged that it might have been spun from Seth's own loom.

She had bathed herself, as usual, and her black hair shone like the fertile earth against the rugged brown landscape she traversed. In her arms she carried a platter of the freshly cooked gazelle and over her shoulder she had slung her bow. As she walked up the hill to the temple, she kept vigilant watch, as if she expected a challenge.

Intef's heart squeezed. In the four months he had been watching her, she had not been visited by a single soul. There was no one to challenge her or even to befriend her in these empty hills. Not even wandering dogs or curious cats from the village ventured this deep into the desert. Aya was utterly alone.

At last she arrived at the old temple of Aten, the ancient sun god that Akhenaten had lifted above all others. She stepped up to the gate between two crumbling pylons and bowed, then walked into the courtyard—though with only two walls standing he would not have even called it that.

She kept her pace slow and even, her bearing stiff and formal. She was acting as if she were in a real temple, as if she imagined brightly painted walls and reliefs of the gods all around her.

She stepped between the second set of pylons and into a roofless hall studded with pillars in various stages of decay. Over the months he had watched her clear the rubble from the floor of the space, though there were some pieces of collapsed roof that even she could not manage to move.

She walked around them gracefully now, then disappeared into the sanctuary, where she would remain for about an hour. Then she would return to her tiny hut and go about her midday chores, returning to the temple again at sunset. He hoped, however, that on this day she would not be returning to the temple at all.

He tightened the straps of his sandals and started off down the hill. His heart was beating wildly. He had been labouring for months to prepare his apology and had no idea if she would even be willing to hear it. Part of him feared for his life. There was nobody in the world he had wronged more than Aya. He only hoped that if she was going to kill him, she would first allow him to show her what was in his heart.

* * *

By the time he arrived outside the temple, she was already on her way out. He could hear the gravel crunching beneath her feet as she crossed the open courtyard and he pressed himself against the pylon gate, not wanting to startle her. He let out a friendly whistle.

The crunching stopped. He continued to whistle, hoping the crunching would resume. It was a tune that he had whistled before—surely she recognised it. The crunching resumed, but instead of moving towards the source of the noise, it sounded as if it was moving away from it.

She was running back into the temple. Intef rushed to the gate and gazed across the courtyard. He caught sight of her white tunic disappearing behind a giant column inside the pillared hall. 'Aya!' he called.

He ran to the entrance to the pillared hall. 'Aya!'

'Identify yourself!' she called from behind a pillar.

'I am Intef, son of Sharek.'

There was a long silence. He saw her bow emerge from behind a pillar.

'Where are they?' she asked, glancing about the hall.

'Where are who?'

'The other soldiers?'

'There are no other soldiers.'

'I do not believe you.' She stepped out slowly from behind the pillar and his stomach flipped over on itself. It had been so long since he had seen her, yet she looked as beautiful and familiar as the sun itself—and just as dangerous. She stretched back her arrow.

'I am telling the truth. I swear it before the gods,' he said.

'You have come to capture me and take me back to Rameses.'

'That is my fault.'

'What do you mean? What is your fault?'

'That you do not trust me.'

He could see the emotions at war inside her: pain, joy, fear, anger, happiness. And it *was* happiness. He could see it in the way she held her brows high above her eyes, in how her lips seemed to be fighting back a grin.

I see you, he wished to tell her. *I love*...

She set her jaw into a tight line. 'Why are you here?'

'I have come to ask for your forgiveness.'

She cocked her head. 'Fine, you are forgiven. Now go away.' She turned and began walking back into the sanctuary.

'Wait!' cried Intef. He started after her, but she threatened him once again with her arrow.

'I told you to go away,' she said. Sunlight filtered in from above, lighting up her eyes and illuminating the shape of her body beneath the linen. He wanted so badly to embrace her.

'I wish to show you something important,' he said. 'A tomb. It will take us only an hour to reach it.'

'I do not wish to enter any more tombs with you.'

'Please, Aya. It is my own tomb that I wish for you to see.' It was not really a lie.

'You have a tomb?'

'In a sense, yes.' She appeared confused, but at least he had captured her attention. 'Please?' he asked. 'I beg you.'

She had never thought this day would come. Now that it had, she did not trust it. She could not trust it. It was simply too good to be true.

He had come back to her. The only man she had ever loved.

He said he wanted forgiveness. Well, he had it. She had forgiven him the moment he had pressed the arrowhead into her palm and told her to get herself free.

Still, she feared his intentions. It was possible that he had bound himself even more tightly to General Setnakht. Now that he had found the true heir to the Rameses line, he would simply pick her up and take her back to Rameses's harem where she belonged.

She could not decide what to do. She only knew that she wanted to hear his voice a little while longer.

She looked around at the hills surrounding the temple. It was near to midday and not a single creature moved. To the east, lazy plumes of smoke marked the cooking fires of the village. Soon it would be too warm to work and all the residents of Amarna would lie down for their midday rest. Even the birds would cease to fly and the wind would whisper through the abandoned temples and empty buildings like the voices of those long gone.

'Live your life, Aya.'

She slung her bow around her shoulder. 'Go ahead, then,' she told him. 'Lead the way.'

She followed behind him a good twenty paces, for she did not trust that he travelled alone. She scanned the desert continuously, aware that at any moment a whole gang of soldiers could emerge from the hills and drag her away.

She would not go down without a fight. She had her bow and a whole quiver of arrows, and she knew the hills better than anyone. If Intef had come to take her back to Rameses, he would be woefully disappointed.

She would never again fall for his trickery.

Though it seemed that she had quite instantly fallen for his whistle. The moment she had heard it her treacherous heart had leapt with joy. Against her own will, she had smiled—had nearly laughed—and wished for nothing more than to leap into his arms. She was not sure who had betrayed her worse—Intef or her own heart.

What was he doing here and, more importantly, why was she so happy about it? And she was happy—terribly, horribly happy. She had hoped that time passing would make her thoughts of him fade. Instead, they had grown more vivid.

Some nights, she would lie awake on the roof of her hut and gaze up at the formation of the archer sparkling overhead. She would picture herself in that pose, but not alone. He was always behind her, his body pressing against her back, his arms covering her own, guiding them.

When she lifted her bow during a hunt, sometimes she could not even see her prey. She could only indulge in the rosy memory of his arms stretched out over hers, his warm breath on her neck, his deep, masculine voice quietly encouraging her.

She even seemed to miss their arguments. Despite his feigned indifference to her ideas, he always took them seriously. She loved how they sparred—his mocking reveries against her good sense—though of course he did not see her sense as always good.

And she was glad of it. Their differences did not bother her. On the contrary, they made her feel as if the world was somehow larger than she had ever conceived. 'Perhaps you do not know everything,' he loved to tell her.

Perhaps not and thank the gods.

Curse him. He was like the sun—impossible to avoid, warming her wherever she went. She could not rid herself of him, just as she could not rid herself of the desire to eat or sleep or gaze at the stars. They had spent only a few days together, yet she would never be the same. He had awakened her body, inspired her mind and healed her soul. Somehow, he had taken her darkness and brought it into the light.

But then he had betrayed her.

Why did her heart not think about that? He had lied to her about the most important thing in the world—the sanctity of Tausret's tomb. He had not only violated her trust, he had tipped the balance of *ma'at*. He was the very reason Tausret's spirit had nothing now.

Aya was the only thing standing between Tausret's soul and total oblivion. Her tomb had been cleaned out, her name erased. She no longer had a home. It was all Aya could do to keep her alive with offerings of beer and bread inside a crumbling temple at the edge of nowhere.

'Why do you walk so far away?' Intef called.

'Because I do not trust you,' she called back.

'You can mistrust me much more easily by walking beside me.'

He was flashing his handsome grin—yet another reason to keep her distance. Still, if he did plan to try to seize her, he would not be so foolish as to do it in the open. He would wait until they arrived at his so-called tomb.

'How did you escape Rameses?' he called to her. 'Please, I must know.'

'I fashioned a bow,' she called back.

'A what?' he asked.

'A bow!' she cried, holding up her bow. 'I fashioned a bow.'

He shook his head. 'I cannot hear you.'

Finally, she caught up to him. 'I said that I fashioned a bow.'

He resumed walking. 'You are too thin,' he observed, but there was a smile in his voice.

'And you remain as rude and manipulative as ever,' she said.

'How did you fashion a bow?'

'With a curtain pole.'

He laughed. 'A curtain pole? Impossible. And the arrow?'

'The poker of a brazier,' she said. He was trying not to show it, but she knew he was impressed.

'How did you get out of Thebes?'

'I took the river.'

'You hired a boat?' She flashed him a grin. 'You swam?'

She nodded, working to conceal her delight.

'But did you not fear crocodiles?'

'Of course I feared crocodiles, but I loved freedom more.'

'Freedom?' He looked at her and she dared to return the glance. His eyes were more luminous than she remembered and vastly more dangerous.

'Yes, freedom.'

'Is that what you are now…free?' He glanced in the direction of the crumbling temple. 'In the village they say you worship a strange spirit—one you have invented.'

'I worship the spirit of Tausret. I keep her alive.'

'You have given your life for hers, then.'

'It is the duty of a beloved servant.'

'But you are not a servant. You are her daughter.'

They crested a rise and Aya stopped. She gazed down into a cleft between the hills very similar to the valley where Tausret's tomb was located. 'What does it matter if I am Tausret's daughter? What will it change? It will not bring her back from the afterlife. It will not keep her *ka*, her eternal spirit, fed or clothed, or help her *ba* recognise her when it needs to rest. Pharaoh's tomb has been pillaged, her death mask destroyed. I am the only one on this earth left to help support her and protect her in the next life.'

He continued walking. 'You are not the only one left protecting Tausret,' he called behind him.

They descended into the small valley and soon were standing outside an opening in the side of a hill—obviously the entrance to a tomb. He disappeared through the entryway and returned with a torch, and she watched him strike flint to stone. The flame erupted in moments and she felt a wave of yearning for days past.

'Why did you do it?' she asked suddenly.

He bowed his head. 'You already know why, Aya—to save men's lives,' he replied.

'I do not refer to the pillaging of Tausret's tomb. I understand why you did that.'

'Then what?'

'Why did you follow Setnakht in the first place?'

'At first I did it for my father,' Intef explained. 'I had failed him in life and wished to atone for my mistake. But I also believed the stories the priests told us—that Tausret was a weak and corrupt ruler, that she was leading the country to ruin. I was so certain that I was doing right by following General Setnakht that I never thought to question the veracity of those stories—until I met you.'

Aya searched his eyes, looking for the lie. Still she could not find it.

'Now I realise that I cannot trust everything I hear,'

he continued. 'I should not trust the priests, or even Setnakht himself. I am not just a soldier, not just some wooden *ushabti* in somebody else's game of power. I am a man who can think on his own. You have shown me this, Aya. For the past four months, I have been labouring for what I have decided on my own is true and good. Will you not let me show you what it is?'

The first thing she noticed was the walls. Intef flashed his torch across them and she was struck by the intricacy of the scenes, all of which were accompanied by columns of text. In one scene, the sun god in the form of a scarab beetle passed beneath the horizon. In another, the figure of a child sat in a boat, floating past a landscape teeming with plant and animal life.

'These are from the book of what is in the Underworld,' she remarked.

'Do they please you?'

'Of course. But I do not understand. The text of that sacred book is for the tombs of Pharaohs only.'

'I know it is,' said Intef.

'Then why have you placed scenes from that text inside your own tomb?' He was walking away from her again. 'Intef?'

'Come.'

They made their way deeper down the corridor and Aya caught sight of an image of a woman making an offering of incense to Horus, the god of kingship. The woman was clad in a body-shaped tunic adorned with the half-moon of a colourful beaded pectoral over her chest. She might have been beautiful, but her image was distorted by the long dark beard jutting out from her chin: the pharaonic beard of kingship.

A chill travelled across Aya's skin. There was only one person it could have been. Moving further down the hall she began to see more images of the beautiful bearded woman. Then Aya was stepping into a chamber that felt oddly familiar.

Intef lit a lamp at each corner of the space until the room was illuminated with a soft glow. Adorning the walls were the same scenes from the Book of Caverns and the Book of the Earth that had adorned Tausret's own tomb. At the chamber's centre was a giant sarcophagus, its lid propped beside it.

Aya felt a surge of joy as her heart comprehended what her mind was still trying to understand. She crossed to the sarcophagus and peered inside.

'Tausret.' There she was—her beloved Pharaoh. There were her lovely limbs, her long straight hair, her perfect fingernails. And there, atop her head, the splendid mask of death that would allow her spirit to recognise her body in the afterlife. It was Tausret—just as beautiful and whole as the day she had been laid to rest.

Aya burst into tears.

Chapter Twenty-Eight

'How did you—what did you—?' She was sputtering with emotion.

'It has been my labour for these past four months—me and a whole gang of workmen, that is,' Intef said. 'And a rather large bag of gold.'

She looked around the chamber once again, as if seeing it anew. She pointed to a corner. 'A storage room?'

'Fully stocked: bread, beer, wine. A nine-year-old vintage.' He grinned self-consciously, then motioned to the other three rooms—one at each corner of the chamber. 'I have included everything she may need: clothing, medicines, furniture, even a cosmetics kit, and there are hundreds of *ushabtis* to aid her in whatever work is required. I have also hired two priests from the village to leave offerings for her daily. I pray it will be enough.'

Tears streamed down Aya's face. 'It is more than enough.' She ran her hand down Tausret's long, desiccated arm. 'My Pharaoh,' she whispered. 'My mother.'

She gently took Tausret's hand in hers. Her whole being seemed to fill with light. 'How can I ever thank you for this?'

'It was my duty,' Intef said, then added, 'and my honour.' He had never felt so light of heart. For the first time in his life, he had done his duty and also managed to protect the one he loved. 'She was a great ruler,' he said.

'Do you truly believe that?' Aya asked.

Intef took her free hand. 'I do and promise that I will never lie to you again.'

There they were—the three of them—their hands intertwined and also their fates. And also, perhaps, their hearts. He sensed that he had only begun to mend the damage that he had done. He only wished he could spend the rest of his life trying.

Aya walked beside him all the way home, though it felt more as though she was floating. She could not feel the rocky ground beneath her sandals. She did not suffer beneath the midday heat. She could only see colours—so many colours! The vibrant blue of the sky against the orange hilltops. The endless variety of hues reflected in the dusty rocks: sepia, grey, henna, agouti. How had she never noticed all the colours?

She noticed the living things, too. There was so much life in the desert. The stalwart bushes and intrepid lizards. The industrious scarabs lurking among the rocks. Overhead, an ancient vulture stretched his wide wings as if in praise. 'Look at the world!' he seemed to be saying. 'How wondrous it is!'

They stopped at the temple to retrieve the offering of meat she had made that morning. As with all offerings, the leavings would ultimately be consumed to help ensure that the living always had reason to thank the dead.

Aya and Intef returned to the hut and sat down to feast. 'Is gazelle all you have to eat?'

'Is it not enough?'

'Do you not have a garden or a field? Somewhere to grow things?'

'I am all alone. I do not find myself wanting…for food,' she said. She popped a chunk of gazelle between her lips and slipped him a clever grin.

He swallowed his meat and stared at her, thankful he did not choke. Had she just suggested what he thought she had suggested? Wondrous woman. She had surprised him once again and it occurred to him that she would always surprise him. It was something he knew as certainly as his own footprint. He could stare across the table at her for all eternity and never grow bored.

'Is there something besides food for which you are wanting?' he asked boldly, taking another bite. His heart thumped.

'Perhaps.' Her gaze shifted to the empty bucket of water in the corner of the hut and she sighed. 'Today I find myself wanting a bath.'

Now he did choke. He coughed and gagged until his half-chewed, half-swallowed gazelle finally went down the right pipe.

'Would you like some more beer?'

'No, thank you,' he replied, feeling himself flush.

'Well, in that case I will leave you with your gazelle. I am going down to the well to bathe.'

She walked down the path to the well, trying to control her blush. She did not know what had made her so bold. Perhaps she had spent too much time alone in the desert. Or perhaps the long hours inside her tiny hut had given her a better appreciation for the nature of time. Sometimes it dragged past. Other times it was as if many months had passed in a day. Today was one of those days. Already the sun was dipping towards the horizon and she feared his plans. She did not know if he would go or stay.

She wanted him to stay.

Still, it was possible that at this very moment he was slipping away into the dusk, never to return. And why not? He had done his penance. He had given back that which he had taken from her and restored the *ma'at* between them.

Indeed, now he could finally move forward with his life—a marvellous life for certain. He was the Hero of Thebes after all. By now he had surely found himself a beautiful wife and a high post in the new Pharaoh's army. He would want to get back to them and she did not wish to stop him. Her quick departure for a bath would at least give him the opportunity to escape.

She arrived at the well and quickly disrobed. The sun god was low on the horizon, but his rays still warmed her skin. She cranked the handle and raised up the bucket, then tilted it over her head and let the cool water pour over her limbs. She felt better already.

If he did not return, she would be fine. She would miss him, of course, but she was accustomed to missing the ones she loved. She would allow herself no regrets but one—that she had failed to thank him. By saving Tausret's afterlife, he had also saved Aya's current life.

Thanks to Intef, she was no longer bound to this place. Her mistress—her mother—was provisioned now. Her death mask was restored. She would live and thrive in the afterlife, giving Aya the opportunity to live and thrive in this one. She would be able to live the life that her mother had always wanted for her.

'Thank you, Intef,' she murmured to the muddy ground. She missed him already. She pictured him making his way down the trail to Amarna. She had lived by herself for years now and never once felt this alone.

She lowered the bucket again into the well and poured it over her head. Yes, much better. The water splattered to the ground, mixing with the sound of bird-song coming from the birds flitting among the nearby boulders. She shook out her head and reached for the pot of salt and oil.

The birds were getting louder with Ra's retreat. One in particular was making quite a bit of noise. Its whistle sounded almost like a tune she knew. She turned to look for the feathered creature among the rocks, but what she discovered was something more wonderful by far. He was no bird, though the sound of his silly whistle made her heart fly.

'Intef!'

He watched the colour rise to her cheeks and knew he had done well. He had decided to remove his clothes at the last moment, in retaliation for her suggestive departure. If she could surprise him, he could very well surprise her in return.

'I have realised that I am also in great need of a bath,' he said casually, as if he had just arrived fully clothed to a banquet. He only wished he had arrived a few minutes sooner so that he might have seen her pour water over her equally unclad skin. As it was he could hardly keep his eyes above her neckline.

He stood beside her and peered down into the well, feigning great interest in it. He let the bucket fall and cranked it back up again. Then he stepped in front of her, positioning her between himself and the rim of the well.

'Please tell me that you at least own some decent scrubbing salts.'

'I would not be a one-woman temple if I did not,' she said and reached for a clay pot full of salt and oil that had been resting on the lip of the well. 'I traded for it in the village.'

'With gazelle meat, I assume?' He rolled his eyes.

She shot him a scolding look. 'Gazelle is a highly valuable commodity! And the hides are incredibly soft, though rather difficult to clean.'

'I would like to clean your hide,' he said, stepping forward.

'That would be a laborious task.' She stepped backwards, closer to the well. She appeared to be reaching for something behind her. 'Cleaning hides is much more difficult than chiselling through stone.'

'Is it really?' he asked. 'Well, you will have to teach me, then.' And in that moment he felt a torrent of cold water pour down over his head.

'Barbarian woman!' he shouted. He dipped his hand into the pot and came up with a palmful of the salt and oil. 'Now you will feel the heat of my palm!'

It was the most welcome threat that had ever been made to her and she sighed as he wrapped himself around her in order to carry it out. He began by rubbing the mixture up and down her back, but instead of moving on to her limbs, he squeezed her in his embrace.

'I feared this moment would never come,' he said, exhaling. She could feel his wet skin against hers, the subtle rise and fall of his breaths. She rested her head on his chest and he pushed his fingers into her hair. 'I started searching for you the moment you disappeared.'

She tilted her head and gazed up at him. 'How did you know I disappeared?'

'I met your replacement. She responds to the name Aya quite naturally.'

'My replacement?'

'She looks very little like you, except through the eyes. They are also blue.'

It took her a moment to apprehend the news. After Aya had disappeared on their wedding night, it seemed that Rameses had quickly found a replacement for her. It was a clever thing to do. As long as the people believed his wife to be the granddaughter of Rameses the Great Ancestor, she was.

Which meant that Aya no longer had any reason to hide. Like Tausret herself, she had been erased. She paused and waited for the anger to come. Instead, relief washed over her. In truth, she had never felt so very free.

'Perhaps now Great Egypt will be at peace,' she said.

Intef's voice was full of heavy stones. 'I thought I had lost you for ever.'

She opened her mouth to speak and felt the crush of his lips on hers. All the gods in all the heavens, how wonderful it was to feel his lips again! She kissed him back urgently, as if she had a message that she had been waiting years to tell him. Only she had not been waiting years, she realised. She had been waiting her whole life.

'Intef, I—'

He placed his tongue between the gap in her front teeth, making her giggle. 'I have wanted to do that from the first time I saw you grin,' he said. Meanwhile, his hands moved up and down her back, rubbing in the salt and oil.

'Aya, how I have missed you,' he said. 'I cannot count

the times I have dreamed of touching you again…these arms…' he dipped his hand into the pot once again and began rubbing the mixture on her shoulders and arms '…this stomach, these hips…' he massaged the mixture into her stomach, then down over her hips '…these legs, these feet.' His hands rioted over her legs and feet, but he soon returned to standing.

'This—'

He wrapped his hands around her backside. 'Ahh, Aya,' he said. He massaged her flanks in long, loving strokes. And then she forgot what she was going to say entirely, for their lips met once again.

It was a hungry, desperate kiss. It was not simply that he found her lips arousing. In kissing them, he had the feeling of imminent arrival—as if he had been floating in a vast ocean and had finally sighted land.

He wanted her elementally, the way he wanted water or air. He yearned to taste her and smell her and take in the sight of her, but that was not all he wanted. He wanted the invisible things, too. The things she had shown him in the dark.

She was the most wondrous woman he had ever known: an arrow-shooting, tomb-chiselling, latrine-digging, life-saving wonder and he loved her beyond words.

He stepped back from her. 'I think it is time to rinse,' he said. He was nearly panting and his desire throbbed painfully. He let the bucket plunge into the well and cranked it up again, but she stole it from his grasp.

'I think it is you who needs the rinse.' She poured the cool water over his burning flesh and laughed.

'How dare you!' he shouted. He plunged the bucket back into the well and cranked it up.

'Intef, I— *Ack!*' she cried as the water went pouring over her head. He repeated the rinse twice more until all her limbs were clean and she was standing like a goddess in the diminishing light.

'I did not think it possible, but after all these months, I believe you are even more beautiful,' he remarked.

'And you have become even more outrageous.'

'Outrageous?' he said. 'Not at all.' Then he lifted her off her feet.

'What are you doing?'

'Do you have a bed mat on the roof?'

'Of course.'

'Then I am taking you to it immediately.'

'But why?'

'Unfinished business.'

Soon they were lying on her bed mat, staring up at a sky full of stars. 'Remember the painted stars that decorated the false chamber?' Aya asked.

'They are all I see most nights,' said Intef. 'I hardly perceive the real ones any more.'

'I think of them, too,' Aya said. 'Far too often.' She sat up and gasped. 'The temple! The evening ritual— I forgot!'

'Shall we go there now?' asked Intef.

'Too late. It must take place in the first hour of night, just as the sun goes down.'

'It is my fault,' said Intef. 'I distracted you from your duty.'

'Not at all,' she said. Now that Tausret was safe inside a provisioned tomb with dedicated priests, she would no longer require Aya's constant attention. Finally, Tausret could rest, which meant that Aya could rest, too.

'Can you ever forgive me, Aya?' Intef asked.

'Forgive you? Without you I would have never discovered my true identity. There would have been a war. Thousands of lives would have been destroyed.'

'And instead two lives were,' said Intef.

'Rameses could never destroy my life. I would not let him.'

'I could not help you escape him.'

'But you did help me escape him.' She lifted her other wrist and held it before his eyes. 'Do you see the object woven into my bracelet?'

He stared at the bracelet in wonder. 'Is that the arrowhead?'

She felt her eyes filling with tears. 'It was all I had left of you.'

She had longed for him, too. She could finally admit it. She had dreamed of embracing him from the moment he had flashed her his wicked grin. It was something she had tried to deny, for surely it was some trick of the gods. How could it be that this impudent, heretical tomb robber had somehow stolen her heart?

Yet he had. Curse him, he had. It belonged to him, to do with what he would. She could feel it even now, beating out its wild enthusiasm.

He pulled away from her and touched her face. He gently arranged her hair, placing its errant locks behind her ear. 'It is strange, but I feel I can see you, even in the darkness,' he said.

'And I you,' she said.

In every way imaginable. She could see the skilled archer and the clever teacher, the loyal soldier and the scheming spy. She could see the blood-soaked plains of battle, where he had grown hard and cold and lost his fire. And she could see the small precious part of him that remained smouldering still.

She sensed that small fire was trained on her. Perhaps it had been for a long while. She would have never dreamed it possible that a man such as he could want a woman such as she. Yet she could feel his liquid dark eyes watching her. She could imagine their dangerous glint, the yearning in them. Even in the dark, they were sending arrows through her.

'I never would have stopped searching for you, Aya,' he said. 'You are my Isis and I am your Osiris. You brought me back from the dead.'

'But your breath never left you.'

'That is not what I mean.'

'I know it is not.'

She rested her head on his chest. His heartbeats were so strong and true, like music. She wanted to dance to those heartbeats for the rest of her life.

He traced her lip with his thumb. 'There is another debt I wish to pay, you know. I promised I would show you the marshes.'

'And you did,' said Aya. 'I think about it often.'

'We may have wandered the marshes that last night in the tomb, but I was the only one who went swimming.'

'Swimming?' There was only one thing he could be referring to. The women at court spoke of it often, but only indirectly and with a twinkle in their eyes. 'I am afraid I have never...swum. How does one achieve such a thing?'

He had neglected her once, but never again. She claimed to have enjoyed the pleasures of the flesh in the past, but he had a strong suspicion she had only ever gone through the motions. Perhaps she had even pleasured herself on occasion, but it still was not the same.

He would show her what pleasure could be when combined with the kinds of feelings they shared. On this first night of her freedom, he would help her find her way to bliss. 'Well, one must first relax one's muscles,' he said.

'And how does one do that?' He motioned for her to roll on to her stomach and she obeyed.

He arranged the bed sheet so that it folded over the bump of her bottom. 'One must also relax one's mind,' he said. He thought of the most distracting question he could conceive. 'Tell me, were there other Libyans in Tausret's court?'

'Why do you ask?'

'I am helping you relax.' He lifted his leg and straddled her, finding his seat just atop her covered bottom. Slowly, he began to rub up and down her back.

'There are many Libyans serving in Pharaoh's court,' she replied. 'Oh, that feels wondrous.'

'Did not Pharaoh Merneptah defeat many Libyans during his reign?'

'He did indeed,' said Aya. 'He took over eight thousand of them to till the fields of the Delta. They worked alongside Egyptians and married them. What is that you are doing?'

'I am simply removing the knots you have developed in your neck from all your hard work.'

Meanwhile, he had begun to move himself gently atop her bottom.

'Oh, well, it feels very good.'

'It is my hope to have you completely relax,' he said. 'Please tell me more about the North. I know it poorly.'

'The North of Egypt is very…different from the

South,' she said and he made his way slowly down the length of her back until he was rubbing her tailbone gently.

'In what way?'

'Well, there are many different peoples in the North.'

'Like whom?' he asked. He gently began to knead her bottom.

'Like the Asiatics,' she said. 'And the Libyans. There are Nubians, too… Oh gods, what are you doing?'

'It is just part of the massage,' he said. 'Which Asiatic tribes?'

'Oh, there are Canaanites and Babylonians and Hittites… What are you doing now?'

'I am just going to massage the inside of your thighs a little. Is that all right? Tell me, why do northerners tolerate foreigners so well?' He moved her legs apart and slipped two fingers inside her.

'Oh, Intef…' She sighed.

'Tell me,' he insisted. 'Why are they so…open?'

'Northerners appreciate people who are different,' she breathed. 'Better ways of doing things, new ideas.'

Keeping his fingers inside her, he lay down atop her. He whispered in her ear, 'And yet every great unifier of Egypt has come from the South.' He was throbbing with his need for her, but he kept his desire tucked inside his loincloth.

This was her moment, not his. 'Why do Egypt's great leaders always come from the South?' he repeated.

He pushed his fingers inside her a little more.

'Perhaps because the South needs the North,' she said. 'And thus is always trying to join with it.'

It was a terrible choice of words, though they certainly belied what was in her heart. From the moment she had seen him walking towards the well that evening she had been yearning for him.

And now this—sweet torture. He was doing what she had always done to herself but was somehow more skilled at it than she. Far more skilled.

He was like an expert mason working his wonders on flesh instead of rock. 'I believe it is the other way around,' he whispered in her ear. 'I believe it is the North that needs the South.'

'Oh, yes?'

'Quite badly.'

'And what exactly does the North need the South for?'

'Roll over and I will show you,' he commanded and she could do nothing but obey.

She was lying naked on her back in the starlight's soft glow and he was gazing at her with such admiration that she had no desire to cover herself. She pursed her lips together as if to send him a kiss.

His grin turned dangerous. She glanced down at his desire and felt her eyes become wide at the sight.

She quickly returned her gaze to his, but it was too late—he had caught her appraising him. She blushed and he shook his head as if to scold her.

Which only made her blushing worse.

She was desperately aroused. She wondered what he planned for her. Nothing about this man could be predicted. The last time they had done this, he had caught her unaware, sneaking into her like a thief.

His clandestine invasion had been her undoing. Never in her life had she felt such a surprise, followed by such an amazement, followed by such a delicious, all-consuming pleasure.

Since then, her body seemed to have been missing his and no more so than right now.

She sat up on her arms and reached for him. He swatted her hand away and pushed her gently back on to the bed mat.

'If you do that, then it will no longer be about you,' he said. 'This is about you.'

He watched her closely as he slipped his fingers inside her once again. 'Oh, Intef,' she muttered. He was coaxing her lust, conjuring it into life. He gazed down at her womanhood as if charting the course of a journey.

She knew where he was going, where he was going to take them both—south.

Slowly, wickedly, he kissed a path downwards to her desire. He continued moving his fingers until his mouth arrived at her entrance. Finally, he pushed his tongue inside her and tasted her.

Egypt was in drought, the Sea Peoples were on the march and the new dynasty might not survive, but lying here beneath Intef there was only the slow susurrations of his breath, the delicious movements of his mouth and fingers, and nothing at all to do but feel.

His tongue. His evil, wicked tongue. It was a terrible magician and she was trapped beneath its spell. And his fingers—two wretched minions that were making her whole body ache. 'More, Intef, please,' she begged.

Small tremors were rumbling through her. He was pushing his magic fingers inside her, his speed increasing with her need. His tongue licked and toyed with her and she no longer knew where she was.

Until, suddenly, there she was, bursting through the sky, pulsing with sensation, a streak of ecstasy in the night. She cried out and tears of emotion filled her eyes as her body writhed and trembled and then went slack.

She lay there for many moments, breathing through the aftershocks. 'What did you just do to me?'

He crawled up her body and lay atop her. 'Those, my love, were the marshes,' he stated with pride. 'And you just went swimming.'

They lay there for many moments, breathing together, and it was as if all the spinning parts of her finally came to a stop and all the burdens she bore were no longer hers alone.

A surprising idea came into her mind: that it might be possible in this life not only to serve, but to be served. To protect and to be protected. To love and to be loved.

He propped himself on his elbow beside her. 'How do you feel?'

'As if I am a heavy stone who has suddenly exploded into a cloud of dust.'

He wove his hand with hers and studied her bracelet. 'There is one more thing I have neglected to tell you,' he said, touching the small sharp stone. 'And I hope you will forgive me for keeping it from you all this time.'

She composed herself. What other thing could there possibly be? Whatever it was, she would endure it. No one was worth more to her than him. 'What is it, Intef?'

He lifted her hand to his lips and kissed it. 'I love you.'

'What?'

'I love you, Aya. I will love you for ever.'

She looked down and studied the place where he had kissed her hand. It was as if he had made a mark there, a relief he had chiselled into her flesh, never to be erased.

'And I love you,' she said. 'I have been trying to tell you all day.'

'You have?'

She sat up and straddled him. 'You were so intent

on kissing me that I did not have a chance. But now I have you beneath my command and it is your turn to go swimming.'

'Is it indeed?' He grinned wickedly.

She bent down to kiss his lips, fully intending to kiss her way down his belly, only to feel him moving himself into her. 'Thief!' she cried out.

The sensation was almost too pleasurable to bear and she moaned as they began to move together as one. 'I believe it is both our turn,' he said.

She had once wondered what it would feel like to be divine. Now she knew, for in that moment they ceased to be human. They were two gods at the beginning of time, wandering through the darkness, casting their glorious light.

* * * * *

*If you enjoyed this book, be sure to
check out these other great reads
by Greta Gilbert*

The Spaniard's Innocent Maiden
In Thrall to the Enemy Commander
Forbidden to the Gladiator
Seduced by Her Rebel Warrior